The Dark Prince of Lazera

The Dark Prince of Lazera

Rachel E. Croxton

Contents

Prologue

The Dark Castle loomed like a grotesque shadow in the distance across the snowy plains. The wind blew bitterly cold air across the land, and gray clouds rolled above.

A set of feet crunched across the snow, leaving a trail of boot prints. He knew he didn't have to walk. It was true. He possessed a much faster form of transportation that didn't require moving. But he liked walking. He enjoyed the snow and cold weather. It never really bothered him.

Cold air breezed through his clothes, bristling through his hair. He liked to feel the chill on his skin flowing through him. Little wispy snowflakes fluttered around him, sprinkling his hair like sprinkles on a cake.

He gazed across the land, taking in the magnificent, wonderful landscape covered in glistening blue snow. *This land will be my kingdom someday,* he thought with satisfaction. He smiled at that.

Closing his eyes, he opened his arms, spreading them wide on either side of him. He tilted his face in the wind. He leaned forward, swaying slightly, and fell face-first into the snow.

One

How did legends come about? They had to be based on something, something that existed. They had to come from somewhere unless someone made them up. But aren't legends based on real-life facts? This topic was confusing.

The entire concept of legends left Simina pondering it day and night. Legends became her main focus. She didn't understand how the people who wrote and told legends got their information or apparent facts. Simina knew of legends because she loved to read books. She mainly read books about legends.

Most people thought legends were related to fairy tales. But Simina did not believe it was true. She read fairy tales, oh yes, but they sounded very different from legends. They were nothing alike and had few similarities, if any. Legends kept Simina intrigued. She fantasized about them and the magic described in legends.

Legends must be the darker part of fairy tales that the authors didn't write about. Simina enjoyed many fictional stories, but something drew her to mythical legends and folktales. Anything pertaining to or about the supernatural, she loved. It fascinated Simina to no end. She positively adored fairytales. She loved stories detailing the bravery of valiant young princes heroically trekking through all sorts of danger just to save the love of their life, the princess.

Simina wished very childishly that someone would love her like that, love her enough to save her from imminent danger. She longed to be a beautiful princess, loved and cherished by all who knew her. Simina never really believed in all of that; she knew stuff like that had never really happened. Handsome young princes didn't exist, and neither did princesses, evil witches who conjured up terrible spells, werewolves that changed during the full moon, vampires that sucked blood out of their victims, fairy godmothers who helped the princess during a time of desperate need, fairies themselves that possessed magical wands, little elves with pointy ears, or warlocks.

But Simina still liked to dream. Without dreams, what would she have? Nothing. Her mind would be empty—her life would be empty. If she wasn't at school or reading a book, she was daydreaming about all the magnificent things previously mentioned.

Because of her fascination with such things, her father constantly told her to get her head out of the clouds and start living down on the planet where reality existed. Her father highly disapproved of her reading these books but never said much to her about them. Simina knew reading about such things was one thing, but speaking of them was on a whole other level. Talking about such things in front of other people, the common public, was forbidden.

Things like that evoked a sense of fear in others because they didn't understand. People often are afraid of things they don't understand, but Simina thought nothing was odd about discussing legends. However, it completely freaked other people out. She didn't know why, though, even though these myths and legends weren't real. If these common people didn't believe such things existed, why were they so afraid? Simina knew what was real: disease, plague, famine. Those were real problems, ones she could actually physically see and not just read about. A few years ago, when Simina was much younger, the plague ravaged rampantly through her small village of Lazera. Her mother was still alive back then, but not for much longer.

A little after the plague hit the village, Simina's mother got sick from working in the Sick House, trying to nurse other people back to health. However, Simina, too, became dreadfully ill with the plague. Now, her father carried the burden of caring for them both by himself.

Simina didn't remember much during that time. The memory of her sickly, labored breathing, and the sluggish thump-bump of her heart pumping sick blood through her veins made Simina think once more of her near-death experience. She vaguely remembered dreaming of dark things moving and forming into grotesque shapes. Her feverish skin burned hot to the touch, and Simina was sure she would die.

But somehow, she survived. The rashes on her skin did not leave scars, they went away on their own, and her fever broke. Her mother, however, was not so lucky. Her mother succumbed to the disease and sadly passed. Simina grieved for the longest time, wishing it had been her to die instead of her mother, wishing she could have taken her mother's place.

But that had been five years ago, and Simina had long since moved on. She still missed her mother, but had gotten over the intense grief she used to feel at her loss. Since her mother's death, Simina's father has never been the same. Even after five years, he's never tried to remarry, though Simina has tried to persuade him to meet other women.

Simina's coping mechanism was reading books, and all those interesting stories made her feel better after her mother died. She didn't know if her father knew that, but oh well, she figured.

One of Simina's deepest secrets was to experience adventure. She secretly wished for adventure and to explore all over the planet. Other times, when Simina couldn't read, she'd go outside in her yard and pretend she was a princess, a damsel in distress in need of saving, and play with her friend Ernest, who would dress up like a prince and pretend to save her. Or he'd play the witch and try to capture her.

Despite being the age of twenty, Simina still acted like a child. She never wanted to grow; she always wanted to stay a child. She never wanted to take on the responsibilities of a grown adult woman. But her father kept telling her to grow up and stop being so childish. She had to grow up someday so she could mature. He told her to stop acting like such a child and to start acting like a proper young lady who'd get married someday and perhaps have children.

Simina was still young and wanted to act as a child for as long as possible. Even though she was twenty, she acted more like a twelve-year-old, and many village elders disapproved of her antics. Simina still wanted to be able to dream and fantasize about things. Sometimes, because of this, her father would take away all her books and not allow her to read them until she acted like a proper young lady. Usually, when this happened, she'd go find Ernest, and they'd play a game called "The Prince and The Princess." That just happened to be what she was doing right about now.

Simina ran through the woods, splashing through puddles of mud. She held the folds of her skirt as she ran, giggling like mad. Ernest chased behind her, wielding a long wooden stick as a sword.

"Come back here, princess! I won't let you get away!" he shouted. This just made Simina laugh harder. Air rushed into her lungs as the wind caressed her hair. Spots of muddy water splattered all over her legs. The soft grass tickled in between her bare toes as the fresh, earthy soil caked up in the gentle creases of her skin.

"You can't catch me! My prince will save me!" she yelled back mockingly. Ernest cackled after her.

"He can't save you; I've captured your precious prince!" Ernest wailed in a high-pitched voice; which was supposed to be a witch's voice, but a poor imitation. Simina looked over her shoulder to see Ernest gaining on her. She tried to run faster but couldn't do it in a dress.

A twig sticking out of the ground, sharp and fresh from a young tree, snagged on her skirt and tore the hem of her dress, shredding through the fabric like butter. Simina kept running, not caring that she tore it. Brief concern for her dress slipped in her mind, but then she decided to sew it up in her free time. Her father would disapprove. But Simina wasn't striving for his approval, nor anyone else's, for that matter.

"My prince will escape! He will come for me!" Simina swore, voice swelling with a fake loyalty. In the midst of her running, she jumped over a rotten, dead log of a long-ago fallen tree. She turned back to see Ernest stumble and lose his balance, but he kept going at a slower pace.

Simina slipped behind the trunk of a large oak tree, hiding from Ernest. She peeked around the side of the tree, both hands placed on either side of its large wooden trunk. Ernest had stopped running. He stood in quite a strange stance, with his legs far apart, only half standing, holding a long stick in his right hand. He squinted.

"Where'd you go, my pretty? Hm? Come out, come out, wherever you are," Ernest said in his poor witch imitation voice. Simina hid, her heart beating fast. The snapping of twigs and the crunching of dead leaves announced Ernest's approach. Simina did not move a muscle. Ernest's footsteps stopped. Simina peeked around the tree's trunk. He wasn't there. Simina widened her eyes in curiosity.

"Ernest?" she called out his name, feeling worried. As soon as she said his name, something jumped out of a tree beside her. She squealed with fright. It was Ernest, arms raised in a creepy fashion above his head, and he growled at her like a wild animal. Simina screamed and stumbled back as Ernest tackled her playfully to the ground. They rolled around for a bit, Simina giggling until Ernest finally let up. He stared at her with a wide, playful grin.

"Gotcha," he said, "I win." Simina nodded, giving up, knowing it was time to concede defeat.

"Okay, you win, you barbarian. Now get off," Simina said, shoving him in the chest as she tried to hide the smile in her voice. Ernest rolled off her and onto the ground. He huffed a huge breath of relief and began panting. Simina lay next to him, her legs too worn out and achy to get up. Simina groaned and stared up at the beautiful beams of sunlight snaking through every small crevice and gaps of the leaves of the trees around them.

Simina took a deep breath, swallowing a mouthful of fresh air. They lay there for a while just panting, catching their breath, until Ernest finally moved. He sat up and rolled to his feet. Simina sat up but did not stand. She watched Ernest climb up the base of an apple tree like a monkey to the top. He picked two apples and, with great agility, jumped down to land on his feet. Ernest plopped on the grass, flicking his wild red curls out of his eyes.

He tossed Simina an apple, which she caught with both hands. Ernest chomped into his with a crispy, satisfying crunch. Juice dribbled down his lips and chin as he draped his arm across a propped-up knee.

Simina daintily took a bite out of her apple, letting its sweet juice run across the surface of her tongue. The tartness came as a pleasant surprise as it mixed with the sweetness, creating a combination of flavors that was just right. She heard Ernest slurp his apple, and she looked up. His wide, boyish grin arrived with a set of dimples on both cheeks.

"We should play a different game sometime," Ernest suggested with a worn-out voice. He took another bite of the apple as Simina chewed and swallowed.

"What do you mean?" she asked.

He shrugged.

"I don't know. Maybe we should consider growing up," Ernest told her. He dodged the glare Simina gave him. He enjoyed playing along with Simina and her games, but was growing tired of playing these childish games over and over again every time they met. Ernest knew that some physical and emotional change had come over him. He began to develop different feelings for Simina than just childlike feelings.

He noticed Simina had also undergone some physical changes lately. She looked the same as always, but something about her seemed suddenly different. He noticed her face wasn't as round as before, the sides of her body not so straight, and the swelling of her chest. Her body curved now.

Ernest noticed these changes in her but wondered if Simina also noticed them. Ernest didn't know how to explain these feelings, but he found her rather pretty. He'd heard of puberty and knew he was going through it; he just didn't know what it fully meant. Simina, however, had never heard of puberty. She didn't know what it was.

She did notice that her body was changing but paid it no mind. She also tried to ignore these new feelings and emotions she'd started feeling about herself, and the wild thoughts she often had.

Simina, ignoring Ernest's previous statement, tossed away her now-finished apple core, and wiped off her mouth as Ernest dropped his apple to the ground. Simina scooted closer to Ernest and crossed her legs.

"Can you show me again?" she asked.

He smiled and cupped his hands. "Sure."

Simina grinned eagerly as his brow knitted in concentration. Slowly, two wispy, puppet-like figures materialized in his hands. The puppet dolls resembled Simina and Ernest. The Simina doll jumped out of his hand and trotted over to her, a soft white light trailing behind her small form. Simina giggled as it jumped into her hand and waved. It squeaked, as if trying to talk, but failed.

Frowning, the little doll jumped to the ground. The mini Ernest tapped her on the back, and then the two began to dance. Simina stared in awe at Ernest's creations. He could make miniature doll versions of people with his magic. At first, when Ernest was around twelve, he could only make strange, faceless lumps with odd and bulky limbs. But after some years of practice and frequent use of his magic, he is now able to make them look more like people. Simina believed that much later he could possibly create full-sized, realistic looking people.

The mini Ernest and Simina danced for a while, but as Ernest twirled her around, they vanished in a puff of white mist. Real Ernest groaned, fatigue clouding his young features.

"I haven't eaten much today, so my stamina is low," he sighed.

"I wish I could do that," Simina huffed, picking at the dirt.

"You still can't do any magic?" Ernest looked surprised.

She shook her head. "None. Is there something wrong with me?"

Ernest patted her shoulder reassuringly. "You'll get yours. You're just a late bloomer."

"But my mother and father both had magic. My dad can help plants grow and move the ground. My mom...well, she could heal the sick..." Thinking solemnly about her mother, she wondered why her powers didn't allow her to heal herself.

"Be patient. Everything happens for a reason."

Simina opened her mouth to reply, but a familiar shout made her pause.

"Simina!!" her father called out to her. She jumped to her feet urgently.

"That's my father. I have to go."

"Bye!" Ernest called after her as she trotted away.

Simina skipped home, humming to herself as she twirled her skirt around. It grazed the tips of the flowers and grass below her. The air was pleasantly warm, the perfect temperature. Not too cold or too hot. Just right. Giggling, she swung around a tree trunk.

But then there came a snap of a twig and the crunch of brush, and Simina halted. Her neck hairs stood on end, all of her senses tingling. She didn't see anyone, but Simina knew someone was there. A cold and harsh breeze danced around her, the warmth from mere minutes ago now gone. She glanced around cautiously, a lump forming in her throat. A mysterious, cloaked figure moved between the trees, almost like it was floating. A strange, purple mist trailed after it, its movements quick and jagged.

Spooked, Simina picked up her pace. Above her the sky birthed dark and ominous gray clouds. A loud thunder rumbled and purple lightning cracked across the sky. Then the clouds released a heavy and unrelenting torrent of rain, the drops pelting down angrily. Gasping, Simina ran as fast as she could, a great terror seizing her heart. Drenched within seconds, Simina's dress clung to her skin, her feet splashing in pools of mud. Even though her bones ached and her chest burned, Simina did not stop until she arrived safely at her small cottage.

Upon entering, she slammed the wooden slat board across the door, bolting it shut. She pulled back the curtain on the small, square window and peeked out. The gloomy, bleak forest revealed nothing but soggy trees and muddy grounds.

Taking a deep breath, Simina calmed her racing heart. *It was probably nothing,* she told herself. Glancing down at the floor, she realized that in her haste, she'd tracked dirt and mud all over the floor from her bare feet. Spinning her head about madly, checking to make sure her father wasn't coming, she quickly scurried to the washroom to wash up and change her clothes.

Before Simina got the chance to do anything, however, she heard her father shout. Her body lurched to a stop. *Darn.*

"Simina, what is this mess you've tracked on the floor?! Come here, this instant!" he ordered. Simina, sulking, hung her head and droopingly walked back into the front room to her father to stand before him. She didn't dare look at him. He tapped an angry foot against the floor.

"Just look at yourself. You've soiled your nice clothes and made a mess of the house!" he scolded. Her father left for a second and returned a moment later with a bucket and a sponge. He snapped his fingers and pointed at the floor.

"Clean it up, now," he said. Forgetting all about her spooky experience in the woods, Simina spent the next few hours scrubbing up the floor.

Two

The next day, Simina skipped happily through the village, heading toward the village library, wearing a warm dress, a shawl draped around her shoulders, a scarf, and a pair of warm woolen mittens. In her hand, she carried a book with her to return to the librarian. She just finished reading a book about vampires. She wanted to read something new and knew the library wouldn't disappoint.

The small village of Lazera bustled with the noise of crowds during the busy afternoon hours. The clomping of hooves across the cobblestone streets rang in her ears as villagers traveled on horseback. The vendors lined on the streets caught the attention of passersby, belting out sales and discounted prices on their items, and other reasons why their items should be purchased over others. Some sold petty jewels, others fruits. The sound of cracking, splitting wood permeated the air as the lumberjack chopped firewood in preparation for the cold, long winter months.

When Simina arrived at the library, she pushed the little door open. A bell jingled above her head, sounding her arrival as she walked in. Warmth flooded through her as she stepped inside. Before the door fully closed, the cool autumn breeze blew in with bone-chilling numbness. Heat flushed her face. Simina's nose and cheeks turned pink from the autumn chill.

The librarian looked up from where he sat at his desk, just right of the door. The old man smiled cheerily at her, his plump cheeks growing all rosy. A wild tuft of white hair protruded from his head.

"Simina, my dear, how are you? What can I do for you today?" Mr. Blikman asked her with a fond greeting. Simina smiled and waved at him.

"Hello, Mr. Blikman. I'm looking for something new today," she told him, standing at the desk and handing him the finished book. Blikman flipped out a pair of spectacles and put them on, the nosepiece barely resting on his nose's edge.

"Finished already, eh?" He picked the book up with two shaky, wrinkled hands. Simina nodded proudly. She breezed through books like a champ. Well, ones she really liked.

"It was good!" Simina exclaimed, "I just couldn't put it down!" Blikman smiled. He admired Simina's joy in reading. He thought perhaps when she got a bit older, she'd become a schoolteacher. *Real bright girl,* he thought, *real bright. Possesses a very broad mind, too.* He adjusted his glasses.

"Anything in particular you were looking for today?" he asked. Simina wandered to the mythical legends and folklore section. She craned her neck to look up at the highest shelf. She adored the high bookcases that towered to the ceiling, crammed with books and more books as far as the eye could see. Every nook, corner, and cranny housed a book, a sight Simina never tired of.

"No, not really. But I'll snag the first book I see that piques my interest," Simina told Mr. Blikman. She scanned the many rows and shelves of books with very catchy titles, but Simina had already probably read half of them.

Simina stroked her fingers along the spine of each book as her eyes scanned each row. *The Big Bad Wolf, The Legend of Sleepy Hollow, The Brothers' Grimm, Vampires: The Monsters of The Night, Werewolves: Slaves of the Full Moon,* and many more fascinating stories of the supernatural. She'd read all of those, of course. Sometimes, if she really liked a specific book, she'd check it out multiple times and read it many times over.

Most of these stories, however, had been derived from the planet Earth. She didn't mind; Simina enjoyed Earthen tales and Zormonian tales. She'd read an equal amount of both.

Simina had heard of the planet Earth but had never been. She knew that Earth was much, much different than Zormonia and they weren't a magical species. However, Zormonia and Earth frequently traded goods. Most of the goods Zormonia offered to Earth came from the wealthier sectors, like Summerville. She'd read about Summerville in a book. It was very, very far from her small, quaint village of Lazera.

Most Zormonians possessed some sort of magical talent. Despite being born on the planet Zormonia, Simina had yet to show magical affinity. She was unsure if she didn't have any powers, or if they were hidden. The Zormonian species varies from place to place. Some look stranger than others, while some look more like humans, and some can even do strange things with their bodies. They also differ from humans in how they tend to live longer lives. The average Zormonian usually lives about five thousand years. In very rare cases, a Zormonian can live up to fifteen thousand years. Simina read a book once about the oldest Zormonian, who was supposedly over fifteen thousand years old.

Zormonians get their magic from the planet itself. Zormonia's core is a crystal containing pure, unfiltered magical energy. Most Zormonians are able to channel this magic, and most Zormonians gain a distinct magic power during puberty. For a select few, however, this power may develop later or not at all. It's a rare occurrence for a Zormonian to not possess any magic at all. This may be due to genetics; perhaps they are not completely Zormonian. Or, some have theorized that the magic core inside the planet deems some Zormonians "unworthy" of magic, suggesting that the planet has a mind of its own. Otherwise, the reason why some do not possess any magical ability is unknown.

A deity created Zormonia, by the name of Zormon. The Zormonian Religious Texts states that he created the magical core and bestowed magical properties upon the land and its people. Others suggest the moon has something to do with the existence of magic. Strange crystals grow on the surface, and occasionally break off and fall to the planet. They come in four colors: red, pink, blue, and purple. Red has the least power while purple has the highest. When held or used in potions or enchantments, the crystals enhance the effect of the potion and/or the power of the spell or enchantment. These crystals can also be found on Zormonia's surface, in places such as caves, and certain bodies of water such as lakes, rivers, and ponds.

Once a child begins to show signs of possessing a magical ability, the parents train and coach them, or they are sent to a school that specializes in magic training. Not only are they taught how to use and control their powers, they learn about how their society functions, their government, and the history of their planet.

After letting her thoughts wander for a moment, Simina's eyes caught on the spine of a book as she read the title. Her fingers stopped on it. *The Dark Prince,* the spine read, each letter emblazoned in bright, striking gold. Simina carefully stroked her fingers along each word and easily slipped the book from its resting place.

She looked at the cover, which repeated the title. Under the title, it read Lazerian Folklore. She opened the book and read the first page. Before she could even read past the second sentence, Mr. Blikman interrupted her.

"Find anything that interests you yet?" His voice floated across the large room, through the large shelves of books, and into her ears. She looked up and closed the book.

"Hm? Oh yes, I think I have," Simina said and wandered back over to Mr. Blikman's desk, still gazing down at the book. Her fingers itched to turn the pages, eyes yearning to feast upon the words encased within.

Simina looked up, smiled, and handed the book to Mr. Blikman. Applying his spectacles once again, he took it from her and read the title. A very mysterious smile stretched his lips, making Simina's skin crawl. She shivered, brushing her arms as if they were covered in bugs.

"Ah. This is a good one," Mr. Blikman said and opened the book. Simina put her hands behind her back, clasping them. Mr. Blikman had said that about every book she'd ever checked out, but the way he said it this time sounded different. Simina picked up something in his voice that she couldn't quite grasp.

As he closed the book and handed it back to her, he said, "You know, some people say that this story is actually true."

Simina took the book eagerly from his hands.

"But that's just silly. Everyone knows that these stories aren't real," Simina said. Mr. Blikman held up one finger.

"Ah, but how do they know? Just because you've never seen any of these things you read about in stories doesn't mean they don't exist," Mr. Blikman told her. Simina said nothing. He smiled at her.

"You enjoy that book, now," he said with a strange grin and mysterious gleam in his eyes. Simina nodded and walked out. Cool air greeted her once more, tickling her cheeks and sprouting goosebumps all across her flesh.

Curious about what Mr. Blikman said, she wondered if it could be true.

Three

Simina lounged lazily on her bedding with her window open, letting the cool, crisp air float in from the outside as the late afternoon sun leaked through the curtains. She laid on her belly, stretched out across her bed, elbows propped up, holding her face up with her hands. Her legs swung up and down, gently swaying in the air.

Simina hummed to herself as she gazed out the window, watching the bustling village unfold from the confines of her little house. She never tired of hearing the baying of horses and the yapping of various conversations. Every now and then, a cool, gentle breeze wafted in, sweeping soft, windy tendrils across Simina's face. Relaxed, her eyes fell closed.

Simina enjoyed autumn. She found the crisp, chilly breezes of October and November refreshing. (In the Zormonian language, October and November translate to Zobore and Zovere.) Spring and summer were too hot, and winter was too cold, so autumn was the season when the weather was just right. But mostly, she loved watching the leaves change color. She didn't like all the green shrubbery—too much green for her taste.

Simina liked more variety. The lovely autumn colors of red, orange, purple, and yellow blessed her sight each year, painting a beautiful, picturesque, natural work of art. She glanced back down at the page in her book and continued reading the book she'd just received from the library. The yellow pages, crisp and rugged with age, brushed roughly against Simina's fingers, showing the wear and tear from many others before her. Her eyes glued to the words as they scrolled through each sentence, reading:

"The story of the Dark Prince is not an old one. In fact, it's quite new. He's part of Lazerian folklore, recently discovered, which gave me the idea to write this book. Before I continue, I assure you this is not just some legend. The Dark Prince is very real. He's a master of disguise. His dark powers lead you on the path of temptation. Don't dare to seek him out, for the Dark Prince will know. Never wander too far, for the Dark Prince is always at hand.

Do not be deceived by his charm and handsomeness. For he only aims to trick you. The Dark Prince possesses such an evil, dark magic, it'll taint your soul just by being in his presence. When he walks, he leaves a trail of dead flowers in his wake. He leaves a trail of dark, shimmering purple smoke billowing behind him. Never look him in the eye. His eyes are such a mystifying, lavish purple that even one look at them will make you entranced. His eyes are terrifyingly beautiful.

The Dark Prince will lure you in to trick you into doing his evil bidding. Don't be fooled, my friends. Don't be fooled. He has a dark and mystical power that he uses to bestow curses. He's out there somewhere, my reader. Beware, reader. Beware."

Below the passage, just under it, was a hand-drawn picture of a man. The man drawn was indeed very attractive, with stark, ebony hair, very tall, and dressed in some sort of black clothing. A dark feeling crept upon her, winding its fingers through her until it touched her very core. The chill whispered over her, whispering dark words in her mind she couldn't quite hear. She squeezed her arms around herself, rocking back and forth on her bed as the hands of dread clutched at her innards. This wasn't like the naive stories told at bedtime. This book conjured a more foreboding impression.

Any other story she read assured her that it wasn't real. But this book insisted that the Dark Prince's story was real. Simina shook her head and closed the book. *That's just silly,* she told herself. *It can't be real.* It's not real.

Simina knew she shouldn't be scared. Over and over, she told herself it wasn't real, but something inside of her kept contradicting that. She had no idea why, but this "story" didn't feel like just a story. Deep inside, she believed it might be real.

But curious Simina, as always, reopened the book. She wanted to know more. So Simina flipped past chapter one and read on with hunger in her eyes. Simina nervously nibbled on her fingernails, chewing them simultaneously. She figured if the Dark Prince truly existed, she ought to know about him, so she'd be prepared for anything if she ever crossed paths with the Prince. So, she read on.

"The Dark Prince lives on the outskirts of the village Lazera, in the Snowy Hills. His Dark Castle sits upon the largest, tallest snowy hill, towering over everything, casting a shadow over the lands. Inside are the gruesome and grotesque beings of his dark creations.

He prefers to live in cold climates and cloaks himself in all black. This Prince isn't the type you read about in fairytales. The Dark Prince is an evil prince who leaves a dark path of destruction.

He seems to appear out of nowhere suddenly. The Dark Prince can appear and disappear anywhere, just like teleportation. He arrives in a swirl of dark purple smoke and disappears in a puff of more dark purple smoke.

No other man can best him in combat, specifically for this one reason: He wields an enchanted sword only meant for his use. If ever wielded by another man, the blade will turn on the man wielding it because of its enchantments. Never touch his sword.

The Dark Prince of Lazera is really of royal blood. His title is not false. He comes from a line of wealthy royals going back thousands of years. Once his father, the king, dies, the Prince will inherit the throne, as is his right, by being the eldest son and only child. The Dark Royal Family rules Lazera. Once the Prince takes the throne, Lazera will be his kingdom to rule over until he dies. There is nothing we can do to stop him. He is too powerful.

There are two parts of Lazera. The right side of Lazera, and the left. The left is called Autumnville, where we are. The right is called Winterville. Together, they form the village of Lazera. The Dark Castle is smack in the middle of both parts, but just a tad closer to Winterville than Autumnville. Now, Winterville acknowledges the existence of the Dark Prince and his rule, but Autumnville does not believe in him at all. His rule is not as prominent here as it is there. No one in Autumnville has ever seen him, so therefore, they do not believe he exists.

But, the people of Autumnville will, soon enough, soon enough."

Simina heard her father's tromping footsteps enter the house, but she continued to read, not paying any attention to his feet. He walked toward her room and stopped in her doorway. Simina kept reading, not noticing her father's presence.

"Simina!" He raised his voice. Simina jumped, startled by his shout, and flipped her body around, twisting herself to look at him.

"Yes, Father?" she answered shakily, her mind slightly fuzzy from reading for a really long time.

"Why aren't you doing your chores?" he asked sternly. Simina scratched her head quizzically.

"Um...I was, um...I was reading," Simina stuttered, biting her bottom lip. Her father shook his head, but she saw a hint of a smile on his lips.

"Stop filling your mind with that foul mess! It won't do you any good," her father told her. Simina, leaving the book open, climbed off her bed. She stared at her father expectantly.

"Go take care of Winona," he ordered. With a sigh, Simina walked past her father, and he stepped aside. Before she left, she put on her warm, fuzzy brown cloak with a hood. She clipped it together at her throat and went out into the chilly air.

She walked gaily over to their stables around the side of the house. Winona was their horse, or rather, Simina's horse, since she rode it sometimes. Yes, that was another thing Simina liked to do when she couldn't read, fantasize, or play with Ernest. She liked to ride her horse through the woods, feel the wind in her hair, the breeze on her face.

Her father bought Winona a few months after her mother had passed. He did it to cheer her up, and it worked. Simina would ride Winona every day, but it's been a few years, about five, and Winona is aging. But Winona is still in good health and fit for many more rides.

Simina opened the stables where Winona resided, crunching and munching on hay. Most of the ground was covered in hay. Winona was a smoky gray horse with a fleck of white spotting her skin. She was a pretty horse and Simina really liked her. She walked to Winona and put a hand on her mane.

The horse whinnied and straightened her head, chewing the hay. She picked up her brush from where it hung on the wall and put it on her hand. She gently brushed Winona's fur, removing all the fleas and mange. Simina cleaned her hooves and replaced her horseshoes with new ones. From time to time, her mind would wander. She thought about Ernest and what he would be doing right now. Probably out in the woods, climbing trees.

She yearned to go back inside and read her book. She wanted to dream. She enjoyed sitting isolated in her room, curled up on her bed, reading a good book. Life seemed like one big dream to Simina, just a long dream that she didn't want to wake up from.

After brushing through Winona's fur, she stroked her long, silky mane. It was soft. Simina petted her and laid her head against the horse, hugging her around the neck. Winona huffed and nuzzled Simina lovingly. With a giggle, Simina pulled away and scratched Winona behind the ears.

Before she left, she fed her hay, gave her fresh water, and threw a warm blanket over her to keep her warm for the night. She scratched Winona under her chin and then left the stables. Simina returned to her house, where her father waited for her. Her father was in the washroom right across from her bedroom.

He stood at the pump sink, pumping water out, washing the dirt and grime from his hands. Simina watched as her father splashed water on his face and started sputtering. Simina started laughing, trying to hold it back but not succeeding. He looked up at her and narrowed his eyes when he heard her laughing. Simina covered her mouth, stifling her laughter.

He grunted and wiped his face with a clean rag. He tromped toward her. Simina stared at him.

"We need groceries from the market," he grumbled at her. Simina doddled into her room, twiddling her fingers.

"Mmm. Okay." She sat on her bed. Her father stood in her doorway. Simina's hand inched toward her open book.

"Can you go get them?" He handed her a list. Simina quickly snatched it from his hand and stuffed it in her coat pocket without looking at it.

"Yeah. Can I read for a little while?" she asked him, eyeing her book and the black-inked words. Simina wanted to glue her eyes to the words and never remove them from the page. Her father lumbered back into the washroom.

"Uh-huh," he mumbled. Simina turned eagerly to her book and began to read. She'd read at least only a paragraph when her father asked,

"What is it that you're reading anyway?" Simina looked up from the words, surprised that her father would even ask. She noticed he was standing next to her, trying to make out the words on the spine. Simina shrugged.

"Nothing. Just a book." He never paid any attention to anything she read. Simina went back to her reading and casually turned a page, one hand holding her chin up.

"What's it called?" Her father lifted the cover, trying to read what it said, but Simina gently pushed it back down. He'd disturbed the pages and, therefore, disturbed Simina's place in the sentence she was reading. It took her a while to finally respond, but when she did, Simina said, in a dream-like state,

"The Dark Prince." She flipped a page. Her father's face went dead white. Simina, however, paid no mind. Her father, whose name was Gregory, by the way, had heard of the legend. He disapproved of his daughter reading about this sort of thing.

Without a second thought, he snatched the book from under her nose and slammed it shut. Startled, Simina stood in protest. She lunged for the book, but her father held it out of her arm's reach.

"Hey! Give that back!" Simina shrieked. Gregory gave her a look of disapproval.

"Why are you reading such a foul book?" Gregory spat. Simina's lips tightened.

"It's not foul! Now give it back!" She reached for it again, but he would not let her have it.

"You should not taint your soul with such darkness." He looked at the book with revulsion.

Simina frowned. Why does her father suddenly care what she reads? He never cared before; why does he care now?

"Father, please! It's just a book!" Simina protested. Gregory held it in front of her, but still out of reach.

"I forbid you to read this book!" he told Simina. Rage boiled within Simina.

"What's it to you? It's just a stupid book! It isn't even real!" Simina shouted, stomping her foot. Although Simina said it, she didn't know if she really believed it.

Angry and frustrated, Simina took off without another word to her dad, sick of his judgment. *It's just a book!* she thought. *What harm can come out of reading a book?* Shaking her head, she grabbed the grocery basket that she always left sitting by the front door and stormed out of the house.

Huffing, she pulled up the hood of her cloak and stomped through town toward the marketplace. The cool wind blew at her face, whipping through her clothes, chilling her skin. Shivering, Simina pulled her cloak tighter around her shoulders. The cool, refreshing breeze from before disappeared, turning into a snapping, bitter cold chill. Gooseflesh rose on her arms, her skin prickled by the foreboding chill. Rubbing her hands together, she blew out a breath, teeth chattering.

Simina's breath vaporized into the air like a puff of white cloud. Hugging herself, she walked into town.

Four

Tiny snowflakes dotted Simina's cheeks in an icy kiss. She looked up and saw a gray, cloudy sky full of snow clouds. The temperature must have dropped since earlier. Though it's only autumn, it can still get cold enough for snow.

Simina watched each flake flutter down like blue ice crystals. The snow here on Zormonia is different from Earth's. Instead of being white, the snow is a bright, icy crystal blue. Carrying her basket, Simina headed for the market. She was upset about her father. Simina didn't see what the big deal was: It's only a book! An old, lousy, stupid, fictional book meant only to entertain and scare its readers!

Her father always told her that all that stuff wasn't real. If it's not real, why is it so bad to read? Gregory never read books anyway. He only read nonfiction books, like autobiographies, biographies, and documentaries of things that have actually happened.

Simina didn't like all that stuff. She thought it was boring and pointless, and reading boring books gave her headaches. She wanted to be entertained.

Simina reached into her pocket and pulled out the list, then reached into her other pocket to make sure she had her money pouch. Simina always keeps her money pouch in her cloak pocket. She looked at the list. It read:

- 1 Loaf of bread
- 3 Fish
- 1 Bag of orange-flavored grass
- Bottle of Sweet Wine
- 10 Frost apples

Simina nodded. She should have enough for all that. The frost apples weren't too expensive.

I know the items on the list sound odd, but you are an earthling. Zormonia is different. On this planet, there are fruits called frost apples, which grow in colder areas and are icy blue. They taste just like regular apples, except they leave your mouth feeling cold, like a mint, but ten times better. The clashing combination of sweet and tart provides an unforgettable sensation dancing on your tastebuds.

The grass on this planet changes colors with the seasons. In autumn, it's orange; in winter, icy blue; in spring, it's magenta; and in summer, it's green. On Zormonia, the grass is edible and harvested in grass farms, each color having a different flavor. The orange grass tastes like oranges. Blue grass tastes like ice blue raspberries. Pink tastes like strawberry and green tastes like limes. The grass can be walked on, but before being harvested, it must be cleaned and sterilized before consumed.

Once Simina arrived at the little marketplace vendor, she handed the list to the salesman. He nodded and turned to give her the requested items. Simina placed her basket on his vendor stand, waiting patiently with her hand on her money pouch. She watched the little odd-looking man place her requested items into the basket.

Two yellow antennas poked out of his head. Large, round eyes stared back at her, popping out more so from the glasses he wore, which gave him a buggish look. Simina smiled, admiring the man's oddness. She thought it suited him well.

Once he'd placed three fish, a loaf of bread, a bottle of sweet wine, a bag of orange-flavored grass, and ten frost apples in her basket, he adjusted his glasses and fixed a blinky, buggy stare on Simina.

"That'll be seventeen zyros," the man buzzed, his voice high-pitched and nasal. Simina took out her money pouch, untied the string from it, and began to count out the zyros. Absent-mindedly, she picked up the basket. Zyros are the Zormonian form of currency. Zyros are only the coins, while zyro dollars are paper money. The zyros are pink, round coins with an odd person's face stamped on it, though we don't know who. Other Zormonian coins of greater or lesser value are blue or purple. The paper money on Zormonia is pink, blue, and purple, depending on value, instead of just green.

Holding the basket, Simina counted seventeen zyros for the man. In the middle of her counting, she heard a puppy yipping. It sounded close as if it were only a few feet from her. She did not look up, though; she was too focused on counting out the zyros and did not want to break her concentration because if she did, she'd lose count and have to start all over again.

"...fifteen, sixteen, seventeen," Simina finished counting and handed the money to the man. The puppy yipped, jumping up and down at Simina's feet. The little fella caught a whiff of her fresh fish, and its bitty little nose wiggled. He stood on its hind legs, nose reaching up toward Simina's basket of goodies. Simina didn't notice, however, she was preoccupied with talking to the salesman. One fish's fin hung over the basket's side, just within the puppy's reach.

The puppy barked, "Arf!" and lolled out its tongue with satisfaction. It pounced, grabbed the tail fin of the fish, and pulled. Simina didn't notice the puppy was there until there came a tug on her basket. Beside her was a stray puppy with its jaws locked on the tail fin of one of her fish. Simina attempted to swat the puppy away.

"Shoo! Go away!" Simina waved her hand at the puppy, but it didn't listen. Instead, it yanked on the fish, pulling it out of the basket. Simina tried pulling it away from the pup but only worsened it. The puppy tipped her basket over, causing everything in her basket to tumble out all over the ground with multiple thumps going everywhere. The pull of the puppy's jaws was so strong that it pulled the entire basket and its contents out of her hand and onto the ground. Her two other fish fell to the ground with a loud splat. Simina screeched, all of her goodies falling onto the ground. Both hands flew to each side of her face. She gasped.

"Oh no! You bad thing!" she scolded the puppy, who still held the fish in its mouth. The salesman rushed over to help pick up her goods.

"Oh dear," he mumbled nasally. Wagging its tail, the puppy turned and hopped off with her fish. Simina growled.

"Hey! You come back here with that!" she shouted and began to chase the puppy, dropping her basket. By this time, Simina had already disturbed the crowd of villagers. Everyone stared at her as she ran, pushing through the throng of people and merchants, chasing after the dog. The salesman got on his hands and knees and started putting her items back in the basket. He also supplied her with another fish and decided to leave that one free. He picked it back up and placed it on his stand, leaving it there for her when she returned.

Meanwhile, Simina shoved through the crowd, running after the pup. Her breaths puffed heavily into the air, forming little white puffs. Cold, bitter air blew against her cheeks, flushing her face pink.

The little mongrel! Simina thought with great disdain.

"Give that back, you wretched beast!" Simina shrieked. She chased the small dog to the outskirts of the village, into the Snowy Hills at the edge of the Snowy Woods. A terrible wind blew, snow billowing around her in a wild, violent torrent. It wildly blew Simina's hair about her head, hood flying off, cloak flowing out behind her.

Panting and shivering, Simina stopped, ankle deep in snow, feet standing on something slippery and firm. But when Simina arrived here, she didn't see the puppy anywhere. It was gone. She only saw her fish lying on a mound of snow like it had been dropped, and puppy paw-prints ran into the woods in the other direction. Simina shook her head. *That wretched thing!* A howling wind made her teeth chatter.

Simina was about to turn around and head back home, but something odd caught her eye. A few feet before her, she saw a trail of wispy, glittering dark purple smoke. Her eyes followed the trail to what it led up to. Standing at least ten feet away, she saw the figure of a man, standing tall and sure, his back turned to her.

Squinting, Simina took two steps forward to get a better look. Snow crunched under her feet. Who is that? Indeed, it was a man. From what Simina could see, he wore all black. He wore an expensive-looking trench coat that fell to his ankles but did not touch the ground. His hair was also black, ruffled by the wild wind.

She stared curiously at him, wondering who he was and why he was standing out in the middle of a mini snowstorm. Simina reached out a hand toward the glittering, dark purple mist, trying to touch it. Her hand went right through it. Oddly though, it wisped and curled around her right index finger, like a swirl. Simina's jaw dropped and quickly took her hand away. She looked back at the man.

She saw his head slightly turned, and the man moved. In one swift movement, he turned and faced her. A pair of glimmering, purple eyes met hers, and Simina froze. She swore her heart stopped beating.

He had such a beautiful face that his beauty was simply indescribable. His skin was a pale olive complexion, and he had a sharp, curved jawline with a prominent, striking jaw. Long, black lashes swooned over his eyes, giving him a beguiling look.

Simina knew of only one person with purple eyes. Her eyes widened in fear. He wore all black, had black hair, and skin as pale as a ghost. Lavishly purple eyes...Simina fell in love with his eyes at first sight but shook herself out of it to keep herself thinking straight. Yes, sure, purple smoke explains everything. He looks exactly like the drawing in the book.

Simina had already thought about the words before she said them. Her lips moved to form the words.

"Dark Prince..." Simina breathed out in a gasp, fear choking the breath out of her lungs. And much to her chagrin, he was, like the book said, quite handsome. Quite, however, was an understatement.

The Prince stared curiously at Simina, wondering why this girl was out and about in these parts. He'd never seen this girl before, though he usually never saw anyone out here. He observed her keenly. She looked young, with wavy, chocolate-brown curls blowing about her head in the wind. Her cheeks were pink from the cold, eyes popping open wide in astonishment and fearful.

The Prince was used to that reaction. He just didn't think a girl so pretty could look so scared. He wanted to know her name.

"D-Dark Prince..." he heard her say a second time. Simina was completely freaking out. The Prince blinked at her. *She knows who I am,* he thought, *how intriguing.* Simina raised her arm, pointing a finger at him.

"Dark Prince! You're the Dark Prince!" she shrieked over the wind's howling. An amused smile slightly lifted the corners of his lips. The Prince stepped toward her. Simina jumped backward.

"Don't you come near me!" Simina shouted. Fear shook her body from top to bottom.

The Prince stood still. He stared at her with intense intrigue. *What is she so afraid of?* The Dark Prince wondered. *I'm not going to hurt her.* Her entire body shook, chilled to the bone, teeth clattering and chattering.

She'll get sick if she stays out here any longer in this weather. He looked down at her feet. The Prince noticed she stood on a thin sheet of ice, and a small crack formed up the middle. He pointed at her feet and spoke.

"You're standing on ice. It's cracking," he said.

Simina almost failed to hear him speak. He'd only just stood and stared at her, giving her odd looks and now he speaks? She didn't think he could speak.

Simina, however, did look down at her feet. She was standing on ice that was cracking and splitting in two between her feet. She looked fearfully back up at the Prince, who smiled strangely at her.

"You should move," he told her. With a leap, Simina jumped off the ice and into a pile of snow, falling onto her knees. The Prince watched her. She was entertaining to watch. Struggling and in a hurry, the girl flung herself up in a weird way, slinging snow about, and took off in the opposite direction, running like hell.

The Prince watched her run away and moved his eyes back to the spot she'd previously been standing. He cocked his head to the side, staring at the cracked ice and disturbed snow.

"That's odd. Why did she run away?" the Prince said aloud, not talking to anyone in particular, but rather, asking it to the spot where the girl had previously been standing.

Five

Fear overwhelmed Simina as she fled through town, her heart pounding with terror. She had just seen the Dark Prince, a figure she had believed to be nothing more than a myth. Now, she knew he was real—the stories weren't just folklore.

Remembering her groceries, she ran back to the sales vendor, grabbed her basket, and continued running home. Simina didn't dare to stop. Maybe the Dark Prince would follow her and try to put a curse on her; just like the book said. Her father was right, she should've listened to him.

All she wanted was to go home to her father, where she knew she'd be safe. She couldn't believe her eyes. The Dark Prince looked exactly like his drawing in that book. It was him. The author must have seen him before; that's where he got the idea. He told her it was true. Why hadn't she believed him?

Simina shouldn't have gotten that book. She regretted picking it up. Shivering, she busted through the door of her house, heaving heavy breaths. She set the basket of groceries on the table and looked wildly around for her father, Gregory. She searched her whole house, but Simina could not find him. Trying to hold it all together, Simina ran outside. She found him outside, in the backyard, chopping wood. Desperate, Simina rushed to him.

"Father!" Simina yelped. Gregory looked up to see a terrified Simina running at him. He dropped the axe and turned to her. Simina flung herself on him, and he caught her.

"Simina, what's wrong? What is the matter?" he asked. She grabbed both of his arms, staring up at him with pale terror on her face.

"I saw him, Father, I saw him! He's real!" Simina squeaked. The backs of her eyes began to burn. Gregory was confused. He didn't know what she was talking about.

"Who, Simina? You saw who?" He thought she'd gone crazy. Simina's voice cracked.

"Him!" she cracked, blinking her eyes. Her vision blurred slightly and she sucked in a rattling breath.

"The Dark Prince, Father! The Dark Prince! He's real, Father, he's real!" Her voice trembled. She watched her father's eyes narrow. Did he believe her?

Then, Simina cried. Tears leaked from her eyes, streaming down her cheeks. She buried her face in her father's chest, bawling like a three-year-old. She'd never been so terrified in her life. Confused, her father hugged her to him, petting and stroking her hair. She kept muttering about how she saw someone—the Dark Prince.

"Simina, Simina, stop causing all this fuss. Calm down, my child, it's all right," he spoke soothingly. Gregory knew the Dark Prince wasn't real. He recalled earlier that day how he'd gotten after her about reading it. Perhaps she'd been reading a little too much of it.

He pulled her away slightly to look at her. He wiped her tears. Simina's entire body shook, trembling, and she hiccuped. Her face was flushed red like a cherry from crying.

"Now, Simina, tell me what all this is about, hm?" he asked gently, now that she'd calmed down a bit. Simina nodded and took a deep breath. She licked her lips nervously, her eyes flitting about around the room.

"Well, I'd gone to get the groceries, just like you asked. I was about to go home when a stray puppy came along and pulled the fish out of my basket. I chased it and chased it until I stopped on the outskirts of the village, in the Snowy Hills. The puppy was gone. Ahead, a few feet away, I saw a man. He turned toward me, and I saw his face. He looked just like the book's Dark Prince: I swear to you, Father, I'm telling the truth!"

She looked at her Father to see if he believed her. She could not tell. He looked doubtful but said nothing. Gently, he stroked her hair.

"Simina, I think you've been reading a little too much of that book. It's been a long day; you're tired. Why don't you go to your room and rest, hm?" Gregory suggested. Feeling defeated, she slumped in his arms.

"You go ahead and rest. I'll take care of supper," her father assured. Simina nodded and pulled away. On weak legs, she slouched drearily back into her cabin and shut the front door. She shrugged off her cloak, kicked off her galoshes, and slumped off to her bedroom. Once there, she saw the book, lying overturned and open on the floor, pages bent at the corners.

Heated with rage and anger, Simina picked up the wretched book and threw it across the room with a frustrated yell. It hit the opposite wall and crashed to the floor in a crumpled heap. Then, overcome with fear again, Simina flung herself onto her bed and buried herself under the covers until she fell asleep.

* * *

Simina woke to the wonderful and comforting aroma of food cooking. But that's not what woke her. What woke her was the sound of a heavy fist slamming against the front door of her house. Startled, Simina jolted under the covers, tangled in her blankets until she managed to kick them off. Lying flat on her back, head resting on her pillow, she listened closely. Her door was open, and they didn't live in a very large house so she could hear anything happening inside. She heard her father's footsteps across the kitchen to the door, creaking as he opened the wooden slat door.

"Yes? How may I help you?" her father's polite voice asked. Not one but two pairs of boots entered her house, and the door gently closed with a soft click.

"Are you Gregory Gorchev, the father of Simina Gorchev?" an authoritative voice asked. Simina's heart skipped a beat.

"Yes, yes, I am. What is this about?"

"This is a matter concerning your daughter, Simina Gorchev. Is she available now?" another deeper voice asked this time. A dark, uneasy feeling quelled within Simina. Her father was silent for a moment. Simina hoped he wouldn't call her down there. She did not want to go. From the sound of it, they possibly were Lazerian Officials, otherwise known as soldiers who work for the government. The government hardly interfered with citizens' affairs, let alone peasant affairs. What business could they have with her and her father? They've done nothing wrong, unless a bigger problem is going on than what Simina can surmise.

"She is asleep at the moment. I do not wish to disturb her," her father answered. One official sighed heavily.

"All right," the authoritative voice said, the first voice Simina had heard. Her father cleared his throat.

"What business are you talking about?" he asked the two officials.

"Your daughter is twenty, correct?" She assumed her father nodded because, after a brief pause, the official continued.

"When is she going to be married?" the second, deeper voice asked. After the question, there was a long, tense silence that followed. At the word "married," Simina nearly fell out of bed. She wanted to liquefy herself and melt right into the sheets. Married? Why do they care? *I won't marry until I feel like it,* Simina told herself. *Frankly, it's none of their business!* Simina hadn't even begun to consider the idea of marriage. And even if she had, who would she marry? There was nobody she was particularly interested in. After a long silence, her father responded.

"She isn't," he said, sounding like he'd forced out the words. The officials made sounds of disapproval.

"She has to be married soon. She has come of age. I trust you have been considering some possible suitors for her?" the first voice questioned. Again, another tense silence. Her father huffed a deep breath.

"No, I haven't," he replied sharply—more sounds of disapproval from the officials.

"You do understand the severity of this situation, Mr. Gorchev, correct?" Simina hated how falsely polite they sounded when speaking to her father.

"Yes," her father answered between gritted teeth. Simina shivered.

"She has to be married soon. If you cannot provide her with a proper suitor, then she will have to go elsewhere," the deep voice said, his tone sharp.

"What do you mean, 'Go elsewhere'?" her father snarled, polite manners now gone, replaced with something ruder.

"She will have to leave your care. She has family elsewhere, yes?" the first Official confirmed. Gregory gathered himself, trying to remain respectful.

"Yes, my sister, she lives on the right side of Lazera with her two daughters," he told them.

"Then, if you can't provide her with a proper suitor, that is where she will be sent," the deep-voiced official said. Her father took a deep breath.

"I'd be more comfortable if Simina chose for herself when and whom she should marry. It shouldn't be up to me, you, or anyone else!" Gregory protested. Simina would have liked to see their faces when her father told them that. Both made incredulous sounds.

"Mr. Gorchev, a man has the authority and dominance to choose what is right for their daughters. Women can't choose for themselves! They don't know what's good for them!" the first official said incredulously.

"Are you saying my daughter doesn't know how to choose what's right for her?" Simina heard her father's voice become threatening.

"How does a woman know what's right for her?" the second official said, laughing.

"Anyway, that's beside the point. The point is, you need to find a suitor by the end of the week or we'll send her away to her aunt and cousins," the first official said, getting back to business.

"And, if she is sent away? What will happen to her there?" Gregory asked, fearing the worst. Either way, his daughter would be taken from him no matter what he did, so it really didn't matter.

"What happens to her then is not in our jurisdiction. The government doesn't rule over the Right Side of Lazera," the first official explained. Simina's brow wrinkled. Then who did? Is the Right Side of Lazera under another ruler? Who? Simina's brain flooded with confusion.

"Anyhow, you have a week. Have a good evening," the first voice said, and Simina listened as their tromping footsteps went to the door. She heard the door open with a creak, and they left with a slam. The house fell into uncomfortable silence. Simina breathed a huge sigh of relief now that they were gone. The insides of her gut coiled with unease, writhing like worrisome snakes.

Simina listened to her father grumble and curse under his breath as he slammed around stuff in the kitchen. A seed of despair planted itself deep inside her being at the thought of marriage. A week. She had a week to find someone to marry, or she'd be sent away to live with her aunt and two cousins. She'd met them once but did not know them well. They weren't even at her mother's funeral.

Simina waited to see if her father would go to her room to get her up and tell her what the officials had said. Dinner smelled about ready. Her father sighed, and she listened as he bustled about the kitchen again in a less angry manner. About now, he was probably dousing the fire in the wood stove and taking the pot filled with fish stew from the stove's surface. Simina could feel the wood stove's heat from the kitchen. He bustled about for a few seconds more, setting the table, and Simina finally heard his footsteps approaching her bedroom.

She quickly rolled to her side and closed her eyes, pretending to be asleep. She didn't want her father to think she was worried, and she didn't want him to see her concerned because it would upset him. Gregory stood in Simina's doorway and knocked on her door with a gentle rap. She pretended to be aroused from sleep. She stirred and gazed up at her father, trying to look sleepy-eyed.

"Simina, are you awake? Dinner's ready," he told her in a soft voice. Simina sat, rubbing her eyes. She saw her father's tired, drawn face, with bags under his eyes. Her stomach growled.

"It's ready? Okay, Father, I'll be down." She slid off her bed. Her father nodded and walked away, seeming quite solemn. It hurt Simina's heart to see her father so sad. Sighing, she got up and walked into the kitchen to eat supper with her father.

She sat, facing a bowl of fresh, steaming fish stew that was appealing. A piece of bread sat on a napkin beside her bowl and some orange grass. Quickly, her father said a blessing and they began to eat in silence, the stench of the officials' presence wafting through them, giving them a feeling of staleness. Simina sipped her stew and looked at her father, who hadn't touched his food.

"What's wrong, Father?" Simina asked. Not wanting to worry his daughter, Gregory sighed and shook his head.

"Never you mind, my daughter."

Simina leaned forward and placed a tender hand on his arm in comfort.

"Father, please. What is it?" Simina begged him to tell her. Gregory knew he'd have to tell her sometime and since it concerned her, he thought it fair to explain the situation that arose. With a sigh, he told her.

"Two Lazerian officials were just here…" he explained. Simina already knew, but her father didn't realize she'd listened. The situation seemed much worse after hearing her father tell her. Simina grew weary with her troubles. She did not want to leave her father or be married. Gregory knew this about Simina; he still considered her too young. He was not ready to give up his daughter. *She's still so young, why must she be married now? It isn't quite time yet, not quite time.*

"But, Father, I don't want to get married," Simina protested. Gregory nodded.

"I know, my child. I know. But you have to; it's the law," he told her miserably. He just didn't know what to do. Simina wanted to cry but knew she shouldn't. Either way, she knew she wouldn't get to stay with him. If she married, she'd have to live with her new husband and probably wouldn't get to see her father very often. And if she chose to go to the right side of Lazera to live with her aunt and cousins, she still wouldn't see him.

Simina succumbed to misery. Just the other day, Simina had been overflowing with joy, like everything on the planet was right. Now, she'd have to make a choice that could possibly change her life forever. Simina's father placed his hand over hers.

"Don't worry anymore, child. You go to sleep now. We'll figure this out," Gregory told his daughter, trying to assure her that it wouldn't be so bad.

Simina finished her stew, washed up before bed, and finally laid her worried and tortured soul to rest for the night. Once alone in the confines of her dark room, she finally allowed herself to cry into her pillow.

<h1 style="text-align:center">Six</h1>

An entire week passed, and within that week, Gregory produced many suitors for Simina, but she denied each one. She did not like any of them, so she refused every one. He even recommended her friend Ernest to her, but she still denied him even then. Even though Ernest was her friend, she did not want to marry him. Ernest agreed. Ernest did not want to force anything on Simina that she did not want.

Secretly, Gregory was glad that she'd denied every suitor he offered. He kept this to himself because if the government found out, they would think he was purposefully making her reject the suitors. Simina didn't know any of these men, and Gregory did not want his daughter to marry someone she didn't know and wouldn't be happy with.

Frustrated, Simina was reluctant to make a choice. She did not want to marry anyone, but she did not want to leave her home. She'd lived here her whole life. This is where her mother had lived. This village was the only place she'd ever known. And time was running out. She had to make a choice soon. Depressed, Simina found herself in the stables with Winona. Sighing, she rested her head on her neck.

"What am I going to do, Winona?" Tears threatened to spill like a rushing waterfall. Winona only huffed in response. The stable gate creaked and Simina glanced up, her cheeks flushed and tear stained. Ernest stood there sheepishly and waved.

"Hi," he said cautiously. At the sight of her best friend, Simina cried harder. She ran to him and flung herself into his arms. He squeezed her tightly and Simina inhaled his familiar, comforting scent.

"I'm sorry this is happening," he whispered into her hair.

She shook her head. "It's not your fault."

"I know that," he sighed.

Ernest pulled away from her, smiling sadly. "It's not too late, you know."

Simina sniffled. "What's not too late?"

"To marry me...you can stay here, then," he suggested again. "And it will just be a marriage in name only. You can do what you want, and things won't change. You'd just live with me. We don't have to do all those other things..."

"But that would just be settling," Simina replied. "I don't want that, and I know you don't want that either."

Ernest sighed heavily. "I know...I just wish there was something I could do."

She shrugged. "Maybe it's time I finally had an adventure. I'm always talking about wanting one. This might be it. Maybe this is the start of *my* fairytale."

Ernest knew that Simina was trying to make light of the situation, but her misguided view of the world bothered him. "Life isn't like a fairytale, Simina. This is real."

"I know that..." She scuffed her shoe in the dirt.

"If you change your mind, you know where to find me." With one last hug, Simina watched Ernest wander away one last time.

***

By the end of the week, she'd refused at least over a dozen young men. Sometimes, she'd be offered at least five a day, each man pledging how good he'd be for her. Even if Simina thought one suitor was attractive, she did not want to choose him because she didn't know him. When the officials arrived at the end of the week, Simina hadn't chosen, and she'd already sealed her fate. She knew she'd have to go away to live with her aunt and cousins on the right side of Lazera.

The officials arrived that evening, on the last day of the week, as supper was readying. Simina opened the door for them as they knocked. They stood at the threshold, dressed in all the finest material used to make the finest garments for the people considered to have "high status." Her father ushered them in, and they all sat at the kitchen table. Simina trying to remain unnoticed.

"Good evening to the both of you," the first official greeted. He was a short, stout little man but muscular in build and handsome. She recognized his voice from the other day. The other official was very tall but fat, with balding hair.

"I trust you've produced some suitors?" the first asked. Simina's father nodded.

"Yes. I have." The second one sat up straighter.

"Who has she chosen?" They asked her father like she wasn't even there. Frankly, she didn't want them to notice her. Lazerian officials made her uneasy. Her father shrugged.

"None of them," Gregory said, trying not to let the smile show on his lips. The officials' jaws dropped. Simina had to turn away to avoid laughing and covered her mouth with her hand. The first official managed to gather himself and speak.

"Excuse me? W-what did you say?" he stuttered, flabbergasted. Simina's father tilted his chin confidently.

"She rejected each suitor, each one," he said. The officials gawked at Simina and opened their mouths. The second official spoke this time.

"You turned down every one?" he asked her, finally speaking directly to Simina. Timidly, she nodded.

"Yes, sir," she muttered, quiet as a mouse. The first official looked offended and stood. Following his lead, the second official stood. The first official cleared his throat.

"Well then. She must be taken elsewhere, where she will be better provided. I suggest you start packing your things. Your carriage will be departing tomorrow morning," the first official told Simina. And with that, he tipped his hat.

"Good day to you." And with swift, sure movements, they showed themselves out. Simina slumped in her chair, her posture now slouchy and relaxed. She was so relieved it was over. Simina and her father glanced at each other, her father's eyes filled with sadness. He gave her a small smile. Simina wished he wouldn't look at her like that. It nearly made her cry.

"I suppose we better get packing," her father told her, and stood.

* * *

It didn't take her long to pack. Simina didn't have many things, just some clothes. That was mainly it. After packing, they ate supper in silence and went to bed. Simina rose early the following day to prepare for her long journey. From what she assumed, they'd be taking a sturdy carriage and possibly have to use a sleigh to get through the Snowy Hills. But Simina had heard of carriages with wheels that could conform to blades like ones on a sleigh. They'd have to be changed manually, of course. Since transport was by carriage, and they'd have to travel a long distance, it would take days to arrive at their destination.

She'd packed one parcel of food containing a few slices of bread, some frost apples, and orange grass. That should be plenty for a few days. She put on her cloak, scarf, and shawl for good measure. She stuffed her feet into her galoshes. Simina heard the neighing of the horses and the clop-clop of their hooves on the concrete. She'd already said her goodbyes to Winona earlier this morning. It had only taken her thirty minutes to prepare and another thirty for the carriage to arrive.

Simina turned and gave her father one last tight hug. He squeezed her tight in a comforting way, almost lifting her off her feet. She enjoyed his warm embrace one last time, wishing she didn't have to leave him. But, it was the law. After a good long time, he pulled away to look at her and placed both hands on her shoulders. He tucked a strand of hair behind her ear. Gregory hated seeing his daughter go.

"You be safe now, all right? Be good to your aunt, huh?" he said to her. Tears in her eyes, Simina nodded.

"Okay. I will," she assured.

"Try to stay out of mischief. You write to me every day when you can. Okay?" Simina nodded, not knowing what else to say.

"I promise," was all she could think to say. He pulled her in for one last hug and pulled away.

"I love you," her father said as she pulled away.

"I love you too, Father," she choked out. Someone outside yelled at her to hurry. Quickly, she turned and walked out the door, where the carriage waited.

To her surprise, Simina saw Ernest waiting to say goodbye. She smiled and hugged him.

Ernest hugged her tightly, not wanting to let her go. He sighed a sorrowful, breathless sigh into her ear.

"I'm really going to miss you, Simina," Ernest said sadly once he'd pulled away. Simina smiled.

"I'll miss you too, Ernest," she told him, and planted a small, soft kiss to his cheek. Ernest blushed but said nothing.

"Write to me?" His voice sounded shaky, like he was trying not to cry. She nodded.

"Of course." Hanging his head, Ernest stepped aside. The carriage driver opened the door for her. Holding up her skirt, she climbed in and took a seat, parcel in hand. The driver gently shut the door. Final preparations were made and the driver climbed aboard his horse. He flicked the whip.

"Hee-ya!" he said, and the horse trotted away. The carriage rolled forward. Simina stared out the window, watching solemnly as her father and Ernest waved her goodbye.

<h1 style="text-align:center">Seven</h1>

A few days passed, and they hadn't yet arrived. Simina was sure it had been at least three days since she left.

The driver had to stop once they'd gotten into the real snowy area and change the wheels to blades so it would be a sleigh.

She'd been riding in the sleigh carriage three days straight without stopping, and it was too cold for Simina to pee. Luckily, there was a pee pot in the carriage. But Simina was cramped and tired, and her head hurt. She'd eaten a few frost apples, at least one a day. She was trying to ration and not eat so much because she knew that it would be a long trip.

Simina had sometimes fallen asleep in the carriage but didn't like to because it jostled around too much, and she woke with sore muscles. The carriage was downright uncomfortable. They'd stop to rest for maybe one to two hours a few times, but then kept going. Her uncleanliness bothered her to an extreme extent, as she had not washed for three days. Anyway, it was the fourth night of travel, and the night was cold and dark; the sky matted over with a mass of gray, shutting out the light of the stars. A great, howling wind blew, rocking the carriage dangerously. A flurry of snow billowed through the air. Frost covered the little carriage windows. Simina shivered, her teeth chattering, and pulled her cloak tighter around her shoulders.

They were traveling across a massive embankment of snow, and that's all that there was—just snow upon snow. Simina now understood why they called it the Snowy Hills. It was just huge hills of piled-up snow, a barren wasteland of snow. Nothing was out there at all.

Simina didn't like the sound the wind made. It sounded like creepy whispering voices saying things to her she couldn't understand. She tried to tune it out, but it was just too much. The driver thought about stopping, but he didn't think stopping in the middle of a storm would be wise. He wanted to get through it.

The wind blew violently, and with so much snow going everywhere, it made it hard to see. The horse moved steadily forward, walking carefully through the snow, following the guidance of the driver, who told the horse where to go.

The Snowy Hills weren't just snow. Under the snow, on the lower parts of the hills, was a thin sheet of ice—prone to crack and break at any given time because it covered a stream. They'd just come down from a steep snowy hill, landing with a thump on the ground of the lesser snow-covered area. The horse's hard hoof landed with a heavy thud on the ice underneath.

Suddenly, there was a ferocious lurch as the horse jolted to a stop, which caused Simina to lurch forward in her seat. The horse neighed with panic and Simina heard an earsplitting crack of ice splitting in two. The sound spooked the horse and it started wildly bucking and jerking everywhere. This caused the carriage to sway violently back and forth as the ice under the carriage split. The carriage fell halfway into icy water without support.

The horse caused the carriage to fall and tip over as it broke from its reins and took off into the night. The driver had fallen off and the heavy carriage had dropped on top of him, crushing him beneath it, between the carriage and the ice. Simina was jostled roughly back and forth within the carriage, hitting her head many times. Stars constantly flickered before her eyes, but she didn't black out. However, Simina knew that it might be imminent. While the carriage was jerking, Simina was violently thrown from the carriage, and into the snowy, slushy ice.

She landed roughly on the cold, hard ice. The impact of her body hitting the ice caused it to crack and split under her, revealing freezing water underneath. Simina's body slid against the slick ice, rubbing her skin raw with the burning cold of the ice. Simina's head smacked against the hard ice; she hit her head so hard that it knocked her out cold.

Instant blackness fell over Simina's mind, and she remembered nothing else.

* * *

A dark shadow stretched over Simina's limp body, lying on the ice. Her lips were starting to turn blue from being kissed with the cold. The Dark Prince stared down at the girl's limp form;. his purple eyes glistened with interest. *I've seen her before,* he thought to himself. The Prince looked around the scene. The carriage had tipped over, probably from the jolt of an out-of-control horse and the furious winds.

The wind blew violently around him. The Prince saw the ice open its wide mouth beneath her, ready to swallow. He crouched low to the girl's body and placed two pale fingers on her neck. Her icy skin radiated through the warm tips of his fingers, almost as if she may already be frozen solid. Her gentle, thrumming pulse kicked against his fingers and then The Prince leaned down closer to hear her shallow, labored breathing.

"She's alive," the Prince muttered. *I should probably get her out of here. She might have already gone into hypothermia.* He picked her head up, placing her head on his shoulder, and slipped his other arm under her legs. The Prince slowly eased her up off the ice and into his arms, cradling her small frame against his chest.

Staring down at her face, the Prince brushed a gentle finger across her cold cheek. The Prince vanished with a swirl of dark purple smoke, leaving a trailing puff of purple mist.

Eight

Simina woke many hours later as a pained whimper escaped her. First, the throbbing pain in her skull greeted her, and then came the overall aching of her entire body. As feeling returned to her body, she blinked her eyes open to see a bright light shining. At first, she thought she was dead, but realized that if she were dead, she wouldn't be feeling so much pain.

She laid upon a cloud-like surface, soft and cushiony. Her body melded into it, the strange yet comfortable surface contouring with her. Smooth, silk sheets graced her skin. The place was very unfamiliar. Everything looked ornate and expensive, with stone walls made of black concrete and a marble floor. A small, very pretty crystalline chandelier hung above Simina's head.

Out of the corner of her eye, Simina saw the figure of a man standing by a window, looking out of it. The light made it too bright for her to see, so she squinted. But whoever it was looked as beautiful as an angel. She stared at him. Simina was sure she recognized him: She'd seen him somewhere before.

She tried to move, to shift her position so she could see better, but that only caused her pain in her limbs and torso. Simina cried out sharply, wincing, and settled herself back down again. At this sound, the Prince snapped his head sharply in her direction. A pair of purple eyes met hers. Instant fear flooded her soul at the sight of him. *Oh, my Zormon, not him again. How did he find me?*

The last thing Simina remembered was being flung out of the carriage and into the snow after the driver lost control of the horse. After that, she remembered only black. Simina pushed herself into a sitting position, no longer feeling the pain in her body. She didn't care about that, she just wanted to get away from him. Simina recognized him now. His black hair, pale olive skin, and she could never forget those eyes.

His expression did not change when he saw that she was awake. It remained blank and unreadable. His lips pursed ever so slightly that Simina barely noticed. "Do not be alarmed." His deep, robust voice startled Simina even more. She pulled the blankets tighter around her, feeling they'd somehow provide her with security.

The Prince wore a beige long-sleeved shirt that showed off part of his chest and tight black leather pants. He held himself in a very dignified, graceful manner, with his back straight and his hands folded neatly behind him. He stared at her curiously. Simina had no idea how she had gotten there. "Where am I? How did I get here?" she asked in a frightened voice. The Prince answered her curtly.

"This is my castle. I carried you here." Simina's stomach churned at the image of him carrying her, of her being in his arms. She held her stomach with both hands and wanted to vomit. *He touched her.* Simina shivered and hugged herself, uncomfortable with the violation of his action.

"You carried me?" Simina nearly shouted this at him, about ready to shed off her skin. He nodded.

"It was either that, or let you die," the Prince spat. "Believe me, I considered the latter." He took a few steps toward the foot of the bed. Simina flinched.

"Don't come near me!" she shouted. A sudden fever swept over her, her cheeks flushing.

He sneered at her. "This is the thanks I get for saving your life? I should have let you rot."

He took another step. "Nevertheless, you are under my care. I need to check your wounds."

With a shriek, Simina leaped off the bed, landed on the floor, rolled, and jumped to her feet at the opposite end of the room.

Breathing heavier than usual, Simina sucked in the air as her muscles began to burn. The Prince blinked in surprise, raising his eyebrows. Despite her wounds, she still displayed amazing dexterity. He was impressed. Simina blinked a few times, a worn-down feeling coming over her. She took a deep breath and shook it off. Somehow, she had to escape from him. The Prince treaded carefully towards her. He liked her spirit and couldn't help but smile. She pointed a sharp, wavering finger at him.

"Stay back!" she trilled.

"Do not run," the Prince warned. She'd only be making it harder for herself. Without a second thought, Simina turned right around, swung the door open, and ran, ran for her life.

Annoyed, the Prince rolled his eyes and sighed with exasperation. *There really is no point in running,* he thought. *I can just catch her anyway.*

"Why do they always run?" he muttered.

Simina, on the other hand, was running down a long hallway. She ran until she found a spiraling staircase, her momentum nearly causing her to topple down the grand set. She quickly descended the stairs, arrived in a foyer, and ran out two big double doors. She ran outside, stumbling into the bright blue snow.

Her breath swooped out into the air in little vapor clouds, swirling in curly cues. The biting cold chewed her skin with teeth made of icicles. Simina ran staggering through piles of snow, heading for the Snowy Woods that was easily within her reach. She wanted to get as far from him as possible. *He'll probably come after me.*

Within moments she was out of breath but made it to the trees. Simina slumped against one, terribly out of breath, panting and wheezing. She placed her hand against the tree's trunk, stopping to catch her breath momentarily.

No sooner than when she stopped, she looked up to see the Dark Prince standing three feet from her. Simina choked, and whirled back around to run again, but somehow, he was already in front of her, when a second ago, he was in the opposite direction. Gasping, Simina pressed her back against the tree. *How did he get here so fast?* Simina's head spun. She had to leave; she had to.

"You are not well," the Prince said. Simina couldn't stand it. She had to look anywhere but at those freaky purple eyes. She wanted to scream. Simina observed everywhere but his face. She noticed a sword strapped to his waist. The silver hilt gleamed, studded with diamonds, but embedded in the top was a dark amethyst crystal. It sparkled in the bright light. With a quick, sure movement, Simina slipped the sword from his waist belt, unsheathing it. It's too bad she didn't remember what she read about his sword and its enchantment.

Simina attempted to raise the sword with both hands, but failed. Her small, weak arms strained from the weight. She grunted with the effort, arms shaking and wavering. She pointed the tip of the blade at his torso. Simina wanted to aim for the throat, but it was too heavy for her.

"Stay away," Simina groaned, her voice strained. Sweat rolled down her face in beads. She shivered violently from the cold, almost able to hear her bones chattering and clattering. The Prince grinned and burst out laughing. This angered Simina. *I'm threatening him with his own sword. Why is he laughing?*

"Really?" he asked her, amusement in his voice. Smiling and unafraid, he raised a finger and touched the blade's tip. The sword evaporated from her hands and re-materialized in his hand in a puff of purple smoke. Simina stared at her hands, and her jaw hit the ground. She thought she must be mad.

Simina noticed the tip of the blade pointed at her throat, and she raised her hands in surrender. *I'm done for, he's going to kill me.* With an unwavering arm, he held the sword with one hand, pointing the tip at her throat, under her chin.

The Prince tilted his head confidently and narrowed his eyes. Simina gulped. Her heart thumped heavily and fast. *How did he even do that?* Not once did his hand waver and not once did his arm droop from the weight of his sword. Taut muscles strained beneath the thin fabric of his shirt.

"Are you going to kill me?" Simina asked in a voice that sounded quite foreign to her. The Prince smiled and chuckled. He lowered his sword.

"No," he said. "But I must ask you not to try that again." He sheathed his blade again. Shaking, Simina nodded, slightly bowing her head.

"Y-yes. Your Highness," she said in a wavering voice. The Prince rolled his eyes and sighed with annoyance and exasperation.

"Oh please," he exasperated. "Don't call me that." Simina looked confused. He placed a hand over his chest and bowed his head to her.

"Please, just...call me Nar," The Prince told her. Simina quirked her eyebrows. Nar? What kind of name was Nar? What a strange name. Instantly, fatigue washed over her, wrapping her body in its tiresome embrace. Her knees buckled, and her eyelids fluttered. Her legs gave out under her and her body swayed. Dizziness overwhelmed her.

Simina fainted from exhaustion, and Nar, noticing that she was about to fall, caught her with quick reflexes. She fell limp in his arms, face very pale, and skin hot with fever. He feared she had pneumonia.

Nar took her back into his castle, into his bedroom, where he gently laid her back on his bed. He pulled the covers back over her and let her rest. He had other matters to attend. Nar left his room, took a right, and climbed another set of stairs. These stairs led to the Hall, where many public conferences were held and used for Royal Banquets.

Nar didn't see the point of walking when he could just appear and reappear in different places. But his father, the King, didn't like it much when he did that, and Nar wanted to respect his father's wishes. His father, however, was getting old and tired, and was slowly dying from old age. The King wouldn't be king for much longer and needed someone to take the throne. Of course, Nar was the heir to the throne, as was his right, since he was the King's only son.

Nar did not have any siblings. He was an only child. His mother died when he was young from the plague before his parents could have more children. His father remarried a few times, but never loved any of those wives as much as his first, so he'd divorced them. A few of them Nar killed by accident. At that time, he hadn't really learned how to control his powers properly. But they were mean to him and made him angry. Without his control, his powers would manifest and kill them.

Of course, he didn't mean to; he was only a boy and didn't know how to control it. It wasn't his fault. Multiple times, it was self-defense because they had been hurting him when, or just before, it happened.

Nar arrived in the Hall, where his father sat on his throne opposite the long, vast room. Nar approached on light feet, his footsteps echoing all around. Five long lancet style windows graced each side of the room, sending in streams of early morning light and casting shadows upon the floor and his own.

Nar stopped before his father, the King, knelt and bowed his head respectfully. Nar stared at the floor beneath him, observing its pattern.

"Your majesty," he said humbly to his father. The King grunted, straightened his throne, and went into a coughing fit. Nar did not move; he remained kneeling. Once finished coughing, he spoke.

"Rise, my son," he told him gruffly. Nar rose to his feet with the utmost grace. He cleared his throat.

"So, who's this girl you've brought to the castle?" the King asked.

"She's a guest. Her carriage crashed, and I found her lying in the snow, unconscious. I do not know her name."

"What is wrong with her?" he asked.

"She is ill, Father. If I hadn't found her, she would have died," Nar said. The King stroked his beard.

"It's almost time for you to take the throne, Nar. You must take a maiden or a young princess to be your queen," the King said in a dire voice.

Nar sighed.

"Yes, I know, Father," he said, annoyed. His father had been urging him to find someone to marry for the past week. It was irritating Nar. His father had previously invited many suitable, beautiful young ladies, and Nar met them all, but he didn't like them. They were all too interested in him and tried too hard to get his attention. They were all very pretty, but they just weren't his type.

Nar knew he had to marry soon. The King would not be around much longer.

Nine

Simina came to in the same place. She stared at the chandelier dangling from the ceiling, mouth open. Something monstrous ached in her head. Even with thick blankets piled on top of her, she shivered like she was cold.

She pulled the covers up tighter, curling up and bundling. Simina didn't feel well. Hot and cold clashed in an intense battle inside her. Her entire body hurt and her head was too heavy to lift, like a giant piece of lead. She rolled all around, trying to get comfortable, but she just kept tossing and turning.

"Ugh…" she groaned and massaged her temple. Simina stared across the room at the window. How long has it been? Her aunt would expect her as the government notified her just before she left. Now, she couldn't get there because she was stuck in a stupid castle with a person she didn't even expect to be real.

Simina coughed, feeling quite feverish. Someone knocked lightly at the door. Simina froze. She didn't say anything. It was probably the Prince, and she didn't want to tell him to come in. He gave her the chills. No one said anything, and the door opened. Nar walked in, carrying a silver tray. On top, she saw a steaming bowl of something and a steaming mug. He offered a tight smile as he walked across the room and set the tray on a table beside the bed. Simina narrowed her eyes as he came to stand by her bedside.

"How are you feeling?" Nar asked. Simina looked away. She did not like him and did not want to talk to him. Simina ignored him and acted like he wasn't there. When she said nothing, he spoke.

"Matilda was kind enough to make you some tea and broth." An ache seared through Simina's stomach, and it rumbled. She turned to face him. Though she didn't trust him, she was hungry.

"It's really hot, and my body hurts," she said in a raspy voice. She swallowed and cleared her throat. "My throat hurts too," she added.

He picked up the mug from the tray and offered it to her.

"Drink this," Nar said. Simina pushed herself into a sitting position. Simina peered over the lip to see what was in it. Simina saw a light brown liquid with white bubbles swimming on top. Feeling wary and distrustful, Simina pinned a suspicious glare on Nar. How stupid was she? She can't drink anything from the Dark Prince! He might be trying to poison her!

She shoved it away from her, making the liquid slosh. "I'm not drinking that."

A scowl cut his young features. "Drink it."

He shoved the mug into her hands, forcing her to take it. The heat from it spread warmth throughout her fingertips as she took it from him.

"It's probably poison," she snapped.

Nar narrowed his eyes, offended. "Now why would I poison it?"

"Because you're the Dark Prince, and you're evil!" Simina mumbled groggily with a nasty sneer. Nar cocked his head at her, looking seriously confused as his brow drew together.

"No, I am not."

Simina sniffed indignantly but said nothing. She stared at the brown liquid, displeased.

"Ah yes, I saved you from freezing to death just so I could poison you," said Prince Nar sarcastically. Simina frowned at his snide comment, but she raised the rim to her lips. She blew on it to cool it and daintily took an experimental sip.

A bitter, stale taste assaulted her tongue, burnt and dusty like hundred-year-old dead herbs. It coated her mouth with a thin, grimy, unpleasant sensation. Unable to fathom such a nasty taste, she spat it out, the liquid spewing out of her mouth, some spraying on Nar. Because of this, Nar stepped aside with a disgruntled expression.

Simina coughed, choking on the liquid as little droplets dribbled down her lips and trickled down her chin. She wiped her mouth on her sleeve, running her tongue across her teeth, trying to get the harsh, lingering, medicinal aftertaste out of her mouth.

"Bluk! What is that? It's disgusting!" Simina stuck her tongue out and set the mug on the tray. Nar gave her an agitated look.

"It's a medicinal tea; it isn't supposed to taste good," he said irritably. Simina stuck her tongue out and crossed her arms over her chest.

"Well, I won't drink it!" she said stubbornly.

Nar shrugged. "Fine. Don't drink it. See if I care."

Simina growled and said nothing. Simina picked up the mug, raised it to her lips, and took a considerable gulp to prove that she could drink it and would get better.

Forcing it down, Simina guzzled it, drinking it gulp after gulp, even though her reflex told her to throw it back up because it tasted so nasty. Despite that, though, she forced it down, letting it burn the back of her throat. Once she emptied the mug, Simina breathed heavily, groaning with disgust. She set it back down.

Nar looked amused, and he chuckled. Simina shivered, trying to shake off the bad taste. Surprisingly, after drinking that, she noticed significant improvement. Her body and muscles still ached, but her head didn't hurt anymore, and neither did her throat.

"Feel any better?" he asked, voice slightly mocking. Even though she did, Simina didn't want to admit that, so instead, she said, "No." Simina defiantly set her jaw. She thought about her aunt again.

"How long have I been here?"

The Prince walked over to the window and gazed out of it.

"About two days."

"Two days!?" Nar grimaced at her loud, screechy voice. He nodded.

"Yes. You were asleep for a long time," he explained. Simina did not like this. She did not know what to say, so there was a moment of silence where neither spoke.

Nar broke the silence. "Who are you exactly?"

Simina glared at him. "Leave me alone."

Nar said nothing; just took a deep breath. He bowed in a very respectful way.

"As you wish," said Nar, swiftly leaving the room in a few graceful strides and closing the door behind him. A shuddering breath escaped Simina's lips. His absence provided her some much needed solace. Hands bunching in her tousled hair, her skin crawled with his powerful, lingering presence. He had yet to display any dark powers. But the image from the book and the author's dire warnings...they stuck to her like cobwebs. Now alone, Simina drank the bowl of broth, quenching her hunger.

* * *

A few hours later, while Simina was pacing the room, trying to ease the pain in her muscles by moving, someone knocked on the door. Simina stopped and turned to the door. Should she say something? She hoped it wasn't the Prince again. She gulped.

"Who is it?" she called. An unfamiliar woman's voice answered her.

"Matilda, the handmaiden dear," the woman answered kindly. Simina breathed out.

"Come in," she said. The door opened, and a young, stout little woman entered. She was young but looked a few years older than Simina. Her auburn hair was pulled back into a neat, tight bun.

"Good day, miss," she greeted Simina. Simina waved, feeling a little shy.

"Hi," she muttered.

"My master has requested that I escort you to another room," Matilda told Simina. Simina wrung her hands.

"Master?" Simina wondered what she meant by "master."

"Prince Nar, dear," Matilda said.

"Oh." She calls him master? That's a little weird. Matilda held the door open, waiting for Simina to walk out first. Simina walked out and into a hallway. Matilda walked out after her, brushing past Simina and turning left.

"Follow me, please," Matilda called to Simina. Simina followed behind her, taking in the high ceiling, flying buttresses, and foyer below her. They climbed up another set of steep stairs.

"Where are you taking me?" Simina asked.

"You'll see," Matilda chimed. Simina noticed that Matilda waddled rather than walked. Matilda took her through some corridors and turned a few corners until finally stopping at another door. Matilda opened the door for her. Simina walked in. Inside was a smaller room that looked more fit for a girl than the other room. This room was adorned with floral decor, with a fancy bed sporting a lovely canopy. An antique rug sprawled underneath with intricate and unique designs of more strange yet magnificent fauna.

Simina liked this room better and looked around. She walked over and sat on the bed and sank gently into the decadent duvet. Matilda opened a wardrobe, revealing an abundance of gorgeous dresses fit for royalty. She pulled out a long, graceful purple dress with long, fluffy, frilly sleeves and a neck slanted down into a V.

Simina's eyes widened at its beauty, and her jaw dropped in awe. Matilda brought it over, running her hand across the fabric, gazing at it with admiration. She laid it out across the bed next to Simina. Simina stood to get a better look at it.

It was a deep, luscious purple, matching the color of Nar's eyes. Simina stopped for a second. She wondered why her brain had automatically made that comparison between the dress and his eyes. This made Simina angry, and she hated herself for making that comparison.

A gold belt was sewn into the dress around the waist. Simina liked the dress; she just didn't like the fact that it reminded her of Nar's eyes.

"Prince Nar picked this dress for you. He thought you might want some new, fresh clothes after what you've been through," Matilda told her. Simina tensed up. Nar picked out the dress? Why was he picking out her clothes?

She inwardly denied that she secretly appreciated the Prince giving her these clothes. Simina got the sense like she was living in a fairytale in this elaborate castle, just like a princess. She wanted to be treated like a princess, but Simina kept that to herself. Now, guilt ate her up inside for being rude to him earlier, when all he'd been trying to do was help her. Simina immediately dismissed that thought. *Nope. He's the Dark Prince. He's probably using his wicked powers on me to make me think that.*

"There's a washroom right over here." Matilda's voice brought Simina out of her thoughts. She followed Matilda to another door to the room's right, slightly across from the bed. Matilda opened the door and led Simina in.

"Just right in here," Matilda muttered. Simina observed the washroom. It was the strangest and most fancy washroom she'd ever seen. A white porcelain tub stood on golden legs, the sides carved ornately with golden flourishes. Simina had never seen anything like it. Attached to the wall were some strange knobs: one in the middle that had an arrow pointing up or down and two more on either side, one with an H and the other with a C.

Above that was a strange-looking nozzle, aiming down into the tub. *What's that?* She turned to and pointed to the weird nozzle thing.

"What is that?" she asked Matilda. Matilda rushed over to explain. She indicated the knobs and nozzle thing.

"You turn these. Turn the middle one up and that thing up there called a shower nozzle, sprays water into the tub when you wash. It's called a shower," Matilda explained. Simina was absolutely fascinated.

"Ooh, a shower," Simina said with fascination. Matilda pulled out some towels and other bathing materials and set them aside for Simina's use. She bowed to her.

"I will leave you to bathe. If you need any assistance, I will send for Nar," Matilda told Simina. Simina opened her mouth to protest, but Matilda left before she could say anything. Simina did not want any of Prince Nar's "assistance."

* * *

It took Simina a while to get the hang of the shower. Luckily, she figured it out just enough to not need any assistance. She wrapped her body in a towel, drying herself, and brushed her wet locks. After she finished, she walked out of the bathroom. The dress was still laid out across the bed.

She put it on in a jiffy, and once thoroughly examining herself in it, she decided that it looked good on her. Simina smiled happily and turned to leave her room. Once she'd exited, she found herself in a dimly lit corridor. Her footsteps echoed with each step across the narrow hall. There were two hallways. One that went to the left from where she was standing and another directly in front of her. A larger swath of light shone from the latter direction.

She didn't want to be here in the Dark Prince's castle any longer than she had to. Simina was determined to find a way out. She followed the hall until it ended, opening up onto a landing overlooking the foyer. Down below, Simina saw the entrance: two gigantic double doors. Two guards stood in front, blocking them. Even if she did get out of here through the main entrance, Simina would be stuck. There was nothing but rolling hills of snow as far as the eye could see. Leaving on foot wasn't an option. She had to find another way out.

All castles had stables. Since there were guards and soldiers, Simina assumed there had to be horses. Warily, Simina walked to the middle of the landing and stopped. She glanced back down at the guards. They didn't seem to be paying her any attention. Breathing out, she turned away, coming face to face with two double doors. Two guards stood at attention, blocking her access.

Exhaling slowly, Simina quickly turned and walked back the way she came. Not remembering which room she originally came out of, Simina went straight until the hall broke off in two directions again: left and right. Simina went right and stopped at the first door she saw. Her skin registered the cool, metallic touch of the curved, delicate handle. She turned it, and much to her surprise, it opened. Nervously, Simina pushed the door open. The room was dimly lit with candles and their small, flickering flames cast eerie shadows on the walls. It caught the light of a crystal chandelier hanging above and Simina wondered why that wasn't being used for lighting instead. Electricity was clearly more effective.

One candle rested carefully on a sturdy desk that sat in the far end of the room. The wall behind it was lined with bookshelves, and to the left sat a small, cozy armchair. Carefully, Simina stepped inside. The soft texture of the floor threw her off and she stumbled. There must be a rug or a carpet. There was a rustling sound, like fabric, and suddenly the dim room was awash with bright light.

Simina threw her arms up to shield her eyes from the unexpected onslaught, squinting. The Dark Prince stood by a window, the snowy landscape outside complimenting his pale, fair features. His poet's blouse hung loosely off his lithe frame, the tassels untied and left opened, exposing his chest.

"What are you doing in here?" he seethed, purple eyes aflame. Simina's heart dropped into her stomach, and every muscle told her to run, but his dark gaze pinned her to the spot.

"Well, I-"

"Did I say that you could leave your room?" In a puff of deep, rich violet smoke, Nar appeared in front of her instantly. Simina shrieked and attempted to run, but it was too late. He grabbed her roughly by the arm and dragged her out back into the corridor.

"Let me go!" she screamed as she attempted to escape, but he held her arm in a tight, unrelenting vice grip.

Stumbling, Simina somehow managed to keep her feet under her. Her arm ached, but she fought with all her might to get free. He dragged her, kicking and screaming, back to her room. Nar opened the door and unceremoniously threw her in. Her cheek skidded on the rug, burning her face. Leaping back to her feet as quickly as possible, Simina charged the door. Nar slammed it shut with a bang just as she reached it, and there was the loud and ominous sound of the lock clicking into place.

"No!" she shouted, grasping the knob. It didn't move. Panic overwhelming her, Simina's chest heaved with sobs. She rattled and pulled at the knob, but the door held strong. It wouldn't budge an inch.

"Let me out of here!" she screamed as loud as her lungs would allow. She pounded her fists on the door. "Let me out!"

Simina's mind reeled, her chest heaving. Now she definitely had to find a way out of here. Zormon be damned if she was about to stay in a castle with the most vile, evil person alive. How could anyone be so cruel? Simina pounded on the door and screamed until her voice went hoarse, and her knuckles were raw. No one came, and the door stubbornly stayed locked. After about an hour or two, Simina finally gave up and slowly sank to the floor, her back against the door. She sobbed, feeling hopeless and trapped. Weeping, Simina crawled across the room and onto the bed, where she cried herself to sleep.

Ten

Simina awoke the next morning with a renewed sense of determination. She sat up in bed, stomach rumbling. The aroma of seared meat and toasted bread filled her nose. Her eyes landed on a silver tray sitting in front of the door. Nostrils flaring, Simina leapt over to the tray and devoured the food in minutes.

Now, after gaining proper nourishment, Simina began looking for a way out. First, she started at the window. One glance told her that it would be impossible to escape via the window. The height alone was dizzying and even if there were foot holds along the wall, only one slip and it would be over. Simina wasn't willing to take that risk. Her physical capabilities wouldn't allow something of that magnitude. She needed to go outside and find the stables. But guards waited everywhere.

Simina thought about her aunt. If there was just some way to contact her, let her know where she was...she could come for her. A letter. There was a slanted writing desk by the window, with paper and pens. Simina sat down and quickly composed a letter to her aunt, explaining her dire situation. Then she hastily folded it and stuffed it into an envelope. Now how would she get it there? If she had magic, she could talk to animals and lure a bird to the window. But she didn't. However, every building had some place where post was received and delivered.

In order to do that, though, Simina needed to find a way out of this room first. A quick jiggle of the knob let her know that the door was indeed still locked. Using the pen, Simina tried to pick the lock. She gave up a half an hour later, frustrated with her lack of progress. Huffing, Simina threw the pen to the floor. Simina refused to be trapped here.

She thought about Ernest and recalled his words. *You might just be a late bloomer...* She'd never attempted to use magic before, or even tried to channel it. But that's because she thought she couldn't. However, maybe that's the problem. Ernest was able to do more magic and for longer periods of time after eating. Maybe it was the same for her.

Simina took a deep breath and placed her hand flat against the keyhole. She closed her eyes, trying to imagine magical energy coursing through her body. She pictured it as a huge, golden ball of light in her chest, and imagined it spreading out. It stretched into her legs and flowed through her arms and into her hands. She focused on the goal she wanted to achieve, and that was to unlock the door.

"Unlock," she said, determination in her voice. She waited a few moments and then opened her eyes. Simina twisted the knob, but the lock held fast. It hadn't worked. Frustrated, she kicked the door. Simina forced herself to calm down, and tried once more. And this time, when Simina imagined the magic coursing through her, she experienced something she'd never experienced before. A surge. A pulsing, electrical warmth spread through her entire body.

"UNLOCK," Simina said again, with more power in her voice. There was a soft, but clear, click of the door unlocking. Simina's eyes flew open in surprise. Has it actually worked? Had she really used magic to unlock the door? Only one way to find out.

Simina grabbed the knob and turned. It opened smoothly without a sound. Giddy, Simina stepped out into the hall with a huge grin. There was some magic in her after all. It may not be a lot. But it was there. Her celebration was cut short by a sudden and unexpected wave of fatigue. Her steps faltered, Simina's knees buckled and she slumped weakly against the wall. Ernest was right. Using magic, even such a small amount, must have sapped a lot of Simina's physical energy.

Nevertheless, Simina pressed on. After several minutes of hobbling around, she found herself back on the landing, in the foyer. The guards remained at their post. But the other doors on the landing had been left unguarded. Simina quietly slipped in after making sure the guards weren't paying her any attention.

She'd entered a very vast room. Simina looked all around, taking in all the details. On each wall, there were five lancet windows, so long that they went from the floor to the ceiling. At least three glorious chandeliers hung from the ceiling, dazzling bright in all of their beauty, filling the room with light. The exquisite, marble floor was polished so well that Simina could see her reflection when she looked down.

There were lots of chairs in this room, lots of chairs, lined up neatly on either side of the wall. Taking in all the detailed beauty of this large room, she slowly walked across the floor, footsteps echoing loudly, bouncing all around on the walls. Simina's eyes landed on a man's figure sitting in a chair across the room. He sat relaxed, with one leg propped up on his knee. He rested his head on his fist, his expression broody. A long, dark trench coat framed his limber body. Upon realizing that it was the Dark Prince, Simina spun on her heel and started walking back towards the door.

"Stop," he grumbled with a heavy sigh. Simina froze. He appeared in front of her in a swirl of purple smoke. Simina held the letter behind her back.

Prince Nar glared at her. "How did you get out of your room?"

Simina said nothing. She cast her eyes to the floor, avoiding his dark gaze.

"Did Matilda let you out?"

Simina shook her head. "No."

"Then how did you get out?" he asked again.

Simina looked up and met his gaze. "Maybe you forgot to lock the door," she quipped, curling her lips.

Prince Nar's eyes flashed with fury. "How *dare* you...what have you got there?"

He must have noticed the letter somehow.

"Nothing," she said quickly, but Nar snatched the letter from her hands.

"Please, it's just a letter to my aunt!" Simina cried. "I was supposed to arrive two days ago, she's probably wondering where I am!"

He was silent as he peeked the envelope open and took out the note.

"Just let me send it."

"Quiet," he snapped, holding up a hand. Simina's heart hammered as she watched his eyes read every line. After a brief hesitation, he finally spoke.

"Simina, is it?" Prince Nar said, her name flowing from his lips. It was a lovely name, and unique. He'd never heard such a name before.

"Simina," he repeated slowly, sounding out every syllable. His voice, seemingly emanating an aura, sounded as if he was casting a spell.

The way he said her name sent chills down her spine. It was unnerving yet attractive. Simina didn't know how to feel.

Breathing in, Prince Nar promptly tore the letter in half. Then he carefully tore the rest of it into tiny, useless pieces and dropped them. They fluttered down to the floor at Simina's feet.

Frowning at the pieces of parchment, tears burned in the backs of her eyes, like liquid fire. "How could you..."

She glared at him, eyes full of tears. "I wish to leave!"

"You will leave when I say you can leave!" he shouted, taking a step closer to her.

"Am I to be your prisoner, then?"

This time, the Prince remained silent. Simina went on.

"That book was right. You *are* evil," she hissed.

This took him by surprise. His eyes widened, jaw dropping. "What book? What are you talking about?"

"I found a book. About you. You are just as vile and despicable as the book says!" Simina's words lashed at him like a whip. Anger and hurt swelled within him, mixing into something dangerous.

"You know *nothing* of me," Prince Nar spat, his face inches from hers.

Simina whimpered in fear, but held his gaze. "I know enough. In fairytales, princes are good. Not evil."

He smiled mirthlessly. "My dear, this isn't a fairy tale."

Sadness enveloped her at this revelation. No. This wasn't a fairytale.

"Why can't you be good?" she whispered.

Much to Simina's surprise, Prince Nar's eyes softened. Maybe it was a trick of the light? Or an evil trick? But maybe not. Simina didn't see cruelty, or evil...only sadness. He tilted up her chin with a finger, staring deep into her eyes. Simina expected his hand to be cold, a reflection of his dark personality, but instead it was warm. And being so close to him, Simina found that his scent was so very inviting. He smiled of lilac and gentle musk.

"Because if I was, I wouldn't be," he murmured. As soon as the words left his lips, his face blanched with astonishment.

"How did you do that?" Prince Nar exclaimed, flabbergasted.

"Do what?" Simina stared at him, confused. What was he talking about?

His vulnerable expression vanished in the blink of an eye, and his face hardened. It happened so fast that Simina wasn't sure what she'd seen. He abruptly shoved her away, roughly, and she fell to the floor.

"Aaah!" she screamed, pain shooting through her small body at the impact.

"Get away from me!" he roared, purple eyes glowing.

The room began to shake, and the floor shifted significantly beneath her. A loud rumbling filled her ears, and all of the walls and ceiling shook. Dust and debris rained down, and the chandeliers swung precariously. Long, jagged cracks snaked up the walls like vines, the sound of the stone breaking deafening.

Gasping, Simina struggled to find her footing. Nar was overcome with rage, his shoulders heaving. A chandelier was torn from the ceiling and came crashing down in a dazzling but dangerous display of smashed, glittering crystal. Simina screamed and dove out of the way to avoid it just in time. Heart pounding, Simina made a beeline for the doors.

How could she let herself falter? The Dark Prince was exactly that: *dark.* Why had she even entertained the thought that he might be good? No one good could do something like this.

Reaching the doors, Simina shoved them open with her entire body and kept running. As she ran down the steps, she saw the two guards at the exit running up them to check out the commotion. Refusing to stop, Simina burst out of the castle and into the cold, snowy landscape. Nearly falling over, she gathered up her dress and ran as fast as she could around the castle, searching desperately for the stables.

Panting, Simina shivered as the cold air bit into her bare skin, ankles deep in the snow. It glistened blindingly in the bright sun. By the time she found the stables, she'd run halfway around the castle. Her face was numb and she could barely feel her toes. The only horse in the stables was midnight black, with a silky mane. Without hesitating, Simina leapt on, grabbing the reins.

"Hiya!" she shouted, and the horse neighed. The horse galloped away, carrying her on its back. Just as she passed the castle, the doors burst open, releasing a gigantic, cascading wave of dark violet smoke. As it cleared, Simina saw the Dark Prince standing there, two guards flanking him. But Simina kept going, and his eyes followed her until she disappeared into the snowy woods.

Prince Nar seethed with unfiltered anger as he watched the peasant girl ride off with his horse, Night Rider. There's no way she should've been able to ride it, it's enchanted. Only he should be able to ride that horse. Nar would have stopped her, but the enchantment protects the rider from being harmed.

"My liege, she's just stolen your horse!" one of the guards shouted.

Nar whipped his head towards the incompetent guard, purple eyes aflame. "I know, I just saw."

"What do you want us to do, your highness?"

He gritted his teeth. "Find her and bring her to me."

There was something odd about that girl and he intended to find out what.

Eleven

It took at least another two days for Simina to arrive at the right side of Lazera, known as Winterville. She trotted through town with the stolen horse, looking for her aunt's house. She noticed that this part of town seemed quite different. Homes here were much better built and looked sturdier. Things didn't look as shabby as they did on the left side, in Autumnville.

There weren't any vendors. Instead, there were actual buildings with little signs next to them. There was even a bakery and a butcher's shop selling meat. There was only one vendor selling fruits and vegetables. Even the people's clothing looked finer. Simina concluded that this part of Lazera was much wealthier than the other part.

But Simina didn't feel like paying too much attention to it. She was tired from riding for two days without food or sleep. She wanted to hurry and find her aunt's house, so she could rest. Simina scanned each house she passed, reading each address to see if it matched her aunt's. She found it and stopped. Simina dismounted the horse, put it in the stables, and staggered to the front door, where she knocked. Simina waited for someone to answer. The door opened, and Aunt Lyda appeared.

Aunt Lyda recognized the girl standing in her doorway as her niece, Gregory's daughter, Simina. Her eyes widened at how terrible she looked.

"Simina! You made it! Please come in!" Aunt Lyda ushered Simina in and shut the door. Simina hugged Aunt Lyda. Behind Aunt Lyda, Simina saw two girls descending a small set of stairs. Simina's vision blurred at the edges. Sleepiness swept over her. All of a sudden, her legs weakened, and her eyelids were too heavy to lift. Simina groaned and collapsed from fatigue, blacking out.

* * *

Simina woke hours later to the delicious smell of food. Her nose wiggled, and her eyes snapped open sharply. Simina looked around. A bowl sat on a bedside table with a glass of water next to it. Simina sat up and stretched, feeling a lot better since she'd gotten some sleep. She peered over the bowl, the steam rising into her face. She sniffed it. It smelled good, and her stomach growled. It was chili. Simina could tell from the beans and the thick broth.

Simina snatched the bowl up, seized it, and devoured it. After she'd finished, she grabbed the glass of water and drained it with only a few gulps. She set down the glass, gasping, and wiped the wetness from her lips. Simina's eyes observed her surroundings. She recognized the room. She'd been to her aunt's house a long time ago before her mom died. Simina was surprised she remembered since it had been so long since the last time she was here. From what she could tell, not much about this room had changed.

The room seemed smaller than she remembered. But maybe that was because she'd been much smaller the last time she was here. The walls were still the same light colored wood she remembered, just like the girly pink dresser with chipped paint in the corner and the flowery little lamp atop its surface.

The creak of the opening door drew Simina's attention away from the room's interior. Simina saw her aunt peeking through the door. Seeing Simina awake, she walked in and approached the bed.

"How are you feeling, sweetie?" she asked kindly.

Simina shrugged. She didn't feel like anything.

"I'm fine," she said plainly.

"You were supposed to arrive four days ago," Aunt Lyda said. "What happened?"

"Well…" Simina wasn't sure how to explain her encounter with Prince Nar. So, she embellished a little bit.

She explained everything from the marriage issues to the accident and about Nar, but omitted the significant details. She also left out the part where she stole his horse. After their conversation, a great weight lifted off her. She belonged here, like a missing part of a puzzle. Everything was right. For now.

Twelve

Within the next few days, Simina spent time with her two cousins, Olivia and Gloria. She'd met them before, but it was so long ago that she didn't remember them much. Gloria was the older of the two sisters. Her skin was fair, like her mother's, with light curly hair below her shoulders and dull green eyes. She was older than Simina and had a sly, pouty look.

Olivia's skin was tan, and her hair was shorter and olive-brown. Her eyes were darker green, and her face was rounder, with an innocent look that held a touch of mischievousness behind said innocence. Olivia was shorter, too, but not as skinny. They'd forgotten Simina's name.

"What's your name?" Gloria asked Simina.

"Simina," Simina told her. Gloria fouled up her nose, hating that her name sounded prettier than hers. Simina saw jealousy flash in Gloria's eyes, but Simina didn't know why.

Simina curtsied. "Pleased to meet you," she greeted kindly. An envious, nasty scowl cut into Gloria's face as her eyes glared with distaste at Simina. She hated Simina's dress just because it looked prettier and more expensive than hers. Gloria was curious about where she'd gotten it and wanted it. The dress Simina was wearing was the one Prince Nar had given her, and it was the only one she had besides her peasant dress. All of the other clothes she'd packed to take with her were lost in the accident, along with a few of her personal items.

Olivia approached her and gave Simina a hug. Simina was confused by her action. Olivia squealed and pulled back, placing her hands on Simina's shoulders.

"We should take you shopping sometime! I can pick dresses out for you!" Olivia offered Simina, overly excited that she was there. Simina nodded and smiled.

"Thanks. That'll be great!" Simina was delighted at this idea. Gloria shoved a sharp elbow into Olivia's side and gave her a warning look. Like a kicked puppy, Olivia stepped away from Simina and lowered her eyes. Gloria's reaction puzzled and uneased her.

Later that evening, Simina, Gloria, and Olivia spent time in Simina's new bedroom. Gloria leaned her arms on the edge of the bed. Olivia actually sat on Simina's bed, crisscrossed. Gloria picked at her nails, while Olivia ogled Simina.

"So what's it like on the Left?" Gloria asked, even though she sounded like she didn't care.

Simina shrugged.

"It's...small," she said, remembering her little village. She missed it. She missed the marketplace, the library, the quaint little cottages, but most of all, Simina missed her home. She missed her father, the loud way he tramped through the little house and the gruff way he spoke. She also missed her horse, Winona. Simina thought it had been ages since she'd been there. Her father probably missed her dearly.

"It's nothing like this on the Left," Simina told them.

Olivia's eyes were wild with excitement.

"Have you met the Prince?" Olivia squealed. Simina's stomach turned, and she became uncomfortable. *I hope she doesn't mean "that" Prince.*

"Uh...Prince? You mean the Dark Prince?" she asked timidly, not wanting to say his name. Olivia shook her head.

"No, silly! That's not what we call him!" Olivia giggled. Gloria looked up at Simina, then glanced at Olivia. A dreamy look fell over Olivia's face.

"Prince Nar," Olivia sighed dreamily. Simina fouled up her face with a disturbed look. Both girls swooned at the thought of him.

"He's gorgeous," Olivia and Gloria said in unison. Simina made the most terrible face. *That's it, now I've officially gone mad.* Simina thought Prince Nar was attractive, but she'd never swoon over him like these girls. They clearly had no idea of how he truly was. Simina shook her head.

"Uh...yeah. I've met him. Once," Simina said hesitantly. Olivia's eyes clouded with envy. Gloria looked doubtful. Olivia placed two hands over her heart.

"Oh, you're so lucky!" Olivia sighed with yearning. Simina gave Olivia an annoyed look. *Not really.* Gloria tossed her hair and batted her eyelashes.

"*You've* met the Prince?" Gloria asked, sounding doubtful, tone full of scorn. Simina recalled her moments with him, when she'd spoken to him. He was harsh, rude and cruel to her. What kind of Prince locks an innocent girl in a room? He wouldn't let her leave, and his rage induced antics nearly killed her.

Simina looked back up at Gloria, who stared at her inquisitively. "Yes. I've met him once," she said simply. Simina didn't want to go into detail about what happened. Gloria seemed like the jealous type.

"I've seen him in the town sometimes, walking around, just observing. I like how he walks and how his lovely purple eyes glint as they take in everything." Olivia looked ready to hyperventilate.

"Oh, he's so handsome," Olivia gushed. Simina rolled her eyes. *Could this girl be any more dramatic?*

Simina never really took a particular interest in guys, but she wondered about Nar. He'd gotten her attention, that was for sure. No matter how often Simina tried to will him from her mind, he always floated back in.

"Oh, hey, do you have any magic?" Olivia wondered, changing the subject.

Thankful that they were off the topic of Nar, Simina breathed out in relief. "I'm not sure...I haven't noticed any magic..."

She decided not to tell them about that moment in Nar's castle.

Gloria picked at her nails, a smug smile curling her lips. "Then that means you probably don't have any."

Olivia glared at her sister and quickly turned back to Simina with a bright smile.

"That's okay!" she said. "You might just be a late bloomer! It happens."

"Okay..." Simina didn't care about magic. She was tired of hearing that late bloomer line.

"What magic do you have?" She looked at Olivia.

"I can make plants grow," she replied, smiling. "I can also create plants too, but I'm not so good at it yet. The most I can make right now is a leaf."

"I'm sure you'll get better if you keep practicing." Simina smiled encouragingly. "What about you, Gloria?"

"I can create mist. It's like a thick fog. Watch." She held out her hands, spreading her arms out. White mist leaked out of her palms in slow, thick waves. It spread through the room, clouding everything in a haze until Simina could barely see anything.

"Eeeh!" Olivia whined. "I can't see anything, make it stop!"

Gloria laughed, and the mist dissipated. "Bet you wish you could do that. Loser."

* * *

That night as Simina slept, she dreamed of Nar. She saw his glowing eyes and heard his deep, demanding voice. Simina didn't know what the dream was about, just that she kept seeing him for some reason. This irked her later when she woke up, which produced a bit of grumpiness in her. Gloria and Olivia took her to town to shop for clothes the next day. Gloria didn't seem to care much, but Olivia wanted to get Simina new garments. This town looked considerably wealthier. The streets and roads were in much better condition and better made. People here looked more affluent and healthier. These people were also noticeably thicker in build because of better eating; people here were better fed.

Lampposts lined the streets, and at the top of each lamppost waved a white banner with a black-stemmed rose. The banner waved from each lamppost for all to see. While walking through town, Simina pointed at them.

"What's that banner?" Simina asked Gloria and Olivia. Olivia answered.

"It's Prince Nar's. It's his flag. It symbolizes his rule. Technically, the King still rules, but he's too old and sick to do anything, so the Prince takes care of everything," Olivia explained to Simina. Simina got an uneasy feeling every time his name was mentioned.

Now Simina understood what the Lazerian Officials had meant by, "not in our jurisdiction." The Right side of Lazera was under the rule of the Dark Royal Family. And Prince Nar was the heir to rule the throne. Simina remembered now what the book said: The Dark Prince is more prominent in Winterville, and the Left side, Autumnville, doesn't know he exists. The book was right. Well, about a few things.

"Why doesn't the Prince take over the throne for the King?" Simina asks. Olivia leaned in close to Simina's ear.

"Because the Prince isn't married yet. And his coronation hasn't been held yet, either," Olivia whispered. Simina wasn't surprised about him not being married yet. What girl would want to marry such a horrible person? However, Simina was sure that girls would overlook his behavior due to his good looks.

Gloria nudged Olivia. "Let's take her to Princess Attire." The name of that place perked Simina's interest.

"What's that?" Simina asked curiously.

"It's a clothing shop for girls," Olivia told her.

When Simina entered the shop, her mind was blown. Mannequins posed wearing various dresses, flaunting how the dress might look on a woman. Racks spilled over with more, some with ruffles, some with tulle and taffeta. She'd never seen so many clothes in one place in all her life, so many pretty dresses. Her mouth opened in awe.

"Oh my gosh..." she gasped, speechless. Simina saw many dresses she liked. *How could I ever buy one?* Simina's heart sank. She had no money.

Olivia chose a sparkly blue dress with long floaty sleeves and a fluffy skirt. She held it up to Simina.

"This would look great on you," Olivia crooned. She made Simina take it.

"Try it on," she insisted. Startled, Simina took the dress.

"But I...I don't have any money," Simina breathed out, feeling winded suddenly. Olivia wasn't listening. She kept picking out dresses and throwing them into Simina's arms to try on.

"Hey..." Simina tried to say but was cut off by the fabric of a dress.

"Wait!" Simina shouted. "I don't have any money!" Olivia turned to her.

"Nonsense. We'll buy some dresses for you. My mom doesn't mind," Olivia assured. She shoved Simina away toward the fitting rooms.

"Go, go, try them on." She shoved Simina. As she walked by, she caught a glimpse of Gloria's face. She glared at her, jealous that Olivia was giving her so much attention. Simina hadn't even been there for a day yet, and Gloria already hated her.

* * *

Simina had never tried on so many dresses in her life. She liked a lot of them and soon began to enjoy herself, despite Gloria's sour expression toward her. Olivia loved how Simina looked in every dress, but Gloria never gave a nice comment to her once. She once said, "No, that dress doesn't look good on you. It doesn't match with your complexion." Simina thought her voice sounded so bitchy. She also noticed when Olivia got too close to her, Gloria would pull Olivia away, or elbow her in the side. Simina quickly realized that Gloria was the controlling type.

Gloria never said one thing nice about her. She never gave Simina even one compliment. Olivia didn't seem to have a problem with her, though. Olivia actually liked Simina. Olivia was happy that she finally had a friend to dress up in pretty clothes. Simina was fun.

That day, she returned to the house with so many new clothes that Olivia picked out for her. Simina didn't know what to do with herself; she was so giddy. She'd had a good first day, despite Gloria's rudeness.

* * *

Three days later, Simina was getting used to living at her aunt's. It wasn't so bad. Today, her aunt told the girls that she wanted them to get outside and enjoy the weather, so Aunt Lyda gave each girl a basket and told them to go to the orchard to pick some apples. Simina wore her sparkly red dress for this occasion and put on her cloak, since it was a bit nippy outside.

Simina had never been to the orchard, so Gloria and Olivia (mainly Olivia) showed her the way. She noticed something in the sky that caught her attention as they walked. She turned her head and looked up. The Dark Castle, looming above the little town, cast a dark shadow that seemed to stretch on forever. The sharp, pointed spires towered ominously towards the cloudy sky. The sight sent a shiver down Simina's spine, and thoughts of the Prince entered her mind.

Simina thought he'd probably figured out by now that she'd stolen his horse. *He'll probably come after me.* Simina wanted to crawl under a rock and hide from him, so he couldn't find her. Somehow though it seemed he was watching her from everywhere.

Olivia tugged on her arm, tugging her mind out of these thoughts. "Come on, Simina!" Olivia urged. The two girls led Simina into the woods, down a little trail that opened into a clearing filled with apple trees. Orange and red leaves rained down from the trees. It was so very pretty.

Simina liked how the early sun shone through the leaves, reflecting their lovely colors. She loved autumn's beauty; it was clearly her favorite season. Some apples littered the ground. Holding her basket, she bent down and picked them up. She put them in her basket. Simina stood under a tree and looked up for some apples.

Enjoying the crisp, fresh air, she plucked one from a branch. Dead leaves crunched under her feet with each step. As Simina picked these apples, she thought of Ernest. A wave of nostalgia drenched her and she fell into a deep melancholy, a whirlpool of distraught emotions she didn't know how to manage. She missed Ernest. She missed playing those games with him, where they chased each other through the woods. She wondered how he was doing. Perhaps Simina should write to him sometime.

Simina reached up to pick another apple. Something hard whacked the back of her head. Simina winced and rubbed her head. She turned as an apple thumped to the ground. It would have made sense if the apple hit the top of her head. If an apple fell, it wouldn't hit the back of her head. It came from behind her. Simina turned around.

She saw Gloria giggling and Olivia glaring at Gloria. Simina scowled. She had reason to believe that Gloria threw an apple at the back of her head. Boy, she does know how to ruin someone's day. Simina, feeling vengeful, reached down, picked up an apple, and threw it at the back of Gloria's head to see how she liked it. It whacked Gloria on the head with a cracking splat and Simina turned back around, acting like she hadn't done anything. She continued picking apples.

Gloria gasped in shock and said, "Ow!" Simina smiled triumphantly as she placed another apple into her basket. She heard Olivia giggling and snorting behind her, but she held back her own laughter.

* * *

Simina learned that when you lived on the Right side, you had to go to school. At the start of next week, Aunt Lyda enrolled Simina in Etiquette School, so she'd learn to be a proper, dainty young lady.

Her first day was humiliating. While practicing to walk in heels, Simina staggered and tripped, falling flat on her face in front of the entire school. The rest of the girls there laughed at her, and Simina's face reddened terribly. But she got back up and kept walking, even though she wobbled.

When she returned to the house that day, her aunt approached her, holding a parcel. Simina stared at the parcel in her aunt's hands. Aunt Lyda handed it to her, but Simina didn't take it.

"Your father sent this for you," Aunt Lyda told Simina. "You must have forgotten something."

Simina took the parcel. "Thank you."

She sat down at the kitchen table and opened it. Inside there were a few zyros, and her mother's necklace. Misty eyed, Simina carefully held it up. How could she have forgotten this?

"Is that a gift?" her aunt asked.

"No," Simina sniffled. "It was my mother's."

Aunt Lyda walked over to Simina and stood next to her chair. "Would you like some help putting it on?"

Wiping away some tears, Simina nodded and handed her the necklace. Aunt Lyda carefully unclasped the chain and fastened it around her niece's neck. She then smoothed her hair out, letting it fan around her shoulders.

"There you go." Smiling, she patted her shoulder. Then she walked back over to the basin to wash dishes.

Simina remained at the table, admiring her mother's necklace.

"So, how are you settling in?" Aunt Lyda asked.

Simina smiled tightly. "Fine. It takes some getting used to."

Her aunt nodded, and said nothing else in response.

Simina wondered why Aunt Lyda hadn't stayed in Autumnville with Gregory. After all, they were brother and sister. Perhaps they didn't get along?

"Aunt Lyda?"

"Yes?" She carefully put an intricately decorated plate in the cupboard by the wash basin.

"Why didn't you stay in Autumnville with my father?"

"Simple." Aunt Lyda twirled around to face her, her flaming red hair bobbing. "I met my husband. He was from here. Of course, I married him and then moved here. The rest...is history."

Since Aunt Lyda had lived here for many years, Simina figured that she must have knowledge of The Dark Prince. Simina loathed him, yet she was curious to know more about him. She wanted to know as much as possible.

"Aunt Lyda?" she asked again.

"Yes?"

"What do you know...about...er, Prince Nar?"

"Not much," she said. "He's a bit of a recluse. Rarely leaves the castle."

"Is he...evil?"

Aunt Lyda rose a quizzical brow. "I don't think so. He's a bit odd, I think, but not evil. Why would you ask that?"

* * *

Another week passed, and Simina became accustomed to living on the Right and attending Etiquette School. She didn't like it, but she managed. She also wrote a letter to her father and Ernest just to see how they were doing. Simina was worried about them.

Simina had begun a daily routine. It consisted of getting up, getting dressed, going to school, coming home, doing chores, making dinner, eating, bathing, and going to bed. The only time she had free time was on Sundays.

Throughout the last week, Simina had noticed many soldiers around the town. They weren't marching in formation. They seemed to be looking for something. Every time Simina saw soldiers, she ducked back into the house and hid. She didn't know why these soldiers were here.

One day, while walking home from Etiquette School, Simina saw a picture tacked to a post. The boldness of the letters caught her eye. She stopped and looked at it.

WANTED

Girl, young, brown hair, wanted for thievery, stole Prince Nar's black stallion. One thousand zyro dollars reward regarding her arrest. Please notify a royal guard if you've seen this girl in your local area. Thank you.

Below that was a black-and-white picture of Simina's face. Simina's stomach turned, threatening to spill its grueling contents to the ground. So, he was looking for her. Helplessness threatened to squeeze the life right out of her. *Oh my goodness.* Simina looked around to ensure no one was watching and ripped the picture from the post. She stuffed it into her pocket and quickly ran back to her house.

Once in her room, she hid the wanted poster in her top dresser drawer, daring not to tell her aunt. She slammed the drawer shut, ran over to her bed, and hid under the covers.

* * *

The next day, Saturday afternoon, Simina was outside in her aunt's stables, brushing the stolen horse. Caution urged her, but she figured that she'd do this since she did this every day and didn't want to look suspicious.

She did not notice the soldier walking up behind her, however. She brushed through the horse's fur, stroking its mane. The soldier behind her thought she looked like the girl on the poster. He also thought that the horse looked a lot like Nar's. The soldier approached.

"Excuse me," a man's voice called from behind Simina. Goosebumps sprouted all over her body. Simina's skin prickled; it was as if her innermost darkest secrets were laid bare. Taking a deep breath, Simina turned and smiled politely.

"Yes, sir?" Simina responded. She wanted to freak now that she saw it was a Royal Guard. He wore armor and a fine silver tunic with the royal emblem on the front. He pointed at the horse.

"That's a really nice horse you got there," the soldier told her. Simina smiled.

"Thank you." She wanted to melt. Every fiber in her body told her to run, but Simina knew she couldn't do that, for it would look suspicious.

"Where'd you get it?" he asked her. He was suspicious. Her throat dried up.

"I...I..." Simina didn't know what to say. Her throat clinched. Her tongue attempted to form words in her mouth, but it flopped all around uselessly. The guard placed two hands on his hips.

"Perhaps you stole it," he stated. Simina gulped and stopped, trying to speak. Her polite composure had faltered. Simina shook her head.

"N-No," she stuttered, "I...um..." Simina was tongue-tied. Her blood drained from her face. The guard looked a little triumphant.

"Ma'am, what's your name?" he asked. Simina did not stick around to respond. She dropped the brush, turned, and ran.

"Come back here!" the guard yelled and chased her. Simina ran around the house and into town. She didn't get far. Unfortunately, Simina ran right into another Royal Guard. She gasped and tried to wriggle away, but he'd caught her.

"Let go of me!" Simina shouted, wrestling with the guard.

"Now you see here, miss," the guard grunted. Simina heard the other guard from before coming up behind her. She heard the clinking and clanking of a pair of shackles.

"You think this is the girl?" the one behind her asked the one restraining her. Simina fought the guard's restraint, struggling to get away, twisting and writhing. The guard tightened his grip on her.

"Yeah, it looks like her," he grunted. He growled at Simina. "Will you keep still!"

Simina saw her aunt and two cousins coming out of the house because of all the commotion. Aunt Lyda's face whitened at the sight of Simina in the hands of two guards.

"Aunt Lyda!" Simina shouted in hopes she'd help. The guard restraining Simina shook her.

"Quiet," he hissed sharply. Aunt Lyda rushed over to see what all this was about.

"By Zormon, what is going on?" Aunt Lyda asked, startled. The second guard raised a hand, stopping Aunt Lyda in her tracks.

"Please ma'am, don't interfere. This is royal business," he said monotonously. Aunt Lyda told Gloria and Olivia to go back inside.

"What has she done?" Aunt Lyda asked the guards.

"This girl has stolen Prince Nar's royal horse. She is to be arrested and taken to the castle for thievery, where the Prince will decide her fate," the guard with the shackles explained.

The guard grabbed Simina's arms, pulled them around and snapped the shackles around Simina's wrists, binding her. Simina struggled, trying to free herself from bondage. Aunt Lyda tried to protest, but the guard shushed her.

"I told you not to interfere. She was caught in possession of the stolen horse. Please. Step back," he ordered sternly. In compliance, Aunt Lyda held up her hands and stepped back.

Each guard taking an arm, they grabbed her and drug her away. Simina hung her head, wanting to cry, but the tears never came.

Thirteen

The guards shoved Simina into a carriage, and they rode out of town. One guard rode in the carriage with her while the other drove. Simina hung her head low. Doom possessed her every fiber. They were taking her to the Dark Prince Nar, and she could do nothing about it. What was he going to do to her? Simina shivered at the thought. She could only imagine. What if he put a curse on her? Or worse, what if he killed her? Simina tried not to think about it.

The ride to the castle was long and dreadful. Or at least it seemed that way, but it really didn't take that long for them to get there. A few minutes later, the sleigh pulled up in front of the castle. Dread washed over Simina at the sight. In an instant, the guards pulled her out of the carriage and into the cold. Holding Simina firmly by the arms, they trudged through the snow up to the castle doors.

Simina shook her head. She did not want to go inside. She stared at the castle with terrified eyes as her heart pounded rapidly in her chest, and she fought against the guards.

"No! No!" Simina kicked, flailing her limbs. She shook her head wildly about, neck spinning. "Don't take me there! Please don't take me there!" Simina shrieked, panic overwhelming her. The guards shoved her forward, shoving her hard in the back.

"Get moving, girl! We don't have time for this today!" the guard yelled at her. The hardness of his voice intimidated Simina and she shut up. Lip quivering, she slumped her head forward. With limp legs, She trudged forward through the snow.

Once directly in front of the doors, one guard pushed the grand double doors open with a heave. They walked in and the doors slammed shut behind them with a loud BANG!!! Simina was dragged up the grand set of stairs that went up to the landing, to the set of double doors she'd run out of just a few weeks ago.

Simina recalled the events that occurred in this room. This is the room he destroyed, where he'd almost killed her. Upon entering, she looked wildly about. The destruction of a few weeks ago was gone, like it had never happened. Everything was perfect and pristine. There was nary a crack in the walls to be seen. And above her, the chandelier hung beautifully, secured safely to the ceiling.

How could they have repaired such damage in such a short amount of time? It was impossible. Even with magic, a feat of that magnitude would be difficult. Someone would have to be very powerful in order to channel and use that amount of magic. Was the Dark Prince really that powerful?

Up ahead of her, Simina saw the throne, and it was occupied.

Simina saw him sitting there on his throne, just like last time. He sat relaxed, with his legs slightly spread apart. Simina wondered how someone so evil could look so elegant and beautiful. Much to her chagrin, a giant tidal wave of admiration swelled inside of her. She hated it.

Even though Simina admired him, she was also frightened of him in a way beyond belief. Nar saw the guards bringing her forth, so he stood with a grand flourish. Finally, Simina stood before him but turned her face away, willing herself not to look in his eyes. The guards forced Simina to her knees, and she grunted.

"Here she is, your majesty. Is this the young lass who stole your royal stead?" the guards asked, bowing his head. Simina stared at the floor beneath her, listening to her mouth panting out each of her breaths.

A gentle hand tilted up her chin. Nar lifted her face so he could see her and Simina found herself staring into his beautiful amethyst eyes. Simina lost her breath and a strangled gasp blew from her. A whimper shuddered out from between her lips as their beauty entranced her.

Nar stared at her face and observed her for what seemed like the longest time to Simina. His purple eyes saw right into her soul, tearing it apart, ripping it to shreds.

He stroked a finger down her cheek, gently brushing the side of her face. His touch, soft as a feather; she almost leaned into it. Simina wanted to. Her eyes fluttered. Nar smirked, beguiling eyes seeing her innermost desire.

"Yes. She is the one," Nar whispered. He stepped away from her, putting at least a foot of space between them. Simina blinked, knocked out of her daze, her mind cleared of its fogginess.

"What do you want us to do with her, your majesty?" the guard asked Nar. Nar smiled, eyes mischievous and glimmering.

"Take her…" He seemed to think about it for a while. "To the dungeon." Nar didn't once take his eyes from her. As soon as the words left his mouth, the guards began dragging her off. Rage filled Simina and she lunged at him, but the guards held her back. Simina growled at Nar's receding face.

They dragged her away, back the way they came. Back in the foyer, they turned right down a dark and dank corridor Simina hadn't noticed before. The guards pulled up a barred caged door on the floor. Its rusty hinges creaked and groaned from old age, the sound grating in Simina's ears. A set of old, cracking concrete stairs led down, down, down, down, until arriving in a terrible, odorous gray concrete room.

The odor of rotting bodies and fecal matter eroded her nostrils, magnified by the dank quality of the air. Her nose crinkled, the mustiness seizing her lungs as the strong odor slowly made it difficult to breathe. Simina coughed. The guards undid her shackles. Attached to the wall were cuffs for the wrists. Bound by another set of cuffs was a real skeleton, cuffed to the wall. Simina screamed. She knew it wasn't alive, but it still frightened Simina nonetheless.

The guards shoved her against the wall and made her sit. They lifted her arms, put her wrists in the cuffs and fastened them. They were tight around Simina's wrists and she winced from the rigid confines. Without doing or saying anything else, they left her there, going back through the barred cage door.

Simina sat there alone, wallowing in sorrow. She hung her head low, so low that her chin touched her chest. The backs of her eyes burned until finally, the tears came and Simina wept.

* * *

Simina was locked in the dungeon for a little over an hour and spent the entire time weeping and feeling sorry for herself. She sniffled, cheeks feeling quite sticky from her tear stains. Her stomach growled with hunger. A sad little whimper escaped Simina.

The creak of the caged door perked Simina's ears. A moment later, she heard footsteps walking down. Simina did not look up. She didn't feel like it. Nar entered the dungeon and came to stand before Simina. For a moment, Nar thought she might be sleeping because of how she held herself. Then he heard her sniffle, as if she'd been crying.

Nar crouched down in front of her, but she did not lift her head. Nar raised a hand toward her and lifted her chin. When Simina saw Nar in front of her, she no longer possessed the energy to hate him or feel anger. Nar took in her sad, sorrowful expression. Her eyes were red from crying, her cheeks held a pinkish blush, and her lips were turned down, sad and pouty.

Nar brushed a few gentle fingertips across her jawline. Nar admired her beauty. *She's too pretty to cry.*

"Answer something for me." Nar kept his voice soft. Simina stared at him, saying nothing. Nar continued.

"How were you, of all people, able to mount and ride my horse?" His voice sounded calm but also slightly unnerved. Simina didn't understand the question he posed to her. She swallowed and licked her lips.

"W-what do you mean?" Simina's voice trembled, scared as a mouse.

"My horse is enchanted with a spell. No one else can mount my horse without being thrown from it. My only question is how you could ride my enchanted horse," Nar explained.

Simina just shook her head.

"I just got on it and rode it like any other horse."

She swallowed, and her body shook. Simina didn't feel good. Her wrists hurt, and she whimpered. Simina stared at Nar with pleading, desperate eyes.

"Are you going to kill me?" Her lip quivered and tears brimmed in her eyes. Her chest began to heave, and Nar watched a tear leak from her eye and trickle down her cheek. Simina looked so pitiful, Nar garnered a touch of sympathy for her. He brushed a tear away with his thumb.

He chuckled darkly, amused. "Do not be absurd. Why would I kill a perfectly good servant?"

Goosebumps sprouted all over Simina's body at his words. "W-what?"

"In exchange for your freedom, you will work for me. You will help Matilda maintain the castle," he stated.

"For how long?"

"As long as I say."

Gulping, Simina nodded. "Okay. I'll do it."

"You have to. There is no choice in the matter. Do not try to run away. I *will* find you," Nar said, voice eerily calm. "And next time, I may not be so forgiving. Do you understand?"

"Yes, I understand. I won't run. Just please let me go," Simina begged him. Nar smiled. Hearing her beg was a pleasure, and she looked especially pretty when she did so. Nar stood and released the cuffs on her wrists, unbinding her. Once free, Simina sighed in relief and rubbed the sore red marks on her wrists.

"Thank you so much," Simina breathed. She stood and stretched herself.

"I will send a royal carriage for you every day, providing safe passage to my castle with protection from my Royal Guards," Nar told her. "You start tomorrow."

"Follow me. My guards will escort you back home," Nar said. Simina went with him, leaving the dungeon. He took her out to a waiting carriage, where two guards also waited. Simina got in and soon they rode away.

Fourteen

When Simina arrived home a few hours later, she told her Aunt Lyda and her cousins what had happened.

Gloria's jaw dropped, and her eyes immediately filled with jealousy. She turned her nose up as if she'd just smelled something foul and frowned. *She did it on purpose just to see the Prince.*

Olivia, on the other hand, wasn't jealous. She was just shocked.

Simina thought she'd let down her father by doing this. He told her to stay out of trouble, and now look at what she'd done. She'd stolen a Prince's horse and been arrested, and now she had to be his cleaning maid just to pay for her freedom from the dungeon. Simina's mind filled with terrible thoughts about herself and wanted to cry, but figured it wouldn't do her any good. She realized that she was only taking the punishment for the consequence of stealing his horse.

That evening, she made sure to eat a hearty supper and take a nice shower, so she'd feel clean the next morning after a refreshing night of sleep. Simina thought that she'd be doing some back-breaking work since the castle was pretty big.

As Simina walked to her room after her shower, she passed Gloria's bedroom. She heard someone speaking. It was Gloria's harsh, snapping voice, which Simina had come to recognize. It sounded so mean and nasty that Simina stopped. Her ears perked. The door was slightly ajar, so she leaned closer to the opened door and listened.

"I can't stand her, Olivia. I just can't stand her," Simina heard Gloria's voice say snobbishly. She figured Gloria must be talking about her, since there could be no one else Gloria meant. Simina also assumed this because of the mean, envious looks Gloria always gave her.

"Well, what has she done to you?" Olivia questioned.

"Oh, so now you're going to take her side?" Gloria said accusingly.

Olivia sighed.

"No, Gloria, that's not what I'm saying. I'm not taking anyone's side. I'm just saying she hasn't done anything to you," Olivia protested.

Gloria sniffed indignantly.

"Yes, she has. She makes herself prettier on purpose just to be prettier than me!" Gloria shouted, and Simina heard her stomp her foot. Simina rolled her eyes. *That is ridiculous.* Simina never did anything on purpose to hurt anybody.

"And she probably got herself arrested on purpose, just to see the Prince, so she can marry him and get rich! That's not going to happen! I'm marrying the Prince! Not her!" Gloria's voice turned into a screech. Simina couldn't believe her ears. This girl thought that Simina wanted to marry Prince Nar. She must be out of her mind. Simina didn't have that intention at all. At the time, Simina just wanted to get out of there.

Simina had no interest at all in marrying him. His words and actions confused her, and recently she'd begun second guessing herself. Was he really all that evil? If he were as evil as the book said, he would have surely killed her by now. Why had he saved her from the crash? Why spare her after she'd stolen his beloved horse? Simina shook her head, refusing to let him cloud her judgment. He may not be evil, but he was cruel. He'd locked her in a room, tore up her letter, and nearly killed her.

"You're just jealous, Gloria. She hasn't done anything to you," Olivia told Gloria, defending Simina. Shaking her head, Simina walked away, going to her room. She didn't care what Gloria thought about her. Simina knew the truth about herself, even if other people didn't understand her.

Simina settled into her bed for the night. Once she settled, she clicked off her lamp. Simina laid her head down to her rest and fell peacefully to sleep.

* * *

The next morning, Simina rose early, feeling well-rested from her good night's sleep. She dressed for the occasion, putting on one of her old peasant dresses, which she used to wear most of the time. She brushed through her thick, curly brown locks and tied them up into a ponytail with a ribbon. It took her a half hour to dress and prepare herself. Her Aunt Lyda stopped in her doorway just as Simina grabbed her cloak.

"Your carriage is here. Good luck," Aunt Lyda told her. Simina pulled her cloak around her shoulders and buttoned it at her throat. As Simina approached the front door, she heard the neighing of a horse. She opened the door and walked out, pulling on her hood. She boarded the carriage and rode away to the castle.

* * *

Simina did not know what to expect from this job. She knew she was supposed to clean, but she didn't know if there was a particular way they wanted her to clean. She didn't know if there was a required way of doing things. Unsure, she knocked on the large castle doors. At first, no one answered. But a few seconds later, the doors opened, and from what Simina saw, they opened by themselves. She did not know how this was possible, and it creeped her out. With a weird feeling overtaking her, Simina walked in, taking slow steps.

She looked all around the foyer, feet tapping with sharp, dainty clicks on the floor. Her footsteps echoed throughout the castle. Simina heard the heavy doors slam shut behind her. Startled, she turned to look back at the doors she'd just walked through. No one was there who could have closed them; they'd closed automatically. Simina glanced all around. She didn't see anybody but heard footsteps on the stairs. She glanced toward them.

"So you came." Nar's voice boomed through the foyer, bouncing on and off the walls. Simina saw him standing halfway on the stairs, his right hand resting on the banister. Nar stood with a stature of authority, grandly, with a looseness to his posture. His posture wasn't stiff, tense, or forced. It was simply how he stood that gave him his grace.

"So I did," Simina responded. Her heart fluttered with excitement at the sight of him. Her stomach flipped and nearly catapulted out of her mouth. She cleared her throat, containing herself.

Nar started to walk down the steps, one at a time, moving very elegantly. As he walked, he never once took his eyes from Simina. She liked the graceful way he moved. She liked watching him; she admired him.

"I didn't think you would," Nar said, moving swiftly toward her. Simina tried not to focus too much on his face. Sweeping a strand of hair from her eyes, Simina gazed down at the floor between her feet. Simina didn't know what to say. She was utterly tongue-tied. She swung herself around, making her skirt twirl.

"I don't have a choice," she stated simply. Her nerves got the better of her, twisting and twirling, like a flutterbudget. Nar took in her appearance and smiled. Her beauty was more prominent in ugly peasant clothes because of the contrast. She had a slim waist, swelling breasts, a slender neck, rosy plump cheeks, and a sharp, curving jawline. Nar looked her up and down, enjoying the shape of her developed body. He wondered if her legs were just as beautiful and slender as the rest of her body under that skirt. She was just a mere peasant girl. Nar couldn't fathom why he was so drawn to her. He pictured a roaring, irresistible fire and he was the moth.

"No. You don't," Nar replied with a smirk. Simina saw Matilda rushing down the stairs with two mops, a bucket, and a pair of slippers. She came down right before her and placed the bucket at her feet. It was filled with soapy water. Matilda shoved a mop at Simina, and she was obligated to take it.

"The floor needs some serious cleaning, that's for sure. That's your first job," Matilda told Simina. Nar looked at Simina and smiled.

"Good luck," Nar smirked, and he was gone in a puff of dark purple smoke. Simina shivered, nervous.

"Oh, and you'll need to put these on." Matilda shoved a pair of slippers at her, beige slippers. Simina took them and slipped them on her feet.

"What do I need them for?" Simina wondered.

"So you won't dirty up the floor while you mop. We got work to do. First, you need to mop this whole foyer." Matilda waved her hand over the entire expanse of the foyer. Simina stared at it. She just realized how great the whole thing looked from here. Simina then realized that Matilda was the only servant she'd seen. In a castle this big, it should take a couple dozen people to maintain the cleanliness of it. Was Matilda really doing it all herself?

"You want me to mop this whole floor by myself? That will take an eternity!" Simina fussed.

"Just use your magic, dear," she said.

Simina's frustration grew. "But I...can't use magic."

"No magic?" Matilda balked. "That's certainly interesting."

"Is that how you manage to clean this whole castle by yourself?" Even using magic, it should take more than one person to clean it. Matilda would have to have a great amount of magical stamina to do this, let alone be powerful enough to channel that much magic.

"Yes." Matilda puffed up with pride. "I've been honing my magical prowess since I was a child. Every day, non stop. Since you have no magic, I suppose I could help you."

Simina breathed out in relief. "Oh, thank you."

Matilda dropped the mop she held in her hand, but instead of it clattering to the floor, it floated in mid air. Then, like it had a mind of its own, the mop dunked itself into the soapy bucket of water and began to mop the floor. Simina didn't attempt to keep up with it, as it was going twice the speed she was, but she tried her best.

However, after only a few minutes, Simina's back and arms began to hurt. She had done chores, but nothing like this before. The foyer floor now seemed enormous all of a sudden. Matilda kept Simina hustling, telling her to put some muscle into it. Simina did not like mopping at all. It caused her back pain and overworked her muscles. She was grateful for Matilda's magic mop, as it did most of the work for her, and after thirty minutes, it was finished.

After mopping, Simina was given a few minutes to rest before Matilda made her dust in one of the guest rooms. Those were only a few tasks she had to do today. But by the end of her first day, exhaustion had won and she was completely wiped out. Nar gave Simina her pay of five zyros in a pouch and then sent her away in a royal carriage to return her home.

Simina dreaded having to come back tomorrow.

Fifteen

As the days progressed, Simina slowly got used to her new job. She often helped Matilda dust rooms, mop floors, clean dishes, and much more. After working for a straight week, Simina didn't mind it much. She was getting paid five zyros a day, which made Simina feel a little better about working.

Nar however, was very critical of her work. At the end of each day, before going home, he would come to inspect what she had done. He complained that the floor wasn't quite spotless, pointing out areas that she'd missed. If there was even one speck of dust still lingering, Nar made her stay an extra thirty minutes longer. Despite this, at the end of her first week, he'd raised her pay by two zyros, so now she was getting seven zyros a day. Simina didn't work weekends and was glad about that. Her aunt had also cut her chores since she was cleaning the castle.

Simina didn't do much on weekends since she mainly rested, but this weekend was an exception. This weekend, Sunday to be specific, Simina was out with Gloria and Olivia around the marketplace. Simina was trying to avoid Gloria, so she was alone somewhere else. She wouldn't have minded Olivia with her, but since Gloria was so bossy, Olivia had to follow Gloria around all over the place.

Simina, doing as Aunt Lyda told her, was buying the groceries. Olivia and Gloria were off looking at expensive jewelry they knew they didn't have money for. As Gloria dragged Olivia away, Simina heard Olivia whining about her not wanting to do something. Her words were,

"No, Gloria. I don't want to. Do we have to?" Olivia had whined. Gloria had snapped at Olivia and said that she had to. At the time, Simina didn't really pay much mind.

So now, Simina was humming to herself as she picked out the groceries. She placed a loaf of bread and some orange grass into her basket, eyes skimming over the selection of fresh foods. Astounded by the variety, Simina's jaw nearly fell right off its hinges. Autumnville never produced such a wide selection of foods. Simina grumbled to herself at the price of salted meat. She scowled. *Gee, ten zyros for only a pound? What are they trying to do, rob me blind?* A pound wasn't even that much.

From a little way down the street, Simina heard a ruckus. She turned her head toward the noise. Someone, a man, was yelling. A little way down the street, Simina saw the jewelry shop. The man inside, the salesman, ran outside, screaming.

"You two come back here, you thieves! Guards! Guards!" the man cried. The man was short and bald, wearing glasses that made him look like an owl. The two nearest Royal Guards took off on a run toward the scene. Simina rushed forward to get a better look and craned her neck above the crowd to see.

To Simina's astonishment and great disbelief, she recognized the jewelry thieves as her cousins. Simina's eyes popped out and her mouth hung open so wide she was sure her jaw would fall off. Both girls were running in her direction, but past her they went, shoving through the crowd with their hands full of expensive and precious jewels. They weren't running very fast, and Gloria was wearing a huge, happy smile.

That confused Simina. *Why is she smiling?* Eventually, the guards caught up, surrounded them, and made them drop the jewels. The guards put shackles on Gloria's and Olivia's wrists, roughly grabbing their arms and arresting them. Once the shackles clamped around Gloria's wrists, she smiled so brightly, like never before, her smile brighter than the sun.

Olivia, on the other hand, looked like someone had kicked her puppy. She looked like she didn't want to. Simina thought that Gloria had forced her to steal that jewelry, but she didn't know why. Olivia's eyes drooped, lips pouty, looking ready to cry. As the two girls and the guards passed Simina, Gloria smiled at her. It was much less of a smile and more like a sneer. It was a mighty nasty sneer, and when Gloria turned away, she stuck her nose high into the air, triumphant.

Simina put the puzzle pieces together, her incredulousness growing. Gloria wanted to get arrested. She wanted to. Simina gathered herself, clearing her throat. She shut her mouth and took a breath. Simina took a moment to think. She reflected on Gloria and Olivia's conversation, which she'd overheard about a week ago. Gloria is jealous of Simina because she thinks Simina purposely stole his horse just so she can work there and see the Prince.

Simina knew that wasn't true. She had stolen the horse on purpose, but not just to get arrested so she could go back and see Prince Nar. A light bulb clicked on in Simina's head. She understood now why Gloria did it. Gloria did it on purpose so that she could work in the castle because Gloria liked the Prince. Simina's eyes popped open. Extremely alarmed, Simina walked home to tell her Aunt Lyda about the mess her two daughters had caused.

* * *

Simina told Aunt Lyda the news. When Aunt Lyda heard, boy was she angry. Her eyes flashed and her face flushed red. She got so fired up that Simina was actually scared of her. The two girls returned a few hours later without shackles, Gloria sporting a great big happy smile. They both got yelled at upon arriving by Aunt Lyda and got double chores for a week as punishment.

It turned out that Prince Nar had given her two cousins the same offer he'd given her. This irritated Simina beyond belief since now she'd also have to deal with them at the castle. This displeasure haunted her until they started the following day.

Simina hated this and hated how Gloria looked so freaking happy about this. She'd done it intentionally just to get Nar's attention. Simina doubted it would work, as the Prince was quite aloof. Simina couldn't fathom the thought of Nar possibly being interested in anyone, let alone Gloria. Why would he? She was a brat. The thought of Nar liking Gloria disgusted her, and even made her a little jealous. She didn't know why she thought these things, or had these feelings. Simina definitely had no romantic feelings toward him. She hardly knew him and he was utterly cruel to her; why did she care if he was attracted to another girl? This made Simina feel stupid, and she dreaded going to Nar's castle.

After dinner, Simina spent the rest of the night avoiding Gloria's demeaning stares.

* * *

The next morning, Simina had to ride in the carriage with her two dumb cousins. Simina wanted to slap that smile off Gloria's face because she hated how happy Gloria looked.

When they arrived at the castle, Nar and Matilda stood waiting at the bottom of the stairs. Nar greeted Gloria and Olivia and explained what they'd both be doing. Both girls were to go with Matilda. Gloria looked ready to faint at the sight of Prince Nar and couldn't stop ogling him for the sake of all things sane. This irked Simina's nerves beyond belief.

Nar turned to Simina, dark eyes staring straight into her soul. However, he said nothing and disappeared.

Trusting her experience, Matilda allowed Simina to clean on her own while she supervised Gloria and Olivia. Glad for this, Simina wandered around the castle, cleaning rooms of her choosing at her leisure. It was refreshing not having someone watching her every move like a vulture. While she appreciated Matilda's help, she enjoyed her solitude.

Later that same day, as Simina was wandering the corridors, she overheard two voices talking. Unable to make out the words, Simina quietly crept closer until the voices became clear. It was Matilda and Nar, arguing. They were just around the corner, in a room across the hall. Simina saw a sliver of Nar's back and some of Matilda's front, but she couldn't see her completely due to Nar standing in front of her.

"I don't understand why you're so hard on the girl!" Matilda hissed at Nar.

"She stole my horse!" he spat in response.

"So what? The punishment should fit the crime, in my book," Matilda said matter-of-factly.

"Well, it's not up to you, is it?"

"The poor girl has no magic! You could at least cut her some slack. You don't always have to act so cruel, *Dark Prince.*"

"I'm not acting," he sneered. "I am the Dark Prince."

"Hogwash," she harrumphed. "I see right through you, and I think she does too. You're just scared. Scared of letting people in."

"I'm not scared of *anything,*" he grumbled. "The last time I let someone get close to me...it's better if people stay away from me."

Prince Nar left the room and turned down the hall in Simina's direction. Heart leaping, Simina darted into the room closest to her and quickly shut the door. She waited there until she heard his footsteps fade away.

* * *

The next day, Simina was cleaning in the dining room with Gloria and Olivia. Matilda was berating them about proper cleaning techniques when the door opened and Prince Nar walked in. Simina didn't have to look up to know that he was watching her. Olivia almost fainted at the sight of him, and Gloria giggled. Simina rolled her eyes hard. Ugh. She attempted to look nonchalant and aloof in the hopes that Nar would ignore her. Unfortunately, he did not.

"Simina, won't you come with me, please?" he asked, attempting to sound polite, kind even.

Glancing up at him, Simina frowned. Olivia gasped and Gloria glared.

She heard her whisper to Olivia, "Why is he asking for *her?*"

For once, Simina actually agreed with her. Why was he asking for her?

Prince Nar ignored them, keeping his focus trained squarely on Simina. Reluctantly, Simina dropped her cleaning rag and walked over to him.

"Please follow me," he said, and led her out of the dining hall. Nar took her through a maze of corridors and up three flights of stairs, until he finally stopped in front of a strange door. It was gigantic, with a long, sleek black handle. Murals depicting various historical events were engraved in the stone: The creation of Zormonia, The Steele family enslaving the Darkla race, The Azrian-Steele conflict. That conflict was the shortest, yet bloodiest battle in all of Zormonian history. There were dozens more, but Simina couldn't remember them all.

"Where are you taking me?" A slight fear twinged the back of her mind. Was it some kind of special torture chamber?

Nar did not answer her. Silently, he pushed open the large door, and it opened with a loud groan. A thick layer of dust blew across the floor, disturbed by their entrance. Inside it was dark, but Simina could make out strange shapes and silhouettes.

"This is my father's artifact room," Nar spoke finally, stepping inside. "No one's been in here for many years."

Simina hesitated at the entrance, afraid to step inside. A draft of air blew out, stale and musky. Nar gestured for her to come.

"It's okay," he assured her. "I'm not going to hurt you."

She didn't trust him, but she went with him anyway. Simina followed him in, and the heavy door crashed shut. Nar waved a hand and candles burst to life along the walls, their flames casting dim, but much needed light. Thick dust billowed around her feet as she walked.

The silhouettes were statues and dusty bookshelves lined the back walls. The room was painted an eerie shade of blue, and there were rows and rows of other shelves that held strange items and jars filled with unknown substances. Some of them had things floating in them, and discomfort clawed inside of her at the sight of it. She hoped that she didn't have to clean it.

"Do you want me to clean it?" she asked, wringing her hands.

"No, nothing like that." Prince Nar shook his head. "My father wishes for this room to remain untouched."

"So why bring me here?"

Nar stroked the spine of a book, and then carefully removed it from the shelf. A huge dust cloud pooled in the air in front of him. "All these books are grimoires. Spell books."

"What does any of this have to do with me?" Was he trying to rub it in her face that she didn't have magic?

Simina peered closely at a jar labeled "Mermaid Scales." They were floating in liquid and the scales shimmered beautifully. Simina was mesmerized.

"Everything," Nar answered, and his voice broke Simina from her trance. He walked over to a podium in the center of the room and placed the book on top of it.

Simina became intrigued with an odd-looking plant. The stems were a dark, vibrant green with blood red tendrils snaking up the length of them. The leaves, wide and bountiful, were midnight black, glowing with sparkles. She reached out a hand to touch it.

"Don't touch that!" Nar snapped urgently.

Simina's finger stopped centimeters from the leaf. "Why?"

"It will kill you," he replied, voice dire.

Simina quickly withdrew her hand and turned towards Nar.

"You still haven't told me why you've taken me here."

He glared at her, irritated. "I'm going to try and help you channel magic."

Simina bit her lip in an attempt not to laugh. "You're going to help me? Why are you being so nice to me all of a sudden?"

Prince Nar took a deep breath, sucking his teeth. "We may have gotten off on the wrong foot and I am trying to...amend that."

"Yes, but why?"

"Does it matter?" He ran a frustrated hand through his hair. "I believe that you have untapped magic that, for whatever reason you have difficulty channeling, unlike the rest of us. You claim to not have magic, but I think you managed to use magic to unlock the door."

Simina didn't know how to feel about Prince Nar being nice to her. Or trying to be. Maybe his conversation with Matilda changed his mind.

"Why is this room important?"

"Because this room is filled with magical items and artifacts. Being around magical items and things makes it easier for someone to channel. Come here." Nar ushered her over.

Simina cautiously walked up to him, gulping nervously. Nar held up his hand.

"Put your hand against mine," he instructed. She did as she was told and put her hand against his. His palm was warm, the sensation of their skin to skin contact sending tingles throughout her hand, and Simina's cheeks flushed slightly at the contact.

"Yes, you most definitely do have magic," Nar said. "I can feel it. But it's dormant."

"Dormant? Why?"

"I don't know. Maybe subconsciously you haven't needed it. But I want you to think back to when you unlocked the door. What did you feel? Describe it to me."

"It was like a pulse. A surge of energy flowing through my entire body," she told him, hand still against his.

"Hm, all right." He lowered his hand and took a small pin out of his pocket. "We'll start with something easy."

Resting the pin in the palm of his hand, Nar made it float for a few seconds. Then, it dropped back into his palm, and he handed it to her.

"Now you make it float."

"Um, okay."

Simina tried to do what she did last time. She pictured the pin floating above her hand in her mind and imagined the magical energy flowing through her. She stared at the pin for several seconds, but nothing happened.

Simina frowned. "It's not working."

"Open yourself up to your surroundings," Nar suggested. "There is magic all around you. It's in the artifacts. Inside the planet itself. You are a part of this planet. So the magic flows through you, too. Just relax. Concentrate."

Taking a deep breath, she nodded. Simina relaxed and focused her energy. Closing her eyes, she thought about the items around her and the magic deep inside Zormonia's core. A surge of energy started in her feet. It trickled up her body until it found its way into her hand. Warmth coalesced inside her belly and she opened her eyes. The pin was not floating, but instead wriggling, as if struggling to lift up. Simina pulled on the magical energy around her harder, but the trickle stayed only that; a trickle. It started slipping away, even though she tried to hold on to it. Soon, it vanished completely and the pin went completely still.

"It didn't work," she groaned.

"That's fine," said Nar. "Just try again."

Simina began to start over, but before she could, a gigantic wave of exhaustion washed over her. Eyes drooping, she swayed precariously, off balance. Her limbs turned into noodles, and suddenly she was careening towards the floor.

"Whoa, now," Nar said, catching her. "Really? Doing that little magic made you this tired? Hm, you're weaker than I thought..."

"Shut up..." Simina mumbled, and then she fell unconscious.

***

Simina awoke sometime later back in her own bed. The last thing she remembered was Prince Nar and his artifact room. Startled, she shot up in bed. Simina regretted this immediately as dizziness overtook her, her head pounding.

"Ugghhh..." she groaned, rubbing her temples.

Aunt Lyda was there by her bedside, hands on her shoulders.

"Easy, Simina," she said softly. "You've been through quite the ordeal."

Aunt Lyda slowly pushed her back into a laying down position. "What are you talking about?"

"You almost used up all of your magical energy. You could've died," she explained.

"What?" Simina exclaimed, attempting to sit up again, but her aunt stopped her.

"You didn't know? If you completely deplete your magic energy, you'll die."

Simina huffed, pushing her head back into the soft pillow. "How did I get back here?"

"Prince Nar brought you back. You were unconscious and barely breathing."

This information surprised Simina. He brought her back here? Maybe he wasn't so bad after all...

"How long has it been?"

Aunt Lyda patted her hand. "You've been asleep for a week."

"A week?!" Simina hollered. "What about my duties?"

"You'll be allowed to resume them when you're better. Right now, though, I think we better get something in that stomach." Aunt Lyda picked up a steaming plate of meat and vegetables, covered in a thick, rich and delicious looking brown sauce. Simina took it gratefully and ate it up. Every bite made Simina better, and soon the dizziness and headache went away.

Aunt Lyda took her plate when she was finished.

"Aunt Lyda?"

"Yes, dear?"

"What do you think about fairytales?" Simina asked.

Aunt Lyda shrugged. "Unrealistic."

"How so?"

"Because things like that don't always happen. It seems nice, yes...but if you really think about it, the outcome of those stories are very unrewarding to the character," Aunt Lyda said.

"What do you mean?"

"Well, for one it's not real. Second, they get their happy ending . But that's all they get. True happiness isn't just getting the ending you want. It's about growth, about realizing that real life isn't as black and white, like being good or evil. Real life is more complicated, dramatic, fulfilling, and most of all, *real,*" Aunt Lyda explained.

Simina was silent for a moment, reflecting on her aunt's words. She thought about Prince Nar, and how just because he was a prince, he'd been given the evil title of The Dark Prince. Despite his previous cruel actions towards her, Simina still didn't know the real reason why he held that title.

Aunt Lyda stood, patting Simina on the shoulder. "You rest up, now."

Without another word, her aunt left the room, leaving Simina alone with her thoughts.

The following day, Simina returned to the castle to complete her duties. When she attempted to go with her cousins to clean with them, Matilda stopped her.

"Excuse me Simina, his majesty has another task for you today," she said.

"Like what?"

"You will be cleaning the library today, with our librarian, Oliver," Matilda told her.

Simina gulped with anticipation. *The library.* She could only imagine the vastness of a castle library, the sheer volume of books it could hold. This servant situation was by far not ideal, but cleaning the library was a task Simina looked forward to.

"Follow me, please." Simina nodded and followed Matilda up the staircase. Olivia and Gloria watched them with curiosity, but as they entered the corridor her cousins disappeared from sight.

Matilda led Simina up three flights of stairs, taking her to the third floor. Simina had never been in this part of the castle before. Soon, they stopped in front of two large, silver lined double doors with striking silver handles. Matilda grasped each handle and pulled the great doors open.

Matilda stepped aside, allowing Simina entrance. Simina walked in, gazing all around. The breath left her lungs as she took in the sight of the library. The library was more expansive than any she'd ever seen before. Built-in shelves, overflowing with books, spanned the entire length of each wall, reaching towards the high ceiling. The sheer volume of books was astounding; Simina had never seen so many in one place. Additional shelves were scattered throughout the expansive room, creating a maze of literature. To the right, there was a counter. Behind the counter was an old-looking man with wild white hair, glasses, and a bushy white beard. He held a cane, and he stared at Simina with a strange curiosity. He adjusted his glasses and squinted at her. The wrinkles in his face were prominent, but something in his aging blue eyes looked distinctly youthful.

On the counter sat a huge, thick book, probably holding the records of each book's placement in the library. A little quill pen sat on the corner. Breathless, Simina gazed around, mouth agape.

"Wow," Simina breathed, craning her neck to see the top of the highest shelf. A smile crept across her lips.

"It's beautiful. It's amazing!" Simina exclaimed, arms out on either side of her. She turned around to Matilda, smirking.

"I love your library," she gushed. Matilda smiled knowingly.

"Yes, it's quite magnificent," she agreed. "I come here sometimes to read."

Simina was surprised. "You like to read?"

"Yes, a little here and there when I'm able."

Matilda cleared her throat. "Back to business...you will be helping the bookkeeper sort books and clean the library."

Simina beamed. "With pleasure."

"Well, I'll leave you two to it.."

As soon as Matilda was gone, Oliver started bobbling to Simina, walking with his cane.

"Come on over here, girl. Help me with these books," he drawled with an old, raspy voice. Simina walked over to him.

"All right, now I need all these books re-sorted." Oliver gestured to the whole right side of the library. Surprise jumped into her bones and she gulped. *That's a lot of books.*

"You'll start over here, Section A. On each spine is the letter A and a number. You go through and make sure they're in order. Here." Oliver shoved a giant, musty book in her arms. Simina grunted with effort and set the big book down on the counter. She opened it. Inside was a list of each book, every title, and every book number. Simina looked at Section A and started her sorting.

* * *

An hour later, Simina had hardly gotten any sorting done. Well, she sorted two whole rows of books but was constantly distracted by the books. She'd find a book with an eye-catching title, get interested, open it, and start reading. Simina would keep reading it until Oliver told her to return to work.

Simina had set aside a pile of books for herself to read later, and this pile kept getting larger by the minute. At this rate, Simina could probably read every book in the library. She was standing, reading a book, when she suddenly heard a loud WHACK! Simina looked up from the book she was reading, startled. Simina saw Oliver hobbling around in between the smaller bookshelves, wandering. She watched him. He lifted his cane and whacked the side of a bookshelf. WHACK! She now noticed the dent marks scratching up the bookshelves' sides. *Why was he doing that?*

She shrugged and kept on reading. Again, WHACK! Simina jumped, feeling slightly disgruntled.

"Get back to sortin'!" Oliver yelled. Simina set the book down and continued sorting. She sorted for hours until Oliver told her that she was done. Afterward, Simina gathered her books, found a table, sat, and started reading.

Sixteen

Surrounded by huge piles of books, Simina slept soundly, head lying upon an open book. Nar came in to check up on Simina since she'd been there for a while. He walked in and found her asleep at the table, lying on a book. She slept so soundly that Nar did not want to disturb her. He was about to wake her in a polite manner, but at that instant, Nar heard a loud WHACK!

Simina jolted awake, squeaking. Nar glared at Oliver as he watched him whack another bookshelf with his cane. WHACK! Simina looked all around and realized that she'd fallen asleep while reading. She placed a hand on her head.

"Oh dear…" She yawned sleepily, covering her mouth. Nar cleared his throat.

"Oliver," he said. Oliver turned toward Nar.

"Yep?" Oliver responded.

"I'd appreciate it if you'd stop whacking my bookshelves with your cane," Nar said through gritted teeth.

"Well, whatchu want me to whack 'em with, my hand?" Oliver drawled. Nar sighed irritably.

"No, Oliver, I don't want you to whack the bookshelves at all," Nar said, scowling. Oliver grumbled and strolled away. As he walked away, his cane quickly snapped and whacked one of the bookshelves. WHACK! Nar groaned.

Simina started even more at the sound of Nar's voice behind her. She turned and saw Nar. Immediately she leapt out of the chair, alert.

"Your majesty!" Simina exclaimed, alarmed at his presence.

"I see you've been doing some light reading." Nar's voice dripped with sarcasm. Simina smiled sheepishly, hoping he wasn't going to reprimand her too harshly for sleeping on the job.

"Yeah, um, I uh, enjoy reading. Quite a bit…"

Nar nodded. "I understand that this is your first day back after your…incident. However, could you please…refrain from falling asleep while you're supposed to be working?"

Simina cringed. "I'm sorry, it…it won't happen again. Your majesty."

He pursed his lips. "Stop calling me your majesty. You can just call me Nar."

"Okay…"

Nar sighed heavily, sucking his teeth. He held back the tension growing in his body and took a deep breath. He took something out of his pocket. "I wanted to...give you something."

Simina flinched out of habit, but nothing happened. He placed a small, jagged pink crystal on the table. She picked it up. "What is it?"

The odd little object was cool to the touch, yet warm at the same time. It glittered in the light, sending small, sparkling beams in various directions.

"It's a magic crystal. They come in other colors, like blue and purple....red too. You can use it to help you channel magic," Prince Nar explained.

Simina nodded. "Oh, I see. I remember reading a book about them. I never thought I'd see one up close, though."

"You, um, read a lot?" Cautiously, Nar sat down next to her. He wasn't sure how to feel. He wanted to talk to her, get to know her better, but perhaps he was awkward.

Simina smiled. "Yes. I love reading."

Surprise sparked inside of him. He'd never met a girl who liked to read.

"What do you usually like to read?"

Simina rested her head on her fist. "It varies. But right now, I like folklore and fairytales."

Nar propped an arm on the table, leaning back in a certain way that made him look like he was posing. Nar experienced a strange stirring deep in his chest, something he'd never experienced before. It was weird, yet oddly pleasant as well. Was he starting to like her? Prince Nar was uncomfortable with this unknown emotion, but tried his hardest to keep his composure. The last thing he needed was his magic flaring out of control due to his emotions.

Nar appreciated the fact that she didn't swoon over him like other girls he'd met. She wasn't like them. He admired that she was different. She exhibited intelligence, along with a subtle beauty. She wasn't overly expressive and didn't seem extraordinary in any way, yet Nar was inexplicably drawn to her. He wanted to figure out why. Something was beautiful about the way she held herself, and Nar couldn't take his eyes off her.

"Being here feels like I'm in some sort of fairytale." Simina fidgeted in her seat as she tried to avert her eyes from Nar. Why was he staring at her like that all of a sudden? Her face reddened.

"What do you mean?" Nar's mellow voice was like the softest breeze, pleasant in Simina's ears. Why did he sound so...nice?

"Well, you know...I'm the peasant girl, and you're the prince. Fairy Tales always have a prince..." Simina trailed off.

Nar smiled. "Yes, I guess it seems that way since I also live in a castle."

Simina pulled at a string on her dress. "So...what do you like to read?"

"Anything, really. I enjoy...poetry."

Simina's excitement grew. "Me too!"

Nar held back a smile at her enthusiasm. He wanted to continue to appear aloof. He couldn't let on that he was interested, but he also couldn't help himself. Nar just had to know if she was of suitable marrying age.

" May I ask you a question?" Nar narrowed his eyes.

Simina nodded, feeling a little wary.

"What is your age?"

Simina grew suspicious.

"I'm twenty," she answered, lowering her voice.

 Nar smirked. *Perfect*. He tried to remain inconspicuous. He dropped his gaze. Now, was she already spoken for?

"And are you...married? Or possibly engaged?" Nar gazed back up at her with glowing purple eyes.

 Simina shook her head.

"No, I'm not." She wondered why he was asking her these questions. "That's the reason I came here—because I am not married," Simina explained. Nar was curious and wanted to know more, but before he could ask, he heard the grandfather clock in the library strike four-thirty p.m. Simina heard it, too, and immediately jumped to her feet.

"Oh my goodness! I need to get home! Aunt Lyda will be wondering where I am!" she cried.

Nar also stood.

"Can I borrow a few books?" Simina asked timidly.

"I'll allow you to take only three," he said sternly.

Simina took three, holding them in the crook of her arm.

"I will take you home if you like," Nar offered her. Simina glanced up in surprise and also in confusion.

"Umm...sure," Simina said uncertainly. Nar held out his hand to her. Simina accidentally made eye contact with him.

"Take my hand," Nar said softly. Simina gulped, staring into his open palm, his hand's pale, ivory skin. She raised a slow, tentative hand and gently placed it in his hand. Nar's smile grew wider. The smooth, cool touch of his skin greeted hers with a surprising, but pleasant, softness. Simina's skin tingled. He curled his hand around hers, tugging her slightly closer to him. She squeezed his hand back.

"Are you ready?" he asked Simina. She cocked her head to the side in confusion.

"Ready for what?" Simina didn't know what he was talking about. But she didn't let go of his hand.

"I'm going to transport you to your house instantly. So you might want to hold on," Nar explained. Simina blinked in realization.

"Oh. Okay. I'm ready. Simina prepared herself, feeling jittery and nervous. She breathed out. Nar counted to three.

"One. Two. Three." As soon as the word three left his lips, a swirl of dark, glittering purple mist flurried around them, and her feet left the ground. She gasped as weightlessness enveloped her, completely untethered. Even though there should have been wind, there wasn't any. Wind was nonexistent, and her tresses lay still. But Simina never let go of Nar's hand. She still left her hand clasped in his. Simina was scared to let his hand go. She decided she'd rather not let go for fear of falling.

As Simina looked across the way, she barely made out Nar's shrouded figure, who was cloaked in purple mist. She saw all of this in a matter of seconds because all of it happened in an instant. Within seconds, Simina's feet touched back down on solid ground again.

Relief flooded Simina at the comfort of feeling the solid ground beneath her feet. The glittering purple mist stopped flurrying about them and disappeared. Everything about them cleared. Simina saw her hand still clasped in Nar's. She stared at him standing across from her. His purple eyes glimmered a smile to her.

"You're home," Nar said and gently dropped her hand. Simina took her hand from his and put it back at her side. Cold, harsh reality returned from the absence of his hand clasped in hers. Simina looked around and realized that she stood at the front door of her house. Befuddlement clouded Simina's mind. She looked back at Nar, wondering. How did he do that?

Simina did not ask, however. Her tongue froze in her mouth; she became tongue-tied. She cleared her throat and opened her mouth, and she managed to speak.

"Thank you," Simina croaked.

"You're welcome. Enjoy your evening," Nar bid her kindly.

Simina waved him goodbye just as she watched him disappear in a puff of swirly purple smoke. Simina reached out to touch the smoke with the tips of her fingers, but it dissipated before she could reach it. A little tiny wisp extended toward her finger, but it evaporated.

Sighing, Simina walked toward the front door. She knocked, holding her three books in the crook of her left arm. A few moments later, her aunt opened the door. She looked surprised to see Simina standing on the doorstep.

"Oh. I didn't know you were back, Simina. I didn't hear your carriage pull up," Aunt Lyda said, stepping aside to allow Simina entrance. Simina walked in.

"Uh...Nar took me home," Simina said awkwardly. Before her aunt could say anything else, Simina quickly hurried upstairs to her room to be alone to read her books.

Seventeen

The next day, after completing her book sorting job, Simina finished her work day by mopping with Gloria and Olivia. She didn't like working with Gloria. Gloria would purposely make more messes so that Simina had to clean them. Earlier, when they'd been mopping up the kitchen, Gloria intentionally spilled the flour and made it look like Simina did it, and Matilda made Simina clean it up.

This made Simina angry, so she glared at Gloria as she sauntered by, sneering. Simina huffed, blowing a strand of hair out of her face, slaving away to clean it. Now, Simina was in the foyer, trying to avoid Gloria while mopping. She clutched the crystal in her fist, thinking about what Prince Nar had told her about channeling the magic within it. She could feel the power coursing through the small rock. It pulsed into her hand, and with the smallest ease, the littlest bit of concentration, Simina drew it out.

Magic flowed through her like a rushing river, her entire being the most invigorated it had been in her entire life. She cast her magic upon the mop, and it wriggled from her hands. It spun and danced around the foyer on its own, cleaning the floor with ease. Simina smiled at her achievement, and wondered if this is what it was like for other Zormonians. Gloria watched in astonishment, mouth agape.

"How are you doing that?" she exclaimed, staring in disbelief. "You don't have magic!"

She heard quiet footsteps slowly tapping down the staircase. Simina released the crystal in her pocket and the mop dropped instantly. The magic inside of her vanished. Her ponytail swished around behind her head as she turned. She saw Nar coming down the stairs, but he stopped midway, one hand resting on the banister, the other on his hip.

Nar stood gracefully upon the stairs, not stiff or relaxed but with a posture of flowing, movements. His broad shoulders matched well with his significant height, pronouncing his perfect masculine physique.

Gloria looked up to see Nar next and immediately tried to make herself look good. Olivia, to her left, began to hyperventilate. Simina did not let her eyes linger on him for long and she quickly looked away. Nar let his eyes fall upon each girl, first glancing at Gloria, only allowing his gaze to rest upon her for a mere second before glancing at Olivia, whom he didn't remain on for much longer than Gloria.

Then, his eyes fell upon Simina, for whom he gazed upon the longest. Feeling his gaze, Simina glanced back up and met his eyes. Despite everything in her mind that tried to convince her that he was evil and dark,

Simina could not help but feel a pull in her heart. Behind the anger and chaos, she saw vulnerability in his eyes. Gloria, the everlasting, jealous hussy standing behind Simina, noticed this. A fire brimmed hotter than the hinges of hell within that spitfire, and she clenched her fists at her sides. She hated the fact that Simina attracted Nar's attention, seething.

"Stop staring at him!" Gloria shouted, startling Simina out of her daydream. Simina broke eye contact with Nar and turned to look at Gloria, whose eyes burned with fiery jealousy.

"What?" Simina acted oblivious. Gloria stomped her foot and huffed, fuming. Nar rolled his eyes at this exchange, annoyance swelling inside of him for the cousin. Jealousy was certainly an ugly quality.

Simina ignored Gloria and turned back to face Nar, but did not directly look at him. From under the hood of her thick lashes, she kept stealing quick glances, wondering what he was doing down here. Nar cleared his throat and faced forward again.

"Your work is finished for today. You may go home," Nar informed them. Matilda scurried about, giving each girl her pay. All three put up their mops and turned toward the door to leave. Simina walked to the door, smiling to herself at the fact that she was able to make Gloria so jealous. Before Simina could leave, Nar stopped her.

"Simina," he called out.

Simina stopped. Chills shivered down her spine. Gloria passed Simina another hateful glare before stomping out the door in a huff.

"Yes?"

Simina was unable to read his stoic expression.

"Your duties are not finished," he told her. "You're staying."

Simina did as he said. She stayed while her two cousins left. Nothing more was said until the other girls had left. She approached the stairs where he stood.

"Why have you asked me to stay?" She stopped at the foot of the stairs, staring up at him. Curiosity grew within her.

"I have something to show you. Please follow me." He turned and started walking back up the stairs. She quickly ascended them to catch up to him, ponytail bouncing behind her.

She followed Nar, and neither of them said anything as they walked. Simina recognized the path he was taking. At the end of the corridor, they turned right and he guided her into the first room on the right. This was the room she'd gone to when she first arrived. Simina recalled the desk, the tall bookshelves, and the leather chair by the window. Prince Nar closed the door behind them and walked swiftly to his desk.

"If you'd be willing...I would like to tutor you in magic." His voice was a soft, quiet little murmur. Her nerves fluttered around inside of her, somehow turned into little flitty butterflies. She looked at Nar.

"Have you used the crystal I gave you?"

Simina nodded. "Just once."

"And?" He raised a brow.

"It works very well," she said. "I was able to do magic in an instant. How will this help me?"

"Channeling the crystal will eventually teach you how to channel your own magic within yourself. It should help it become less dormant and more active in your system. Once your own magic isn't dormant anymore, you shouldn't need the crystal and you should be able to use your own magic. Do you understand?"

"So...essentially, using the crystal will help draw my magic out?"

"Correct," he confirmed. "Do you agree to let me train you?"

"Okay." She was still wary of him, but Simina wanted to continue to learn how to use her magic. She didn't want to feel useless anymore, like she was an anomaly because she was the only one who couldn't use magic.

"Then every day after you are finished with your tasks, you will meet me in the artifact room," he said.

Simina agreed.

"Good." Nar slipped a book off the shelf behind his desk, a rather thick book. He brushed off a thick layer of dust and handed it to her.

"Start with this."

Simina took the large book. The cover read: *Magic for Beginners.* The spine cracked as she opened it, the pages yellow with age. They were smooth and feathery, like a well-worn glove. The book was much older than Simina expected, as the language of the title and the words were written in the ancient Zormonian language. This didn't deter her at all, however, as she was well versed in it. Before she finished the first paragraph, the door swung open violently, slamming against the opposite wall.

"Prince Nar," Matilda said, voice urgent.

Nar glared at her, clearly agitated. "Matilda, you should know to knock! Don't you ever enter like that again."

"Apologies, your majesty, but this is an urgent matter," she said. "The King is requesting your presence."

"I'll be there shortly."

Matilda bowed and quietly left the room. Prince Nar sighed heavily.

"Did she say the King?" Simina had been all over the castle, but had yet to lay eyes on him. But if he was sick like Olivia said, then he'd most likely be bedridden.

"Yes, the King," Nar replied. "I'll be back shortly. Will you wait here please?"

"Okay."

Silently, Prince Nar strode out of the room and into the corridor. Simina waited several seconds before following after him, curiosity getting the better of her. Shoving her hand in her pocket, she clutched the crystal and channeled it. She didn't want Nar to know that she was following him, so with the magic of the crystal, she made herself invisible. Simina followed him down the corridor and up a flight of stairs, until he entered a room. She didn't want to risk following him inside the room, so she stayed just outside the entrance and peeked in.

Prince Nar and Matilda stood at the King's bedside. An open curtain let in bright, late afternoon light. Lying delicately in the dark red duvet in the four poster bed, Simina saw a frail, withered old man. His face was full of hard creases and wrinkles, with dark, heavy circles under his eyes.

"I'm here, father," Nar said gently.

"Come closer, my son…" the King rasped. Prince Nar got down on his knees, level with his father's face.

"My days are growing shorter…please tell me you have begun negotiations with Azria…" he wheezed.

"Not yet, but I am scheduled-"

"Silence!" the King snapped harshly, but immediately dissolved into a coughing fit that lasted for several minutes.

"Useless…" the King groaned, dabbing blood from his lip.

Prince Nar pursed his lips. "Negotiations are scheduled to take place soon."

"Have you at least found a proper maiden to take as your Queen?"

Nar was silent.

"Answer me, boy!" his father spat.

"There is…one girl I have taken a bit of an interest in, yes," Nar finally answered.

"Oh? Is she rich? What kingdom is she from? Doesn't have to be royalty, but just as long as she's some sort of nobility…" He trailed off, coughing slightly.

Nar sighed heavily. "She's a peasant."

The King exploded. "A PEASANT!? ARE YOU OUT OF YOUR MIND? HOW-"

Due to the excessive shouting, he started coughing and hacking like mad. Spittle and blood flew everywhere, and his body shook uncontrollably. Nar placed a comforting hand on his shoulder.

"Please don't shout, father," he said.

"I can't believe this!" the King said when he finished coughing. "My own son, interested in a peasant! I didn't raise you this way!"

Nar's jaw tightened, his fists clenching. "You're sick. All this shouting isn't good for your health."

"I can't believe I have to leave the Kingdom of Lazera in your pathetic hands!" he raved. "If only I'd had other sons, before your mother died, but you killed her! And now you've killed me too!"

"Father, please-" Nar gritted his teeth.

"You did this to me! Your darkness!" he went on. "My legacy is dead..."

Purple eyes glowing, Prince Nar snatched the King up by his shirt, jerking his face up towards him.

"Shut up, you old fool," he hissed. The King's eyes bulged with fear as he stared up at his son, whimpering. Nar threw him back down on the bed.

"My kingdom..." the King mumbled, coughing. Without another word, Prince Nar stormed out in a fury; a dense, thick amethyst smoke trailing after him.

In all of the commotion Simina must have let go of her crystal because Nar was staring right at her.

"What are you doing here? You are not supposed to be here!" he shouted at her, his eyes dark and stormy.

Simina flinched at his tone and shied away, clutching the book to her chest. "I'm sorry..."

Nar was immediately guilt-stricken when he saw the hurt and scared expression on her face. He realized that he was unfairly taking his anger out on her and he'd made a promise to himself that he wasn't going to be that kind of person anymore.

"I...I'm sorry," he apologized, sighing. "I shouldn't have yelled at you."

Simina blinked rapidly in surprise. "It's okay..."

"Here, I'll take you home." Prince Nar held out his hand. Simina didn't take it. Instead, she said,

"You don't deserve to be treated that way."

This time, it was Nar's turn to be surprised. "I beg your pardon?"

"Your father. What he said to you...it's wrong," she said. Simina regretted all of the times she'd called him evil. Maybe he was this way because of constant mistreatment from his father. Simina saw from his previous efforts that he was trying to be good.

"Perhaps," Nar said tightly. "But he might be right, I...I destroy everything good around me..."

Simina gently took his hand. "No you don't!"

Nar laughed softly, sadness in his eyes. "You have no idea..."

"You're not pathetic." She squeezed his hand, staring into his teary eyes.

With a heavy sigh, Prince Nar cupped her cheek, stroking her face. "You are a kind person."

Simina leaned into his touch, her heart fluttering. He wasn't evil. Not at all. Someone evil would never show emotion like this. An evil person would have let her die that day in the bitter cold.

"I've never properly thanked you," she said.

"For what?"

She smiled at him. "For saving my life."

A genuine smile raised his lips. "You are welcome, my lady."

Simina wrapped her arms around him and hugged him, pressing her face into his shirt. Nar's breath caught in his throat, utter surprise rendering him speechless. Uncertainly, he returned the embrace, gently stroking her hair. It was pleasantly soft. Without a word, he used his magic to teleport her home, and in seconds, the two of them were standing on her front porch.

"Simina," Nar murmured. She was still hugging him, and hadn't noticed that they'd teleported. "You're home now."

She opened her eyes and pulled back from him. She suddenly realized what she was doing, and blushed. Simina stared at the buttons on his coat, observing his shirt. Had she really just hugged him? Simina suddenly became aware of the warmth of his body against hers. Simina's brain went on overload, and a warning filled her mind. *What am I doing?* she thought incredulously. Immediately, Simina ripped herself away from Nar. She took a few steps back, gathering herself, dropping her gaze away from him. She scuffed the ground with her shoe.

"I'm sorry, I don't know what came over me..." she muttered sheepishly.

"It's quite all right."

She raised her head to meet his gaze once more. "For what it's worth, I think you'll make a great king one day."

Nar smiled and took Simina's hand. "Until tomorrow."

He brought her hand to his lips and kissed it, never taking his eyes from her. Simina's face flushed, and a bashful smile curled her lips. Her heart beat a mile a minute, her spine tingling. After, Nar pulled away and disappeared, leaving Simina speechless and very, very confused. She didn't know how to feel about the Prince now.

Little did Simina know, Gloria had seen it all from her window. The flame of jealousy burned hotter and brighter than ever. So, Gloria began forming a diabolical plan.

Eighteen

Simina found it hard to focus when other things were on her mind. Oliver had her dusting off books, but Matilda wanted her in the kitchen cleaning up dishes. Matilda said she had lots of work to do today. She wanted her to dust the books while Gloria sanded the shelves, which made more work for Simina because of the sandy, dusty stuff created from the sanding. Then, she had to wash the dishes and clean the stables.

Simina hated working with Gloria, but not so much with Olivia. Gloria did everything possible in her power to make more work for her and to make things harder. When washing dishes later, while Olivia dried the others and put them away, Simina saw Gloria purposely drop a dish in a way that made it look like Simina did it. Simina then had to sweep it up and throw away the tiny shards.

Olivia, on the other hand, tried to help Simina as much as she could. She washed Simina's dishes while she swept. Gloria had also tracked mud across the foyer and the carpets. Simina was made to mop it up and bless Olivia's soul, who offered to help. Simina's back started hurting halfway through her day, and gloom hung over her in a sick, funky cloud for the rest of her day.

Today, her thoughts were more preoccupied. This surprised her, though, since she didn't usually have that much to think about. But now she did. She didn't really have "things" on her mind. Instead, it was just one thing—Nar.

She hadn't seen him all day, though she usually would have on any other typical day.

"Matilda, where is Nar today?" Simina asked while cleaning the dining room. Matilda raised a questioning eyebrow. Simina realized that she'd used his first name, which probably wasn't used very much among commoners.

"Oh, I mean, the Prince. Where is the Prince?" Simina reworded her question. Matilda's brow now creased with suspicion.

"He's not here today. The Prince is away taking care of royal business. Why?" Her eyes narrowed at Simina. She blushed and turned her gaze away from Matilda.

"No reason. I was just...wondering," Simina muttered and quickly skittered away from Matilda to continue her chores. She didn't want anyone to suspect that she had an interest in the Prince, but she was sure that Gloria somehow already suspected—;the little wench.

Simina had hoped to see him today. He'd said he'd train her in magic, and she'd spent all night reading the book he'd given her yesterday. She sighed, feeling glum. She wanted to go somewhere quiet where she could be alone. Simina requested this of Matilda, so she granted her request, telling her to clean the stables.

Simina went out to the castle grounds, feet crunching the snow, but did not go directly to the stables. She took a walk through the castle garden. She had never been in the garden before. She thought it magnificent. There were rows of large hedges that were a sparkling, frosty blue .Despite the cold weather, Simina saw beds of blooming flowers all around. The snow-white flowers were coated with a chilly frost that sparkled in the sunlight.

She recalled these flowers as ice flowers, a type of flower that thrived in cold weather. Next to the bed of ice flowers was a bush of frost berries, sparkling like blue crystals, just like the blue snow. Every flower here thrived in cold weather. Without the cold, they'd die.

Simina walked under a canopy of frost bells that hung above her, and they sprinkled little blue sparkles onto her head. She smiled as they landed softly on her nose and cheeks. She saw another bed of flowers, but these next ones were different. These flowers were also a frosty, icy blue, and Simina remembered they were called Frosty Winkles. But Simina's favorite was the black roses. She liked how they sparkled a dark purple, like Nar's mist. Their beauty was indescribable.

Simina thought it beautiful, but did not lollygag for too much longer because she had to clean the stables, so that is what she did. Nar's horse was, of course, there in the stables. Simina cleared out the snow, replaced his hay and water supply, and cleaned out the remains of his feces.

After a while, Simina brushed and cleaned Nar's horse, the same one she'd stolen. She admired his horse's black beauty, petting it and stroking its mane. It neighed to her and nuzzled Simina under her chin. This made her giggle, so she put her arms around the horse's neck and hugged him.

Simina loved horses. This horse reminded her of her old horse, Winona, the horse she missed. She missed the beauty of Winona and riding her. This only made her nostalgic and caused a wave of sadness to overflow her. She missed her quiet town of the Left. She missed her quaint little cottage, her father, and her friend Ernest. Simina really missed the games she and Ernest would play, the pretty woods, the stream they drank from. But most of all, she missed the library and all those books. Simina hugged the horse tightly, gently petting it. She honestly saw no point in why the Lazerian Government sent her to Winterville. She still hadn't gotten married yet, anyhow. Simina sighed and pulled away from the horse.

"I miss my home. I was happy there. I had friends there. Here, I only have one friend," she muttered to the horse. She considered her friend here to be Nar. At least he was kind to her. Besides Olivia, of course. Simina didn't think that she belonged here, in Winterville. She wanted to return to Autumnville, where everything seemed much simpler. There, she didn't have Gloria: A demeaning cousin who made life hard for her. But if she returned home, Nar wouldn't be able to teach her magic.

Simina was so focused on her thoughts that she ignored the sound of footsteps behind her.

"Do you ride?" a familiar voice from behind asked. Simina turned, hoping it was who she thought it was, and she was right.

She smiled. "Your highness. Yes, of course, I ride. I used to before I came here."

She took a few steps closer to him. "I haven't seen you all day. You told me that you'd tutor me. Where have you been?"

Nar's smile vanished. A troubled expression replaced it. "I was...away."

She cocked her head. "Away where?"

Nar looked at her. He found it easy to open up to her and talk to her. He figured he could tell her; Nar didn't see the harm in it.

"There's been some diplomatic issues with another Kingdom. They are refusing to make a trade agreement and form an alliance. I fear we are on the brink of war. The King of Azria wants to share our land, which will soon be mine once I take the throne." She noticed this troubled him very much. Did this have anything to do with the conversation with his father yesterday? The King had mentioned Azria.

"Is there anything I can do to help you?" Simina asked. Nar thought it sweet of her to ask; her concern was charming. He offered her a sad smile.

"My lady, I do not wish to worry you with my troubles." After all, it was none of her concern. What could she do? He became immediately stricken with guilt when he saw the dismissed look in her eyes.

"Walk with me?" he said quickly after.

Simina nodded.

"Sure."

They started to walk, and Simina fell into step beside him. They said nothing for a while. Nar didn't know what to say to her. He thought he might've hurt her feelings. Guilt gnawed at him. Nar figured he should say something. But what? What should he say? Nar screamed internally at himself, thinking that he'd lost his head.

"Do you like my horse?" Nar started.

"Yes, I do. It's a beautiful horse," Simina replied.

Nar grinned. "Is that why you stole it?"

Simina turned to glare at him. "No."

Nar chuckled.

"I like horses. I used to have one before I came here. Her name was Winona."

"What was she like?" Nostalgia crept upon her.

"She was a gray horse with spots and rode like the wind." She sighed. "I wish I had a horse now. I miss Winona."

Simina thought about the King, and wondered why he was sick. In fact, she realized that other than the book she'd found about Nar, she didn't really know that much about him or his family. He was such a mystery.

"How...did your father get sick?" Simina asked.

"He was right about one thing. It was my fault," Nar replied.

"What happened?"

Prince Nar took a deep breath. "From birth, I was gifted with magic. Others don't develop their powers until about five to ten years old. Well, I possessed it as soon as I came out of the womb, which is...quite rare."

"As I grew older, so did my power," Nar went on. "My father hired all kinds of expensive private tutors to train me, sparing no expense. But, see...my magical prowess grew too much and too fast for a young boy to contain...I had trouble controlling it. Needless to say, the tutors stopped coming back. One after the other, they quit, fearing for their lives."

"But why?"

He shook his head. "If I happened to get too angry at one of my tutors, my...magic would lash out, all on its own and...well, bad things started to happen."

"One day, about five years ago, there was an accident. My father attempted a spell to seal away my...dark powers, but the spell backfired. Shortly afterward, he fell ill. He's only gotten worse, no matter the tonics, potions, or spells he'd try. He never got better," Nar explained. "My magic...is slowly killing him."

Simina gulped. "What about...your mother?"

Eyes clouding with sadness, Nar stared up at the sky. "I killed her too."

Simina's stomach turned. "Whatever happened, I'm sure it wasn't your fault."

"Father said that my dark magic gave her the plague," Nar mumbled, voice thick with emotion. He sniffled. "And...she died when I was five. He's always blamed me."

Simina placed a comforting hand on his shoulder. "Nar, I'm sorry. That wasn't your fault. And I'm sure your mother loved you very much."

It made her think of her mother. As they walked, they entered the garden.

"My mother died from the plague too," Simina said. "Lots of people died from it. It was just a disease going around, and your mother happened to catch it. You didn't kill her."

Nar was silent for a long time. Then, he finally said, "I am sorry for your loss."

Simina took a deep breath, feeling the hole in her chest reopen, the part that her mother used to fill. "Thank you. It was really hard without her."

She shook her head.

"I don't want to talk about it. Did your father ever remarry?" She changed the subject.

"After a while, yes. He remarried several times, actually. But the marriages never lasted. Some he divorced, a few of them…died." He hesitated. Simina drew her brow.

"Died?" she wondered. Nar's face changed to stone.

"I killed a few of them," he said emotionlessly. Simina's eyes nearly popped out of her head.

"You killed them?"

"It was an accident. I didn't mean to kill them," Nar said.

"What happened?"

"Some of his wives were mean to me or would hurt me. I got angry. And without my control, my powers unleashed and killed them," Nar explained. Simina thought how terrible it would be to have such power and kill someone by accident.

"That's terrible," Simina muttered. And she complained about going to school when she was that age. He said nothing. Neither did Simina.. Simina stared at the flowers and let a smile stretch her lips. She went over to each bed of flowers and ran her hand across the petals. Simina cupped an ice flower in her hands, bent down, and sniffed it daintily. A cool breeze sucked up her nostrils, filling her nose with the sweet scent of frosted vanilla. She brushed her finger along each petal until moving to the next bed of flowers, which were the frosty winkles.

Nar watched her sniff the flowers and gently caress them, then smile with pleasantness at the beauty of them. Nar liked that the flowers pleased her, and he liked how happy they made her. He wanted to see her happy. Nar smiled. Her beauty was indescribable. Simina's plump cheeks were flushed red from the cold weather, her lovely curly locks of hair draping around her pretty face. Nar liked Simina. Perhaps he could even love her some day, but it was too soon to say. He liked being with her. She made him feel normal. Simina noticed him staring and smiled at him.

"Your garden is beautiful," Simina said admiringly. "I love it." She sniffed the frosty winkles. They smelled like blue raspberries. She stroked the petals.

"Who planted them?"

"I did. Sometimes Matilda helped." Simina stared at Nar with admiring eyes.

"You like flowers?" She meant it to be a statement rather than a question. Nar just couldn't stop smiling when he was around her.

"Yes, of course. I enjoy their undying beauty," Nar said, caressing a flower. Simina squinted with confusion.

"But won't they wilt?" Simina didn't understand what he meant. Nar shook his head.

"They'll never wilt. I enchanted them with everlasting beauty." Simina found that fascinating. She caught sight of the black roses, her favorites, with the purple sparkling glitter floating around them. She touched one, fascinated by their beauty.

"I like these ones the most. I've never seen anything like them before." Her voice sounded enchanting. It was at that moment that Nar realized that he'd do anything she asked of him. While Nar wasn't paying attention, Simina picked up a handful of snow and packed it up into a ball. With a mischievous smile, she threw it at him. It hit him in the shoulder. Nar looked up. Simina snorted, holding back a laugh. She grinned. Nar smirked.

"Oh really?" He cocked an eyebrow. Simina nodded, giggling. Nar bent down and made his own snowball. He threw one back at her, but Simina dodged it. She stuck out her tongue.

"Missed me!" she teased. Nar threw another. It hit her this time.

She gasped. "Oh, no you didn't."

Nar laughed. They kept throwing snowballs back and forth at each other. Nar's heart sang with happiness. Simina's presence filled Nar with a warmth and contentment that had been absent for years, and he reveled in the unfamiliar lightness in his heart.

Simina and Nar kept throwing snowballs at each other until Simina begged him to stop through her laughter. Nar was winning. They stopped, laughing and giggling, rolling in the snow. Finally, they stood, and Simina went to him, no longer resisting the urge to run into his arms. Nar took her in his arms, picked her up, and twirled her around in the air until he put her down, and they hugged each other tight.

Simina laughed as she laid her head on his shoulder and breathed with contentment. She closed her eyes. Nar held her close, petting her hair, stroking his fingers through it. She was so warm and comforting. She smelled like home. Even though he was the happiest man in the world, sadness visited once again, a frequent, unwelcome friend. He couldn't stay with her long; he'd be leaving again tomorrow. He had to settle the dispute in Azria. Nar had no idea how long he'd be gone.

"I must tell you something," Nar said. She must have caught the sad tone of his voice because she looked up.

"Is something wrong?" Worry creased her beautiful young features.

"No. Nothing is wrong," he assured her..

"Then what is it?"

Nar sighed.

"I have to go again."

Her smile faded. "When?"

This disappointed Simina. She didn't want Nar to go anywhere. He had promised to teach her magic.

"Tomorrow. I have to settle this dispute. I have no idea how long I'll be gone. It depends on how long it takes to settle the dispute and the methods used to settle it. But I promise I'll write to you."

Simina shook her head.

"No. You said you'd teach me how to use my magic."

"I know, I'm sorry. But I'll be back soon."

Silently, she nodded and hugged him. Unfamiliar emotions stirred in Simina's chest. She didn't know why, but she didn't want Nar to go. She had a bad feeling about this thing with Azria.

"Please don't go. I have a bad feeling," she whispered into his shirt.

"I think I have something that will put your mind at ease," he said, pulling away. He smiled. Simina looked up at him, curious.

"What?" Nar held out his hand, palm up.

"Watch." Simina looked at his hand. To her amazement, she saw a small flurry of purple glittering sparkles gathering in the middle of his hand. They swirled all around very fast, spiraling like they were making something. She stared in wonder at them. Slowly, a wisp of purple mist joined. The wisp of purple spiraled, and the purple sparkles were absorbed into the purple wisp, forming a bright green stem. Simina opened her mouth and gasped.

"Ooh!" she squealed. Nar smiled at her delight. The purple wisp swirled higher, just as the sparkles gathered in number, glowing brighter—two tiny wisps formed on the stem and made two leaves. The curling purple wisp at the top absorbed the gathered sparkles, transforming into a beautiful, spiraling black rose with many petals. Simina gasped, gaping at its beauty. Purple glitter fluttered around it, and each petal sparkled. It glowed magnificently, levitating in the middle of his palm. Simina's jaw dropped in awe.

"Oh my." Simina was breathless. Smiling, Nar took the rose by the stem. He offered it to her.

"For you," Nar whispered. Unable to speak, Simina took the fragile flower with two delicate hands.

"Oh, Nar, it's beautiful." She brushed a gentle finger along the edge of a petal. She brought her nose to it and sniffed daintily. It smelled like a rose but with the scent of lilac. It smelled like lavender, like Nar. Nar's finger brushed across her jawline. She looked up as Nar tilted up her face to see her. He cupped her chin.

"I've enchanted this flower. As long as I live, this flower shall never wilt. It will only wilt when I start to die. Take it, and keep me with you, always," Nar whispered, letting his hand drop.

Simina smiled at him. "Thank you, Nar." She stood on her tiptoes and kissed his cheek softly. Nar stood stunned at her actions. Besides her hugs, this was her first real sign of affection. After he composed himself, he leaned forward. He buried his nose in her hair, closing his eyes.

"Mmm. Always," he muttered, kissing the top of her head. Simina closed her eyes. As he kissed her, he used his magic to send her home. When Simina opened her eyes, Nar was gone. She stood on her front porch alone, holding his flower.

Nineteen

Simina found an old jar in her aunt's house and put her flower in it. She figured that since it was an enchanted flower, it didn't need any water. She set the jar with the flower on her bedside table and stared at it for the rest of the night.

The next day, she was disappointed. Working at the castle now was boring since Nar was away. She thought about him often. Simina missed him. Every day, she would pick up her flower and hold it for a few minutes. He was different now. He wasn't like that cruel prince she'd met at the beginning. Nar was kind and sweet. He'd only been hiding that part of himself because he was afraid the same thing would happen to her like with his father. Nar wasn't evil; not at all.

One evening, Simina forgot to close her bedroom door, which she usually closed right before she picked up her flower. This time, she didn't. Gloria appeared in Simina's doorway when she was holding it, thinking dreamily about Nar. Simina didn't hear her approach because she was too focused on her flower. Gloria's eyes narrowed as they landed on the extraordinarily beautiful black rose. Gloria had never seen a flower like that before.

Gloria's mouth sloped into a frown. She hated that someone like Simina owned something that beautiful. Her jealousy and hate for Simina boiled over. She hated how pretty Simina was, how she always got what she wanted, how the Prince looked at her, and how he always chose her. Gloria suspected that Simina liked the Prince and wanted to marry him. She didn't want that to happen, considering Gloria liked the Prince and she wanted to be rich.

"Where did you get that?" Simina heard Gloria's voice snap from her doorway. Simina jumped, startled, and looked to see Gloria. She played dumb.

"Hmm? Get what?" Gloria scowled.

"You know what. That, right there, in your hands." Gloria pointed at the black, sparkling rose.

"Oh. Nowhere." Simina shrugged, gazing back at the rose.

"Let me see it," Gloria demanded. Simina held the rose closer to herself, feeling possessive.

"No," Simina denied. She didn't want to let anyone touch her flower, especially Gloria. This rose meant a lot to Simina, since it was from Nar, and he was special to her. Gloria grabbed at it.

"Give it," Gloria ordered. Simina yanked it out of her reach.

"No!" Gloria didn't want Simina to have anything nice if she couldn't have it too. Gloria lunged for the rose, but Simina didn't jump back in time, and Gloria caught the rose by the stem. She managed to snatch it right out of Simina's hands. She held it like she was about to break the stem.

"Nooo!" Simina cried, reaching for it to get it back from Gloria. Gloria held it out of her reach with a sneer.

"Give it back!" Her heart waned, a waterfall of panic flowing over her. Tears brimmed in her eyes. Nar gave that to her! She wouldn't let Gloria have it! It was hers! Hers!

Gloria sniffed it and grabbed a petal between her thumb and forefinger. She smiled maliciously at Simina. Simina didn't like the way Gloria held her rose. She held it dangerously like she wanted to destroy it.

"Tell me where you got it," Gloria demanded to know. She wanted one, too. Simina thought up a lie. She'd destroy it if she told her that she got it from the Prince.

"I...I picked it from the woods. It's a wildflower," Simina lied. Gloria gave her a nasty grin.

"Liar. Tell me where you got it, or I'll tear off all the petals," Gloria threatened. Simina's heart leaped in her throat. This rose was somehow connected to the Prince's life; she didn't know how it might affect him. Gloria grabbed a fistful of petals.

"Fine! The Prince gave it to me!" Simina confessed. Gloria's face contorted into something nasty and ugly.

"What? The Prince?" she scorned. Her face was paper white, before turning cherry red. Gloria looked about ready to explode. Simina grimaced. Gloria's hand loosened on the petals.

"I told you, now give it back!" Simina reached for it again, but Gloria still held it away from her. It took all of Gloria's inner strength not to rip off every petal, break the stem in half, and throw it to the floor. She wanted to, but resisted. Instead, she settled for just throwing it on the floor.

"Fine! Take your stupid, ugly rose! I don't want it anyway!" Gloria threw it down and stomped out of Simina's room in a huff. Once she was gone, Simina rushed to the rose and gently picked it up off the floor, cradling it. She checked it over. It looked perfectly fine, unmarred, and unscathed.

She sat on her bed with it, stroking each petal gently. Just because it was an enchanted flower didn't mean it couldn't be destroyed. Simina then decided that she had to hide it somewhere Gloria wouldn't know. Gloria would ruin it if she got her grubby little paws on it when she wasn't around.

A few minutes later, while Simina was finding a place to hide her rose, Olivia entered. She knocked on the door frame to get her attention. Simina spun around, scared that Gloria might be there again. She breathed out in relief once she saw it was only Olivia.

"Hey, I came to tell you that supper's ready," Olivia told her. Simina nodded.

"Okay, thanks. Be down in a sec," she replied. Simina expected Olivia to leave, but she didn't. Olivia saw the black rose.

"That's a pretty rose," Olivia complimented, gazing at the rose with admiring eyes. Simina gulped.

"Thank you." She hoped that Olivia wouldn't try to do the same thing as Gloria.

"Can I see it?" Olivia noticed Simina's reluctance. "I promise I'll be gentle." She decided that Olivia sounded genuine and handed it over. Olivia was very careful with it, unlike Gloria. She smelled it and smiled.

"It's really pretty. Where'd you get it?" she asked nicely. Simina twirled her skirt around.

"Nar gave it to me," she told Olivia. Olivia smiled.

"That's so romantic." She swooned and gave the rose back to Simina. As Olivia left, Simina rolled her eyes. She went back to finding a good hiding spot. Since she couldn't find one, Simina just settled to put it safely in her top dresser drawer, where she kept all her belongings.

* * *

Simina's first letter came a few days later. While she was sitting on her bed reading one of the books Nar had let her borrow, Aunt Lyda knocked on the door. Simina looked up from her book.

"Come in," she called, voice a light jingle. Aunt Lyda entered, holding a sealed envelope in her hand. She handed it to Simina.

"This came for you," Aunt Lyda said. Simina took it.

"From who?" she asked, looking at the handwriting. She didn't recognize it.

Aunt Lyda shrugged.

"I don't know. Maybe someone from home?"

Simina shrugged and didn't respond. All of her attention focused on the letter. Her aunt left the room, and Simina eagerly tore the envelope open. She opened a piece of paper folded into thirds with words scrawled across it. The handwriting was a flowing, elegant script with fancy cursive and swirling letters that looped. It read:

Dear Simina,

How are you? I hope you are well. I hope to settle this dispute in a month, but things aren't looking too well. So far, the King of Azaria is refusing negotiations because I am a Prince and not a king. I tried to explain to him that I come on behalf of my father, since he is too ill to come himself, but he refuses to listen. I wish to refrain from using brute force. My deepest apologies, Simina; I don't wish to concern you with my troubles. I only wish to have someone to talk to, like you, for instance, where conversation comes naturally. No one here in Azria likes to talk about anything but business and diplomacy. It bores me, and I wish beyond the stars to see you, to speak with you. I often think of you, and will wonder what you are doing while in the middle of a court session about trade nego-

tiations, where the Judge looks like an overgrown rat who drones on and on. Pardon me, I know that is rude and I shouldn't say such things; it isn't princely.

Nonetheless, you occupy the majority of the space in my mind. I constantly try to envision what you could be doing, what you are wearing, what you look like, etc. I wish to know, so please, if you decide to write back to me, tell me in every detail what you've been up to. Meanwhile, I'll be guessing your endeavors from here. I already miss you. If you want to write back, I urge you to please give your letters to Matilda; she will know where to send them.

Sincerely,

Prince Nar.

Simina smiled to herself and giggled at the part where he called the judge an overgrown rat. Meanwhile, she was thrilled that Nar wrote, just like he said he would. She was also thrilled beyond the bits that Nar missed and wanted to see her. She found it sweet. Eagerly, Simina rummaged through the drawers in her bedside table, found a spare ink pen and piece of paper, and began to write back to him. She wrote:

Dear Prince Nar,

It flatters me to know that you miss me and think about me. I think about you often too. The castle seems to be much more boring and empty without your presence of prestige. I am less dapper, so why do you waste time on such a mere peasant as myself? Don't answer that question. I am afraid to hear the answer.

But regarding other matters, I am sorry to read about your troubles in Azria. If I could help you, I would, but I doubt they'd listen to a peasant girl such as myself, a mere trifle of what those higher-ups consider less than nothing. I will leave you to guess the details of my actions. I will not tell you.

I will only tell you this. A few days ago, my spiteful cousin, Gloria, almost viciously destroyed the rose you gave me. Most days, I like to hold your rose and admire it while I think of you. Gloria came into my room that day and saw me holding the rose. She demanded that I let her see it, but I refused. The third time she tried to take it from me, she succeeded. She asked me where I got it. When I wouldn't tell her, she threatened to rip off every petal and break the stem in two. So I told her and afterward, she threw it on the floor.

I don't know what I would have done if she'd destroyed it. That rose is a treasure to me, dear to my heart. Again, I thank you for it. It lets me feel connected to you on a much deeper level. I miss talking to you too, and ever since I came here, you are the only one who talks to me and I enjoy talking with. You are my only friend here, and now that you are gone, I am dreadfully bored. The only entertainment I have is reading and cleaning the castle. By the way, have I served a proper sentence yet for stealing your horse? I impatiently await your return.

Sincerely,

Simina.

Simina found an envelope, folded her letter, and sealed it within. On the back of the envelope, she wrote Prince Nar, not knowing exactly where in Azria he was. When she went to the castle the next day, she gave her letter to Matilda, just as instructed. Impatiently, Simina waited for a reply. She didn't get one until a week later. This one read:

Dear Simina,

Why did Gloria try to destroy the rose I gave you? Luckily, I have made good progress on this dispute. They are willing to listen and finally negotiate with me. However, they are proposing the topic of marriage since the King of Azria has a daughter, the princess. I've only met her once, and her name is Amelia. She's attractive, young, nineteen years old to be exact. I think she's too young, I am twenty-one. She seems nice enough and pretty, but she has buck teeth and looks like a beaver. And besides, my interests lie elsewhere. I don't want to marry her. I hope the King doesn't suggest that as a truce between the Royal Families. Princess Amelia is too polite; she's not natural. She's nothing like you at all. This dispute should be settled within the month. Then I shall return.

Stay well for me. I can't wait to see you again. This place bores me. Take good care of my rose. I also want you to know that it matters not that you are a "peasant." I do not care about such things or such labels. Why label yourself as a peasant when you can be so much more? You mean much more to me than just that. Please, write back to me as soon as possible. Your letters are my only entertainment here.

Your friend,

Prince Nar

P.S. I do hope you are still using that crystal I gave you.

A troubled feeling settled in upon her at his letter. Simina didn't want him to marry Princess Amelia. She didn't want him to. For the first time, jealousy reared its ugly head as Simina became envious of Princess Amelia because she was a princess and Simina was not. So quickly, she wrote back:

Dear Prince Nar,

Oh Nar, why must you fill your letters with so many woes? I don't want you to be troubled. And please, please, for the sake of Zormon, do not marry Princess Amelia. But who am I to tell a Prince what to do? It's your decision, not mine. I hold your rose close to my heart every day, reminding myself of you, the only thing that makes me feel close to you.

Gloria only tried to get rid of it because she is jealous of me. She is jealous that you have given me your attention when she views me as a mere peasant girl, someone below her. I hate how she looks down upon me. I wish to return to my home on the Left, where I was a wild child. I was free there, free to be improper. I'd run through the woods, tear my dresses, climb trees, and skin my knees and legs. I'd play in the mud, dirty my clothes, and then splash in the stream, which irritated my father when I tracked mud throughout my house. Then I'd read, read, and read to no end. Some days, I'd ride my horse Winona and never stop riding until the sun began to set beyond the trees. Take me back to those days, take me back. I wish to return there and stay.

But Government Officials made me leave because I wasn't married yet at the age of twenty and my father hadn't raised me right, so they sent me here, where my life is a struggle. I love my aunt, but I can't stand Gloria. Olivia is fine. My life was simple when I lived on the Left. I didn't have any problems. Now, I do. I don't want to grow up. I never want to grow up. I never ever, ever want to marry, and no one can make me. I just want to live and be free. Write back to me as soon as you get this.

The Girl Who Never Wants to Grow Up,

Simina.

P.S. Yes, I have been using the crystal to channel. I practice every day.

She sealed her letter in an envelope and gave it to Matilda the next day. Later, she received a letter from her father, Gregory, and eagerly opened it to read it.

Dear daughter Simina,

How have you been? I've missed you so much. It has been dull here without you, since I've had no one to fuss at for doing mischievous things. I've taken good care of Winona for you. How are things in Winterville? I want to know everything you've been doing. Don't leave anything out. Write back quickly.

Your Loving Father,

Gregory.

Simina responded quickly to his letter and told him about Winterville and what had happened. Just like he said, she left nothing out, including the Prince, whether or not he believed her. She sent it off once she'd finished.

Finally, a month had passed since Nar had left, but Simina hadn't received any new letters from him. This upset her. She expected to see Nar at the castle, but he wasn't there. Simina thought he'd be back since he said he'd return after a month. When he didn't, Simina checked on her rose. It looked normal and there was nothing wrong with it. There were no signs of wilting. Then Simina got a letter. She opened it up and read it:

Dear Simina,

Okay, so what do you want to hear first, bad news or bad news? All right, bad news it is, then. I'm afraid I have to stay longer than expected. As I predicted, the King offered me Princess Amelia's hand. When I refused, my progress disappeared. I am failing at this diplomacy thing. I am sorry, my lady, I have to stay longer; he is threatening war, threatening to take over what will be my land. Hopefully, I can think of something to fix this. But marriage is out of the question. I do not want to marry Princess Amelia. I told them I was already betrothed, which, of course, is a lie, but my interests lie elsewhere. You can't marry someone when you're in love with someone else, can you? No, you most certainly cannot.

Well, I do have some good news. I'm bringing you back something I hope you'll like. It's a surprise, so I won't tell you what it is. But I'll be gone longer, just a few more months. Hopefully, I will see you soon.

Your friend,

Prince Nar.

For the next few months, Simina wrote and received letters from Nar. The more she read them, the more she fell in love with him. He'd write sweet things to her, telling her how he missed her voice, personality, beauty, and her. Nar joked about marrying her, or Simina thought he was joking because surely a Prince wouldn't want to marry a peasant girl. Once, in a letter, he wrote:

"I dream and wish for my lady, who lives far from me. There she waits for me, but I don't want to return to her unless I know she feels the same way for me in return. Do you, my lady? Don't hold it against me when I say this, but I must. I have fallen in love with you, Simina Gorchev, the peasant girl of Autumnville. If I do not return alive, I'd like to know if my affections are returned. Write back as quickly as you can, my lady, my love.

Love,

Prince Nar.

When Simina read that, she fell to the floor. Literally. She, too, was in love with him, but didn't want to confess it on paper or out loud, not quite yet. She didn't know how to respond or what to say, so she didn't write anything back.

Embarrassment overwhelmed Simina for loving someone, especially a Prince. How could she express her feelings? This emotional territory was unfamiliar and uncomfortable; she had no clue how to take the first step in order to breach this divide. The chasm of emotions was way too deep for her to handle, and she ended up crying several hours later.

Simina read and reread Nar's letter, wanting to love him but not knowing how. Her tears landed on the page, blotching the ink, so she put the letter down and cried silently into her pillow, wishing for Nar's return.

A few days later, Simina was intently watching her rose. Suddenly, the glow around the rose started dimming, and it slowly started wilting. One petal fell and fluttered down to the floor. Simina's eyes widened, and her heart started pounding. She began to panic. She didn't know what that could mean, but she knew that it couldn't mean anything good. Simina ran out of her room and charged out of the house. She needed to see Matilda. She was worried.

Simina borrowed a horse and took off for the Dark Castle at a gallop. At the pace she was going, it didn't take her long to get there. She busted through the great castle doors and looked around the foyer.

"Matilda!" she shouted. She ran up the stairs. Simina looked in each room.

"Matilda!" she called again, urgency filling her voice. Matilda heard Simina yelling from the kitchen and ran down to meet her in the corridor.

"Simina? What are you doing here? Your work is done for the day," Matilda said. Simina shook her head, about to cry.

"No, I'm not here about that."

Matilda was confused.

"Then what?" she asked.

"I think Nar is in trouble. A petal fell from an enchanted rose he gave me. It stays alive as long as he's alive," Simina told her. Matilda looked serious. She believed Simina; Simina didn't have any reason to lie to her.

"Matilda, if you know where he is, then you have to tell me," Simina pleaded. Matilda nodded.

"Follow me. The King will know what to do." Matilda was able to remain calm under pressure while Simina was not.

Twenty

Simina followed Matilda to the King's room. He eyed them both with a dangerous expression.

"What is the meaning of this?" the King croaked. Simina babbled.

"Your majesty, I fear Prince Nar is-"

"Silence!" he bellowed, followed by a long coughing fit. "Did I say you could speak, peasant?"

Simina frowned deeply at him. "Your son is in danger!"

"How do you know this?" The King looked skeptical.

"He gave me an enchanted flower that will never wilt until he starts dying. It started wilting, and a petal fell," she explained.

The King harrumphed, seemingly unconcerned. "What do you want me to do about it?"

Simina gawked at his lack of concern for his son. "Can't you do anything to find him?"

"Why should I? He's nothing but a wretch! Maybe if he dies, I'll finally be free of this curse he put on me!" he hollered.

Fury pulsed through Simina's body and she leaned down close to him, shouting, "You'd let your one and only heir die?"

He shrunk away from her, but still glared. "I have a brother! The Darkla line will continue!"

Furious, Simina yanked a pillow out from under his head.

"Aah!" he cried out in surprise. Simina held the pillow above him.

"Help me find where he is or I swear to Zormon I will kill you," she threatened.

"Simina!" Matilda gasped. "If you attempt such a thing, I will be forced to call the Royal Guard!"

"How *dare* you threaten me..." the King hissed. "Fine! Give me that crystal ball."

He gestured to a desk in the corner, where miscellaneous papers and books sat. Dropping the pillow, Simina ran over and grabbed the crystal ball. She handed it to the King.

The King placed his hand on the ball and poured what little magic he had left into it. It glowed purple.

"Show me Prince Nar," the King boomed and removed his hand from the crystal ball. Simina and Matilda leaned closer to gaze into it. Simina saw the Dark Castle and then the image moved away from the castle to the

Snowy Hills. Lying in the middle of the snow was Nar, passed out. He looked pale, paler than usual, and his lips were turning slightly blue. Simina flipped.

"Nar!" she shrieked, voice cracking up. She didn't even see the blood staining his shirt. Slowly, the image faded, and the crystal ball went dark.

"Send out a search party," the King said to Matilda. Simina didn't wait for anybody else. She ran back the way they came, Matilda trailing behind her and into the snow. Simina ran, the cold wind biting her skin, whipping through her clothes, sprouting goosebumps across her skin. The cold snow pressed against her bare ankles, getting into her shoes. She shivered but continued onward.

"Nar!" she called. "Nar!" Simina didn't want him to die. Guilt sprouted in her heart at her previous reluctance to express herself. If he died, he'd never know how much she cared for him, and she'd never get the chance to love him. She wanted that chance. Simina's chest began to ache. Matilda ran behind her, searching, too. Simina ran until she finally found his limp form lying in the snow.

"Nar!" Simina cried and knelt in the cold snow, shivering. A terrible, strange choking sound burst from her chest as she looked at him. Blood stained the snow around him: fresh, raw, and red. His shirt was torn, and a deep red gash cut sharply into his side, exposing his flesh. Simina gasped, tears streaming down her face.

"No...Nar..." she whimpered. Blood still leaked from his wound. Immediately, she checked him for a pulse. Her hands ran over his cold skin, which was still slightly warm. She placed two shaky fingers on his neck. She checked for a pulse. There was a slight flutter against her fingers. She breathed out with relief, feeling hope arise within her.

"He's still alive," she told Matilda. Simina took his face in her hands, caressing his face. He looked like he was sleeping, but his face was too pale and his lips were blue. Simina heard horses and the murmur of shouting guards and soldiers in the distance.

"Over here!" Matilda shouted to them, standing and waving her arms about wildly. Simina held his head in her lap. He was like ice, cold to the touch. In a jiffy, soldiers rushed to his aid.

"Outta the way!" they shouted and shoved her. Two soldiers picked Nar up from the ground.

"Get a horse!" Another soldier brought a horse, and they helped Nar get on top of it. Simina followed them into the castle as they rushed him up the stairs and into a room. Simina pushed through the soldiers to get to Nar, wanting to make sure he would be okay. Soldiers yelled at her, telling her to go back.

"Get that girl!" one yelled. But Simina kept running. She wouldn't let anyone get her.

"Simina! Come back!" Matilda called to her. Simina didn't listen. She followed the soldiers carrying him into the room, where she saw them lay him on the bed. Through all the chaos, Simina heard his voice.

"Ugh...what's going on?" Nar groaned in pain. He growled. Someone removed his coat and shirt to inspect his wound. Heart aching, Simina pushed forward until she got to his side.

"Nar!" Simina yelled out. Nar heard her and turned his head in the direction of her voice.

"What?" He thought he was hallucinating or hearing things. She knelt at his bedside.

"Nar, Nar, I'm here. It's me," she said softly. Nar turned his head to look at her. His eyes looked glazed.

"Simina?" he croaked out weakly. Simina took his face in her hands. Some color had returned to Nar's face.

"I'm here, Nar," she assured him.

"We need a healer here!" Matilda yelled. She was trying to attend to his wound. Nar breathed out. He brought up a hand and brushed a gentle finger along her jawline. Simina leaned into his touch.

"I'm so glad to see you," Nar whispered hoarsely. Simina smiled sadly, stroking his cheek. He placed a hand over hers. Nar's dimming purple eyes fluttered to a close. He passed out again. A soldier grabbed Simina and shoved her.

"Get the girl out of here! She doesn't need to see this!" a soldier said. Simina spun her head wildly.

"What?" she squeaked. Two soldiers hoisted her up onto her feet and started dragging her away. Nar began to get farther and farther away from her.

"Wait! No! No! Let me go!" She fought against the soldiers restraining her. Simina was shoved out of the room and handed over to two guards. Simina kicked her legs.

"No! No! Take me back!" She wanted to stay with Nar.

"Take her home; there's a carriage waiting outside. Make sure that horse she borrowed gets back to where it belongs," a soldier barked at the guards. They saluted and dragged Simina out of the castle. She was thrown into a waiting carriage and taken away back home. Simina banged on the windows.

"No! No! Driver! Turn back around!" she shrilled. The driver didn't listen. He just went faster.

Twenty-One

Neither Simina nor anyone was allowed into the Dark Castle for a long time. News spread in Lazera that the Prince was injured and the town soon became the center for gossip.

Another two months passed, and Simina hadn't heard a thing from him. She was worried about Nar. The only thing she had that let her know how he was doing was the rose. It wasn't wilting anymore, so it let Simina know that at least Nar was alive and doing better. In some way, the petal that had fallen had grown back.

Simina, Gloria, and Olivia were relieved of their duties as maids. They no longer had to work. The girls were made to go back to Etiquette School. Simina hated it there. All the girls ever did was gossip about the Prince. Simina thought of him often, wanting to see him and know how he was doing. It had been two months since she found him lying in the snow, bloodied and bleeding.

The next day, Simina got what she wished for. Aunt Lyda heard a carriage pull up outside her house. Someone ratted on her door. Aunt Lyda went to the door and opened it. A soldier stood outside on her doorstep. He saluted Aunt Lyda.

"Good evening, madam," he greeted them.

"Good evening," Aunt Lyda greeted him back, nodding her head. "Is there something I can do for you?"

"Does Simina Gorchev live here?" the soldier asked. Aunt Lyda widened her eyes and raised her eyebrows.

"Yes? Why?"

"The Prince has requested her presence at the castle," he told her. Aunt Lyda nearly flipped her lid. She wanted to know what the Prince wanted with Simina, but she didn't ask because she decided it wasn't her business. Was she in trouble?

"Oh. Wait here, please. I'll go get her," Aunt Lyda told the soldier. She went up the stairs and got Simina.

"A soldier is here for you," she whispered. At that, Simina jumped and ran down the stairs to meet the soldier. Panting, she stopped in front of the soldier.

"Yes?" she said, breathless. The soldier bowed.

"The Prince has requested your presence. Won't you please come with me?" the soldier asked politely. Simina nodded. The soldier led her out and into a carriage. Simina wanted to go. She wanted to see him.

She arrived within a few minutes. The soldier took her to the throne room, or the Great Hall, and there Nar sat, waiting on his throne. Nar stood when he saw her and immediately approached. He ushered the soldier away, eyes on Simina. He looked okay. He was dressed normally. Nar bowed to her.

"My lady," he greeted her. Simina resisted the urge to lunge at him and hug him. Instead, she just smiled.

"I've missed you, Nar. I'm so glad you're okay," Simina said. They started walking side by side down the stairs.

"Why didn't you respond to my last letter?" Nar asked, a little disappointed. Simina gulped. Her heart leaped up into her throat.

"I didn't know what to say," she responded in a shaky voice. Nar nodded.

"Ah. I see." Deep melancholy filled his voice. Simina stopped and turned to him. The look of rejection was plastered all over his face. She nearly drowned in a flood of guilt.

"Nar...did you mean what you wrote in that letter?" she asked him, swallowing down the throb in her throat. He turned back to her, extreme hunger burning in his eyes.

"Yes, of course I did. Why would I lie?" Nar's voice was thick with passion. Nar took a step closer to Simina. He threaded his fingers through her hair and stroked a thumb across her cheek.

"I am truly in love with you," Nar confessed zealously. Simina's face reddened with a deep blush, and her stomach tingled with an indescribable sensation. Simina dropped her gaze from his handsome face, bashfully smiling. She let her hair fall to hide her face. Nar cupped her cheek.

"No. Look at me," Nar murmured, lifting her face so she could look at him. He brushed her hair out of her face. Simina stared back into his lovely features, absorbed in his magical purple eyes, falling deeply in love. She was in love with him; she just didn't know how to say it. She didn't want to speak it aloud; she was too embarrassed to tell him.

"Tell me, Simina. Do you love me?" Nar asked. Simina didn't know how to answer. She tried to look away from him, but he wouldn't let her.

"I...I won't say," Simina whispered.

"Why?" Nar swept her hair behind her ear.

Simina took a shuddered breath.

"I don't know how," her voice cracked. Tears swelled in her eyes. "And I'm scared." Her lip quivered.

Nar wiped her tears away. "No, no. Don't cry."

Simina sniffled and dried it up.

"Just take your time," he murmured, smiling. "I have something for you. You're really going to like it."

Simina smiled, curiously.

"What is it?"

Nar took her hand.

"It's a surprise. Come. I'll show you." Nar led her out of the castle and into the snow. He leaned in close to her ear.

"Close your eyes."

"Okay." Simina giggled and closed her eyes. He guided her around to the stables, taking both of her hands in his. Once he put her in the right spot, in front of the two horses, he told her to open them.

"Okay. You can open them." Nar walked over and brought the horse to her. Simina fluttered her eyes open. She opened her mouth in amazement and gasped with surprise. She saw a beautiful, milky white horse with a luscious white mane. The horse wiggled its head, flicked its mane, and neighed.

"Oh, my Zormon…" Simina gawked. She approached the horse slowly and laid a gentle hand on its neck. Nar smiled.

"Do you like it?" he asked. Simina petted the horse's fur and stroked its mane.

"Yes. I love it. It's so beautiful," Simina gushed. Nar was happy that he was able to please Simina. She hugged the horse around its neck and stroked it, snuggling up to it. She scratched under its chin. The horse nuzzled up to Simina, huffing air out through its nostrils.

"Thank you so much, Nar." *He's so sweet.* She turned to Nar, went to him, and enveloped him in a tight hug.

"Thank you," she whispered. Nar hugged her tighter, closed his eyes, and let a soft little sigh break from between his lips. Simina kissed his cheek and quickly pulled away. Nar smirked.

"You want to ride it?" Nar walked over to his horse, Night Rider. Simina nodded.

"Yeah." It was already equipped with a saddle and reins. Simina watched Nar swing himself up smoothly and efficiently onto his horse with ease. He sat grandly upon his steed, agile and light in posture. Nar looked very appealing to Simina's eye. He smirked when he saw how she admired him.

Simina mounted her horse, gripping the reins. "Where do you want to ride to?" Simina asked him and flicked her hair.

"Into the woods, as far as you want." Nar took his reins and trotted his horse forward. "You ready?"

He quirked an eyebrow up at her, a cocky smirk playing on his lips. Simina smiled and nodded.

"Yes," she said. Simina tossed her hair. Nar flicked his reins.

"Ha!" Nar shouted and his horse took off at full speed with a gallop. Simina snapped her reins.

"Ya!" she screeched and took off after Nar. Her horse galloped at full speed behind him, catching up. The wind breezed through Simina's hair, flying behind her. Strength rippled through the horse's muscles as it carried her over the ground, bouncing and jouncing her. They entered the Snowy Woods and Simina caught up to Nar, keeping pace next to him. Simina pushed her horse to go faster.

"Hi-ya!" Simina took off and breezed by Nar. She glanced at him as she passed, laughing, hair billowing in front of her face. Nar smirked, and a cocky grin spread across his lips. He kicked his horse forward to go faster.

Simina's horse jumped over a fallen snowy log, and they kept running, Nar catching up. He glanced over at her through the rushing trees and winked at her. Simina smiled as she rode, whipping through all the trees and branches. Nature caressed her in all its beauty, exhilarating her. This is what it meant to be alive.

She truly missed the feeling of riding. Simina loved this. Happiness returned to her once again, for the first time since she'd been here. She was so glad to have a horse again, so pleased to feel free finally. The cool, brisk air whipped through her clothes, biting her skin. The woods looked like a beautiful winter wonderland of snow, except the snow was an icy, frosty, cool blue.

Nar liked watching her ride. It made her look alive and gave her a wondrous glow around her person. Her lovely hair flowed behind her, bouncing and floating in the air. Simina looked positively radiant. Genuine, sweet, joyful laughter bubbled up from Simina. She enjoyed the way he made her feel free. Simina liked being with him.

They ran and ran until the sun started to set, and then they turned and rode back. Panting, Simina laughed, trotting along on her new horse. She and Nar rode side by side on their horses, breathless and winded.

"That was fun," Simina said. Nar smiled.

"It was," he agreed. Simina looked at him, beaming.

"Thank you again for this beautiful horse." Simina stroked its neck. Nar nodded.

"It's a gift, Simina, for all of your hard work and my love for you," Nar said in a soft voice. Simina blushed at the word love and looked away from him. She gazed at her horse as she petted him.

"I wanna name it. Is it a girl or a boy?" she asked, trying to avoid the topic of love.

"It's a girl," he answered. Simina smiled.

"Then I'll name her...Wind Rider," Simina decided, just like Nar's horse, Night Rider. Nar, changing the subject, said,

"My uncle is coming to town."

Simina stared at Nar.

"Your uncle?" She wondered why he was mentioning this to her.

"Yes. He's coming to town to visit. He heard of my accident," Nar said with tight lips. Simina wondered why he disliked that his uncle was coming to town.

"Oh. When will he be here?" Simina wanted to be prepared when he arrived if she ever met him.

"A few days. Maybe three. I have no idea why he suddenly wants to come here. I hadn't heard from him in a while, and he suddenly wants to visit. I think he wants something," Nar told Simina, troubled by this matter. Simina cocked her head to the side.

"What do you think he wants?" she asked. Nar frowned.

"My throne," he said with distaste, a bitter look staining his young features. Nar sighed and looked at the sky, the wind bristling his hair.

"But you shouldn't worry about that. I don't want to worry you with my troubles," Nar sighed. "On another note...you and Olivia don't have to work in the castle anymore."

"What about Gloria?" Nar hadn't mentioned her.

"She still has to work," Nar responded curtly. Simina sighed and stared with loving eyes at Nar.

"When can I see you again?" Hearing the desperation in her voice, Nar turned to her. Nar saw the wanting look in her eyes, and he knew she loved him. However, Nar did not know how to answer her question. He tried to think of something, but he didn't have an answer.

"I don't know. I don't know." He seemed to struggle with his words. Since neither of them knew what to say, they fell silent. They kept walking until they came to the edge of the woods and could see the castle again. Nar and Simina stopped at the sight of a carriage pulling up in front of the castle. Simina looked at Nar. A confused look fell upon his face. He wasn't expecting anyone today.

A Royal Guard opened the carriage door. Simina saw a vast, black, muddy boot step out into the slushy snow. A second muddy black boot stepped out. A chunky hand then grabbed the side of the carriage. A large, gruff-looking man fully stepped out of the carriage with a thick neck, arms, torso, and gigantic feet. His eyes, a dull, sad lavender, were the only indication of any resemblance to royalty. His thinning, brown hair hung limply, stringy and ugly.

Wrinkles creased his skin, drawing attention to the sunkenness of his eyes. He appeared to be tired, but anxiety filled his expression. Despite not being very tall, his stubby and short limbs rippled with muscle. He adorned himself in fine silk clothes, with a fur cape draped around his shoulders.

The sight of the man startled Simina and gave her the chills. He did not look nice, and frankly, he looked scary. Simina noticed a long, sharp sword strapped to his waist. She gulped, having the urge to hide. Simina glanced over at Nar. He looked just as confused as she did, but for a different reason.

"Uncle?" Nar exclaimed, surprised.

Twenty-Two

The man Nar called uncle looked up at him and cracked a smile. To Simina, it looked more like a sneer.

"Nephew!" he bellowed, spreading his arms out wide. Simina took that to mean that he really was Nar's uncle.

"You're here early. I thought you'd be here a few days later," Nar said. His uncle laughed.

"Wanted to get here as soon as possible, my nephew. It's great to see you!" he drawled. Awkwardness waved the red flag of alarm in her mind, signaling that perhaps she was out of place here.

"I'll see you later, Nar," Simina whispered. She didn't want to talk to his uncle, she didn't want to be noticed. Nar looked at her.

"Goodbye, my lady." Nar bowed his head. Simina hurried off on her horse, galloping away, riding like the wind.

* * *

Nar was not expecting his uncle to arrive so soon. This slightly unnerved him. He was not prepared for this. He knew his uncle was up to something. Nar hadn't heard from his uncle for years, until now, after he had an accident. Of these years, he hasn't bothered to contact him. Now, suddenly, he wanted to "visit." He didn't trust his uncle one bit. Nar dismounted his horse and approached.

"It's good to see you, uncle," Nar said blandly. "It's been a while." Of course, he didn't mean that.

"Give your old Uncle Julian a hug!" He pulled Nar into a bear hug and slapped his back. Nar did not hug back. He pulled away and straightened his jacket. He cleared his throat and put his hands behind his back.

"To business, Uncle. Why have you come here?" Nar asked, getting straight to the point. Julian scowled.

"Damn, you're so stiff! Just like your old man! How is the old man doing anyway?" Julian stroked the rough, scratchy beard on his face. Nar ignored his comment.

"He is not well. My father is dying, in fact," Nar stated plainly. Julian's eyes narrowed, and he sneered.

"Oh, I'm sorry to hear about that...misfortune. I heard about your accident, too, by the way. What happened there?" Nar pursed his lips. His uncle didn't sound sorry at all about his father's illness.

"Yes, that was quite...unfortunate," Nar mused dryly. He tilted his chin, insinuating dominance.

"You see...the King of Azria challenged my throne. We fought. He left me wounded, and I killed him," Nar told Julian, voice calm but scary and intense.

"It's a good thing you didn't die...who would have taken over the throne after your father if you had died?" Uncle Julian asked rhetorically, insinuating something. His insinuation, whatever it may be, did not amuse Nar.

"Yes...it's a good thing I am alive." Nar cursed internally. He wanted nothing to do with his uncle. He hadn't even been there long, and Nar already wanted to be rid of him.

* * *

When Simina arrived home, she went to her room and found Olivia rustling and snooping around in her top dresser drawer. Simina's skin prickled, and her eyes widened. It's a good thing she moved her rose because she figured that's what Olivia was looking for. Simina hid her rose underneath some loose wooden planks in the floorboard. She knew something like this would happen.

"What are you doing!?" Simina screeched. Olivia turned with a startled jump. Her face was surprised. Simina entered the room, perilously approaching Olivia. Olivia twiddled her thumbs nervously.

"I was...um..." she stuttered. Simina clenched her hands into fists, reaching a firm halt, feet rooted to the floor.

"What were you doing with my stuff?" All Olivia could do was stutter. "Answer me!!" Simina shouted. Olivia flinched from Simina's shout.

"I was looking for your rose," Olivia answered quietly, eyes downcast, not meeting Simina's eye. Simina thought as much. She crossed her arms and tapped her foot, containing her anger.

"Why?" Simina snapped. Olivia shook.

"It wasn't my fault. Gloria made me do it," she told Simina. Simina's brow drew.

"What?" Simina didn't understand. She toned the harshness of her voice.

"Gloria told me to do it. She wanted me to find the rose Nar gave you," Olivia explained. Simina shook her head.

"Gloria..." she mumbled distastefully. Simina sucked her teeth with her tongue. She looked back up at Olivia.

"Why do you listen to her?" Simina squinted her eyes at Olivia. She shrugged.

"I don't know," Olivia mumbled, rubbing her arm. Simina put her hands on her hips.

"Olivia, you need to stand up for yourself. You let Gloria boss you around too much."

Olivia shrugged again.

"I don't know how," Olivia whined.

Simina sighed.

"Of course you do. The next time she tells you to do something, say no. It's that easy," Simina said.

Olivia nodded.

"I'll try. I'm sorry about going through your stuff," she apologized. Simina breathed heavily.

"Yeah, just don't do it again," Simina warned. With a shy nod and the expression of a kicked puppy, Olivia skittered out of the room like a nervous spider.

A nerve-frazzled Simina walked to the middle of the floor in her room, leaned down, lifted the floorboards, and took out Nar's rose that stayed hidden and safely tucked away out of harm. She held it delicately as she plopped down on her bed and thought about Nar.

* * *

At least another week later, Simina was preparing the dinner table with Olivia when Gloria rushed in, excited about something. She busted through the door and started yelling about something. Simina saw that Gloria was smiling, and Simina had never seen her smile before with genuine happiness. She'd returned from cleaning at Nar's castle.

"Guess what? Guess what?" Gloria shouted, jumping up and down. Aunt Lyda turned to look at Gloria from where she stood at the stove.

"Gloria, won't you please pipe down? And shut the door; you're letting in quite a draft," Aunt Lyda said, pointing a finger. Gloria shut the door.

"Well, what is it?" Olivia asked curiously. Simina was pretty curious, too, but didn't say anything. She set a plate on the table and the silverware next to it.

"The Prince is going to be hosting a Royal Ball soon!" Gloria squealed. Simina raised her eyebrows in interest. *Really,* she thought. Olivia squinted her eyes.

"How do you know?" Olivia didn't believe Gloria. She thought Gloria was telling one of her usual lies.

"I heard the Prince talking to his uncle about it. He's hosting it to welcome his uncle to town and so he can choose a suitable wife." In the last part, her voice became dreamy, and so did her eyes. Simina snorted. Gloria scowled at Simina but didn't say anything.

Aunt Lyda approached the table and placed a dish on its surface with steam rising from the top.

"Gloria, let's not talk about this now. It's dinnertime. Go wash up, then help us set the table," Aunt Lyda told Gloria, ending the topic. Aunt Lyda didn't care to hear about such matters. Other things were more important.

Huffing, Gloria stomped upstairs, ignoring Aunt Lyda's order to help set up dinner. Simina, however, was intrigued by this news. It excited her, but Simina kept her excitement contained. She wanted to go just to get a chance to see Nar. Simina wondered when the ball was. That way, if she knew beforehand, she'd have plenty of time to prepare if she could go.

* * *

The next day, Gloria was cleaning the castle, mopping up the hallways. She noticed that the door to the Prince's study was slightly ajar. Gloria heard some rustling about. Confused and curious, she wanted to check it out. Still holding the mop, she approached the door. Gloria peeked in through the crack. She saw a person shuffling around inside, messing and looking through things.

Gloria gently pushed the door open. It didn't creak when she pushed it. The person in the room didn't hear her. She quietly padded into the room and saw who it was. It was Prince Nar's Uncle, Julian. He was rummaging through Prince Nar's personal spell books on the bookshelves. He rummaged through little bottles of strange liquid on the shelves and his desk drawers.

Gloria spoke.

"What are you doing?" she asked, wondering why he was going through the Prince's stuff. Julian jumped, startled, and tried to act like he wasn't doing anything. He whirled around, eyes bug-eyed and wide.

"N-nothing," he stuttered and scratched his head nervously. Gloria put a hand on her hip.

"Why are you going through the Prince's stuff?" Gloria snapped. Julian grimaced.

"You don't understand." He shook his head. Gloria blinked in confusion.

"Understand what?" Her hip cocked to the side. Julian sighed.

"Do you know what it's like...to walk in someone's shadow?" He spoke very slowly and clearly. Gloria knew what he meant. She thought of Simina.

"Yeah," Gloria replied.

"No matter what you do, you're never as important as someone else. You never get recognized. You never get the attention, the recognition you deserve. Just because you're not as 'special.' Someone's always better or prettier and gets everything you want. They take it from you, when you know it's supposed to belong to you. Not them. You get that?" Uncle Julian ranted. Gloria nodded, completely understanding.

"Yes. I feel that way about my cousin Simina," Gloria spat, dislike filling her eyes.

"I hate her. Ever since she came here, she's gotten everything she's wanted. She's prettier, she's so deceitful, and she gets the Prince's attention. She gets everything I want," Gloria complained, jealous.

"I want the Prince. I want to be rich," she continued. She only wanted the Prince so she could be rich, and she liked him. Not like Simina did, of course. Simina truly loved Nar and wanted to be with him. Gloria didn't care about all of that. The Uncle smiled.

"Do you wish to rule?" he asked. Gloria nodded vigorously.

"Yes."

"So do I." Uncle Julian looked malicious.

"But you can't. Prince Nar is the heir to the throne, and he's interested in my cousin Simina. He probably wants to marry her." Uncle Julian narrowed his eyes.

"I won't let that happen. The throne should rightfully be mine." He wanted the throne for himself, when it belonged to Nar and whoever Nar chose to marry.

"Nar can't marry her. I don't want Simina on the throne. I must stop her from marrying him," Gloria said, determined. Julian started to formulate a plan.

"Or..." He stroked his bearded chin. Julian looked at Gloria. "We can work together," he suggested, eyes blazing.

"Work together to do what?" She didn't know what he meant.

"Take the throne!" Julian exclaimed. Gloria's eyes widened.

He continued.

"We both want the same thing! We both want to rule, to gain what we rightfully deserve! You don't want to let your cousin get what she wants, do you?" Julian knew he had her under his wing.

"No. I won't let it happen," Gloria vowed. Julian spread his arms.

"Then help me," he offered.

Gloria agreed. "What do you have in mind?"

Julian thought for a moment. "The King, my brother, is dying, so he won't be a problem. But then there's Nar, my nephew, heir to the throne."

Gloria racked her brain. "How do we take it?"

"We have to find a way to get Nar out of the way," Julian said. "That's step one."

"Wait..." Gloria narrowed her eyes. Julian looked up at her.

"What?" Gloria shifted.

"How do I know you won't try to get rid of me when all is said and done?" She was reluctant to trust him.

"Once it's all over, I'll ask for your hand in marriage. You will become my wife and, therefore, my Queen," Julian promised. "I swear to it." He placed a hand over his heart. Satisfied, Gloria nodded and agreed.

"Okay. Continue."

"But that's after the fact if we succeed," Julian said.

Gloria held up a finger.

"There is going to be a ball soon. That could work to our advantage," she suggested.

Julian nodded.

"Yes, that could work." He thought long and hard. Gloria thought too.

"We have to keep this quiet." Julian lowered his voice to a whisper. He pointed behind Gloria to the door.

"Close the door." Gloria listened and shut the door quietly.

"If someone hears of this…we'll be thrown in the dungeon," she said. Her stomach twirled nervously at the thought of the dungeon. She did not want to go there.

"Or worse, executed for treason against the Prince," Julian added. A dark, seething pit formed in Gloria's stomach, and she became queasy.

"You mustn't speak of this to anyone," Julian spoke urgently. Gloria's nerves fired up, electrifying her.

"I swear, I will not speak a word of this. I promise."

"Good."

"How are we going to do it? We have to get rid of the Prince," Gloria whispered. Julian groaned.

"I know, I know." Irritation consumed him. He thought long and hard.

He snapped his fingers. "I've got it!"

Gloria jumped.

"What is it? Tell me!" Julian looked devious.

"We have to kill him and make it look like an accident," Julian hissed. Gloria agreed.

So, they both conspired to overtake the throne by plotting to kill Nar and Simina, and make it look like an accident.

Twenty-Three

"How will we do it?" Gloria wondered, feeling excited, her anxiousness building.

"I was thinking of using a spell from one of these spell books." He indicated the books on the shelves. *Maybe I can curse them,* Julian thought. Gloria nodded.

"We'll figure something out. But I have to get back to work now. Matilda's gonna start suspecting something if I don't come back," Gloria said. Gloria left without saying another word to Julian.

* * *

Gloria spent the next few days thinking up ways to kill Nar and Simina. She rummaged through Nar's library and his study for spell books and read them. She read about curses and spells, but didn't have the suitable materials to do any of them. She talked with Uncle Julian about it daily, in secret.

Later, Gloria managed to find something in a Deadly Potion Book. It was a potion mix, something called The Choking Death Poison. It collapses the lungs and causes them to fail within two hours. The ingredients for this specific potion are:

- Zormonian Death Root

That's a prime ingredient for all poisonous drinks.

- Lung Poison Dust
- Dead Icy Flower Petals, three

Gloria had seen those ingredients on the shelves in Nar's study. Upon finding out this information, Gloria left the house to meet with Julian. It was Saturday, and she had told him to meet her in a far-off alley behind the jewelry shop. This alley led to the darkest, slummiest area of Winterville. No one went there, so it was the perfect spot.

She found Julian in one of the castle's corridors. Gloria told him she'd found something, but she couldn't tell him right then cause it would have been too risky. So she told him to meet her in the alley in the slums, behind the jewelry shop.

Simina was coming home from Etiquette School when she saw Gloria leaving the house. Simina wondered why Gloria was leaving. She noticed Gloria looked suspicious. She wore a dark cloak with the hood pulled up, covering her face. She looked suspicious, jumpy, and kept looking behind her. Simina watched her walk behind the jewelry shop. This confused Simina. Why was she going down there?

Luckily, Gloria didn't see her. Getting a bad feeling, she decided to follow Gloria. She kept a reasonable distance from Gloria, so she wouldn't see her. Simina pulled the hood up on her cloak. She followed Gloria behind the jewelry shop and down a long, dank alleyway.

As Simina walked farther down the alley, things started to look dirty and slummy. The walls were coated in graffiti, trash strewn all over the ground. Gloria turned a few corners, twisting and turning. Simina followed close behind her, but not too close.

After Gloria turned a corner, she suddenly stopped. Simina stopped and peeked around the corner. Gloria was talking quietly with Nar's uncle, whom Simina recognized. Why was Gloria meeting up with Nar's uncle? Simina strained her ears so she could listen.

"What did you find?" Nar's uncle asked. Simina didn't know his uncle's name.

"I found the directions to make a certain potion. Poison," Gloria whispered.

"So you want to poison him?" the uncle responded. Simina wondered who they were talking about.

"Yes. It's called the Choking Death. The instructions are in the Deadly Potion Book. The ingredients are in the Prince's study. I saw them. We can make it!" Gloria said enthusiastically.

"That's a perfect plan, Gloria. Let's do it," Nar's uncle agreed. Gloria giggled.

"We just need to figure out how to get him to drink it," the uncle whispered, thinking. Simina's mind spun. Who were they talking about? Who were they plotting to poison and kill? Simina reeled.

"How about we just give it to him and tell him to drink it?" Gloria inquired. The uncle shook his head.

"No, Nar's smarter than that. I know he already doesn't trust me," he surmised. Simina held back a gasp. She clamped a hand over her mouth. Nar! They were plotting to kill Nar! Simina couldn't believe her ears. But why? Why? Huge worry bloomed inside of her. This is bad. Simina wanted to cry at the thought of Nar dying from drinking poison. It hurt her. *No, not Nar, please, not my Nar.* Simina panicked.

Simina managed to gather herself and keep listening. Gloria gasped and held up a finger.

"Ooh! I know! Since the ball is in a few days, we can do it then! We can just slip it in his drink and give it to him. He'll drink it, and then, bye, bye Prince," Gloria sneered evilly. "And then, we can do the same to my annoying, stupid cousin."

Her heart stuttered in her chest. Her knees buckled. What? They were conspiring to kill her, too? Simina couldn't believe it. She knew Gloria hated her, but she didn't think Gloria hated her so much that she wanted to poison her. Simina wanted to cry but knew she couldn't because her crying would make noise and draw them to her. It upset Simina that someone would hate her enough to want to kill her. Simina had never done anything to Gloria; Gloria was just jealous. Gloria hated her the moment she walked through that door.

"And then the throne will be as good as ours," the uncle said. They laughed deviously.

Simina knew one thing. She wasn't going to let them get away with it. She wouldn't let them. Simina had to tell Nar. Panic set in upon her. Thinking she'd heard enough, she quietly ran away, back the way she came in a hurry. Simina ran back home to the stables. She mounted her horse, Wind Rider, and took off at a gallop for Nar's castle.

"Hiya!" Simina shouted and kicked her horse into high gear. She bounded at full speed, speeding toward the castle. She arrived in a few minutes. The castle came into her view. Simina caught sight of Nar walking through the Snowy Woods. Nar heard a horse galloping toward him at a great speed. He turned to see Simina riding toward him on her horse.

"Nar!" she called out urgently. "Nar!" He noticed her voice sounded panicked.

She skidded to a halt on her horse. She swung off Wind Rider and jumped off, landing on her feet in the snow. Nar liked watching her body move as she jumped off that horse. Her face was flushed and pink and her brown hair wisped about her face in swirly waves, bouncing gaily in the wind.

"Nar," she breathed out once more, out of breath. She ran toward him, air puffing out in short breaths.

"What is it?" Nar asked her, his mellow voice calming her. Simina grabbed his arms.

"Nar, Gloria and your uncle are conspiring to kill you," she warned, voice cracking with panic. Nar somehow wasn't surprised.

"I figured as much. It's my uncle; he isn't to be trusted," Nar told her. Simina put her arms around him.

"They want to kill me too," she whined. Tears started to pool in her eyes.

"How do you know this information?"

"I heard them talking about it privately in a deserted alleyway. Oh please, Nar, you have to believe me," Simina pleaded. A tear leaked from her eye. Nar ignored her tears.

"What did they say?" Nar's voice sounded serious, curt, and tight. Simina gulped, swallowing the throb in her throat.

"They plan to put poison in your drink at the ball, and the same to me. You have to stop them, Nar! Please!" Simina's beautiful face was marred with worry. Nar didn't like her looking like that. She was too pretty to cry and be worried.

"I can't do anything," Nar said plainly. Simina did a little "hmph."

"Why not?" she complained.

"There is no evidence. So far, you are the only witness to this. It's only your word against theirs," Nar explained. Simina squirmed.

"Then at least cancel the ball, Nar; you can't go through with it!" Simina begged. Nar smiled, amused at her concern.

"I can't do that. That would look too suspicious. And it seems unlikely that they'd try to poison me in front of everyone. I'm sure the last thing they want is a spectacle," Nar said.

Simina shook her head. "No! I don't think they care about that! They just want you dead."

He placed a comforting hand on her shoulder. "It's going to be okay. I promise."

She fell silent and let her tears come. She did not feel reassured at all. Simina hugged him and buried her face in the crook of his neck. She cried into his neck, pouring out her sorrows and worry onto him. Simina sobbed and her chest heaved. She cried so hard that her chest hurt. Nar held her and let her cry. He touched her head and stroked her hair, saying nothing. Simina breathed out and sniffed.

"I don't want them to kill you," she whimpered and let out a strangled sob, and then a shaky sigh.

"They will not kill me. I will not let them. Thank you for warning me. Now I know," Nar assured. He pulled away from her and looked closely at her face, which he took in his hands. He offered a small, sweet smile and wiped away her tears with his thumb.

"Oh, Simina," Nar sighed, stroking her cheek. Simina leaned into his hand.

"Walk with me?" He thought a walk through the Snowy Woods might calm her. Smiling slightly, Simina nodded. Nar took her hand, clasping it tightly, and they started walking side by side through the woods. Simina squeezed Nar's hand.

"I'm sorry for crying," she apologized, ashamed of herself for making such a fuss.

"It's okay," he said. Snowy white trees closed in around them as they walked further into the dense forest. Though the snow was a light, frosty blue, sometimes the snow looked white by how the sun shined. Enjoying the forest's beauty, Simina reached up a hand to stroke a tree branch covered in snow. She watched a white bird fly from tree to tree. She watched the Boolu creatures—like Zormonia's version of squirrels, but a lot cuter—run around, chasing each other and playing. Simina smiled. She liked the peaceful tranquility of the Snowy Woods.

"It's very pretty here." She looked at Nar. "Why is there always snow here?" Simina noticed that all year around, it was always cold here, always covered in snow.

"I've enchanted the land, so it'll always be winter here. Winter's my favorite season, mainly because I enjoy the snow," Nar answered. Simina didn't mind winter.

"I like autumn," Simina told him. "I like all the colors." Nar changed the subject.

"I'd like it if you'd come to the ball. I'll send you a personal carriage," Nar whispered softly. Simina took her hand from Nar's and turned to look at him. She looked worried again.

"I don't know now. After I found out they're trying to kill me, I don't think I should go," Simina cried. Nar shook his head.

"They are trying to kill us both, Simina. And you don't have to worry, nothing is going to happen," Nar reassured. Simina leaned back against a tree.

He sighed and brought a hand up to her cheek. He cupped her face with his hand.

"Now I know that you must love me. You warned me of this threat because you care about me. If you didn't love me, why would you care?" Nar surmised, murmuring to Simina. Simina began to blush, and Nar knew that he was right. Even though she didn't say yes, she didn't deny it either.

Nar observed Simina, taking in her beauty. Her cheeks were red from blushing. Snowflakes dotted her hair, landing on her eyelashes. Her eyes were a dark, sugary honey and her lips were plump and bright pink. Nar traced a finger across her bottom lip. He yearned to kiss them.

"Close your eyes, Simina," Nar whispered. A nervous lump rose in her throat, an unwelcome sensation.

"What are you going to do?" Her voice shook.

"Nothing," Nar whispered. Simina obeyed and closed her eyes. She waited. A moment passed. Then, Nar's soft lips pressed gently upon hers as he kissed her.

An alarm started to sound off inside of Simina's head. She wasn't expecting this. She didn't know what to do. Nar moved his lips against hers, and her shoulders relaxed as she grew accustomed to it. Simina kissed him back, feeling a strange but pleasant electrical sensation run through her. Nar cupped her face, pulling her closer, and tilted her head back slightly, deepening his kiss. Simina liked the feeling. Their bodies fit together like two puzzle pieces, perfectly conjoined and matching. She liked Nar being against her.

The heat from his body pulsed into her hand beneath the fabric of his shirt. She liked the feeling of his lips on hers. Simina's breathing turned rapidly, and warmth rose in her cheeks. Nar heard a soft, little squeak of a sigh escape from Simina just as he pulled away. Immediately, guilt rushed into her. She knew her father's opinions about the Dark Prince. Was she betraying him by kissing Nar? He'd lose his head and go nuts if he knew what she was doing right now. But her father wasn't there, was he? Still feeling guilty, Simina slapped Nar. Not hard enough to hurt, just a small, scolding slap.

"You brute," Simina snapped, though there was no heart in it. Nar laughed.

"Stop pretending. I know you kissed me back," Nar mused. Simina saw a twinkle of desire gleaming in his eyes. Simina was shy when it came to expressing her feelings. Instead, she said,

"Kiss me again." Nar smirked and granted her request. He kissed her again, but this time more passionately. Simina put her arms around his neck and pulled him closer. Her fingers threaded through his hair, wisping through each strand. Nar took her by the waist, pulling her close to him so their bodies touched. Simina had never been so physically close to him before. The kissing soon progressed and got hungrier and wilder. Simina never thought it would be possible to want someone until this moment. Their breathing became heavy, and every time their lips broke apart for a short moment, Simina would sigh.

"Nar..." Simina sighed, breathing out his name, caught up in him: his smell, his feel, and his lips. Nar held his lips on hers for a long time before finally breaking away. Nar breathed out, letting out a huge breath, panting. Simina breathed heavily too, feeling winded and very out of breath, face flushed a deep, rosy pink. Their breath puffed out into the air in white vaporized clouds.

"We have to stop," Nar breathed. He licked his lips, the look of arousal in his eyes.

"If we keep going, I...I don't know what will happen." Nar's voice dropped to a low, deep husk. Full of butterflies, her stomach fluttered with a thrill. Simina was also quite aroused and had very intimate thoughts about Nar.

"I should probably get home. My aunt will wonder where I am if I don't hurry along."

Nar pushed away from her. "Okay."

Simina pushed away from the tree. She stood on her tiptoes and gave Nar a goodbye kiss. He sharply inhaled as she did so. Simina gave him a long, sweet kiss. She did not want to pull away from his tempting, juicy lips. It took quite an effort for her to pull away, but she finally did.

"Bye," she breathed against his lips. Simina walked away, toward her horse. Nar watched her. Simina, as she mounted her horse, realized that was her very first kiss. She smiled and blushed. Simina gave Nar one more glance until finally riding away. Nar didn't take his eyes off her until she rode away out of sight.

Once she was gone, Nar straightened, composed himself, and walked briskly back to the castle.

Twenty-Four

Simina arrived back home a little later than usual. Her mind was preoccupied with what happened with Nar in the woods. Gloria was back. Simina didn't know how to act around her now that she knew what she knew. Gloria narrowed her eyes at Simina into dangerous slits.

"Where have you been?" Gloria sniffed. Simina's mind reeled for an answer. She couldn't tell Gloria, or anyone else for that matter, that she'd been in the woods kissing Nar. So she lied.

"I stayed late at Etiquette School," Simina lied. She smiled to herself at her secret. She thought about telling Olivia since Olivia was sort of her friend. Wanting to be alone to think her thoughts and think about Nar, Simina ran away upstairs to hide.

* * *

The very next day, some time in the afternoon, Simina sat at the kitchen table, studying her etiquette books. She hummed happily, thinking of Nar, thoughts of him scrolling through her mind. Simina couldn't really focus too well because her head was in the clouds. Her mind kept replaying the scene with her and Nar in the woods. She kept blushing and smiling at the memory, picturing herself kissing Nar.

Simina tried to remember the feeling of the kiss, the feeling of him, the feeling of everything, and the feeling of all those sensations she had never experienced until now. She didn't know what to call this feeling, but every time she thought about Nar and kissing him, a warm, crazy feeling spilled through every inch of her. She didn't know what to call it, but it was desire.

Aunt Lyda, busy lifting heavy pots and pans onto the stove, had been calling Simina for several minutes. Someone was at the door, and Aunt Lyda couldn't get it. Olivia wasn't in the kitchen at the moment, and Gloria was upstairs, getting ready to come downstairs, alerted by the pounding on the door.

"Simina!" Aunt Lyda shrilled. "Simina!" Simina jumped, startled, finally becoming aware of the pounding on the door.

"Huh?" Dazed, Simina finally tuned back in. Aunt Lyda grunted.

"Open the door!" she shouted. Simina jumped to her feet. Gloria tried to beat her to the door, but Simina got there first. Simina opened it. A Royal Soldier stood at the door. He saluted Simina.

"Good evening, lass," he greeted. Simina bowed her head, wondering why a Royal Soldier was on the porch.

"Hello," Simina greeted in return. She noticed he held something in his hand.

"Are you Simina Gorchev?" he asked her. Simina nodded, curious.

"Yes, I am." He handed her what he was holding. It was a small envelope, addressed to her from Prince Nar.

"The Prince wanted me to give it to you. He said he would have come and delivered it himself, but he's busy," the soldier explained. Simina took it, recognizing Nar's elegant handwriting.

"Thank you," Simina mumbled, staring at the envelope.

"Have a good day," the soldier bid and left. Simina shut the door. Still staring at the envelope, she walked over to the table and sat. Gloria tried to snatch it from her, but Simina slapped her hand away.

"It's addressed to me," Simina snapped and tore the envelope open. She pulled out a neatly folded piece of paper and unfolded it. Around the edge of the paper was a string of black roses. Olivia and Gloria peered over her shoulders as Simina read the letter.

My dearest Simina,

His Royal Highness Prince Nar has invited you to attend the Royal Ball. It's next Saturday, starting at 8 p.m., in the ballroom. It would please me ever so greatly if you would come. Of course, there will be some dancing and hopefully some romancing as well. Wear something lovely. I hope to see you there.

P.S. If you have nothing to wear, please contact Matilda; she will assist you.

Love,

Prince Nar.

Excitement electrified her insides. Nar personally invited her to the Royal Ball. A smile threatened to curl her lips. Gloria, next to her, flared with jealousy and hate. She stomped her foot.

"Of course, *you* get invited!" Gloria blew up, face red. Angry and jealous, she stomped upstairs. Olivia was excited, however. She squealed.

"Ooh, you got invited by the Prince himself!" Simina stood, excited. She did not respond to Olivia. Since the ball was tomorrow, Simina wanted to pick out a dress today. She decided to do what Nar suggested and go to Matilda for a dress.

Simina didn't know how to act around these people here. Suddenly, she was overcome with a strange feeling and didn't know what to call the feeling. She just wanted to be away from them all right now. Olivia kept ogling, Gloria kept being a bitch, and Aunt Lyda was just...a little unsocial. Who could she possibly confide in?

So Simina told her aunt where she was going, that she'd return later, and left. She got on her horse and rode to Nar's castle. She walked in but didn't see Nar. Just like Matilda knew she would be coming, she was in the foyer waiting for Simina. She waved at Matilda.

"Hi, Matilda!" Simina greeted happily. Matilda smiled.

"Hi, Simina. What can I do for you today?" She showed Matilda her invitation.

"I got invited to the ball, and I was hoping you'd help me pick out a dress for it."

"I thought you might come. Please follow me. I have dresses for you to look at," Matilda said and started up the stairs. Simina quickly followed behind Matilda. She took Simina into the dressing room accessed from the parlor.

Inside, there were many wardrobes and racks filled with pretty dresses of all colors, sizes, and styles. It was the loveliest thing she'd ever seen. There were more dresses than at the dress shop. Her eyes widened, and her face showed an expression of astonishment. She gasped.

"Oh wow! This is amazing!" Simina exclaimed. Simina ogled everything. The dresses were so pretty. Simina admired each one, stroking her hand across each gown. Matilda lifted a lovely red gown from a rack. She admired the dress and twirled it around.

"This one is pretty," Matilda said. She held it up to Simina and assessed it closely. After a minute or two of contemplation, she shook her head.

"No, I don't think that one will look good," she said and put the dress back on the rack.

For the next hour or so, Simina looked at and tried on many gowns, many different ones with different colors and styles. Finding her right size was the main issue. Some dresses were too small, and others were too big. Doing this made Simina feel like a queen or a princess. She thought a lot about Nar, and every time she tried on a dress, she wondered if he would like how she looked in it.

Simina wanted Nar's approval. Simina knew he liked the color purple, as did she, so she wanted to wear something purple that matched the color of his eyes. Simina loved his eyes. They enchanted her, entranced her. She regretted all of the mean things she'd said to him and thought to herself. Yes, he was cruel before but he'd changed. He was better now, sweeter and kinder. And now, after everything that they'd been through together over the past year...Simina was sure that she was in love with him.

Simina, tired of thinking and worrying, slumped down into a chair with a sigh.

"I think I'm in love with the Prince," she said and sighed wearily. Matilda stopped what she was doing and gave Simina a wary look. Her eyebrows rose. There was a slight blush on Simina's cheeks and a dreamy, dazed look. Matilda didn't know what to say or to think about that.

"Well..." Matilda exclaimed. She was startled by Simina's words. Simina wondered where he was and what he was doing. She wanted nothing more than to just speak with him and spend time together. But would they even get that chance with the looming threat of Gloria and Julian?

"I don't know what to say about that..." Matilda mumbled. Ignoring what Simina had just said, she continued looking for the right gown for her. Simina sat in the chair, staring into a space filled with Nars.

Matilda, on the other hand, picked out a pretty purple gown off the rack. She smiled in admiration at its beauty. The handmaiden knew that Simina would really like it, so she brought it over to Simina and showed her.

"Simina look, I think you'll like this one," Matilda said, holding up the gown. Simina, coming out of her daze for a moment, looked up. She gasped in awe at the beauty of the dress.

"Oh, Matilda, it's lovely, absolutely lovely," Simina gushed, standing. It was a long gown with ruffles down the skirt, covered in purple glittering sparkles. Along the bottom of the skirt was a string of black roses sewn along at the bottom, on the edge. The dress's bodice was covered in purple sparkling glitter, and more black roses were sewn all along the waist. The front of it drooped down in the shape of an elegant V, and the sleeves were long and covered the shoulders. The gown was exactly the color of Nar's eyes. Simina took it from Matilda, staring at it adoringly.

"Oh, Matilda, may I try it on, please?" Simina begged, yearning. She smiled and nodded.

"Yes, dear, go right ahead," Matilda said. Clutching the gown to her body, feeling the silky fabric beneath her fingertips, Simina went into a fitting room. Thankfully, she had no trouble putting it on and getting into it. The gown went to the floor, covering her feet. Simina enjoyed the feel of the silky-smooth fabric against her skin. It pleased her immensely. At the end of each sleeve, the fabric stopped in the middle of her hand in the shape of an upside-down V.

Simina stepped out of the fitting room to show Matilda. She cheered with delight at the sight of Simina in the dress. Simina found moving in it quite effortless. The color matched her skin tone perfectly. It fit snugly against her body shape, fitting her curves, pronouncing her lovely body shape.

Matilda clapped her hands together with glee, smiling from ear to ear. "Oh, you look marvelous, Simina, just marvelous! The Prince surely won't be able to take his eyes off you in that gown!"

Simina's face blushed pink at the flattery. She never really thought herself that pretty because she never really stopped to look at herself in the mirror. Simina smiled and wondered what Nar might be wearing to the ball. She was sure he'd look so regal and handsome, dashing in all his princely, graceful manner.

"This is the one," said Simina. "I will wear this one." Matilda sighed with a longing look and approached Simina. She placed her hands on Simina's shoulders.

"You look just as beautiful as a queen," Matilda commented, admiring Simina's beauty, stature, and posture. To Matilda, Simina looked like she was made to be royalty, yet she was born a mere peasant.

"Thank you," Simina murmured, at a loss for words. She swallowed. Seeming suddenly timid, Matilda stepped back from her and bowed to Simina.

"If you wish, I will deliver the gown to you tomorrow." Simina nodded.

"I would very much like that. Thank you, Matilda, for your service," Simina said regally. She returned to the fitting room to remove the dress, so Matilda could have it cleaned, pressed, and sent to her. Bidding Matilda another thank you and goodbye, Simina left the castle, dreaming of tomorrow night.

* * *

Without delay, it seemed to Simina, the next night soon arrived. Her excitement was uncontainable. Anxiety coursed through her veins. Nar—or rather the King—invited the rest of the noble populace. That meant Gloria, Olivia, and her aunt were going. Apparently, their father had been some sort of nobleman. But Simina, as far as she knew, was the only person invited by the Prince himself. She was excited but also scared. She kept thinking that something might go wrong. Simina knew that Julian and Gloria were planning to poison them, but it seemed that to her that Nar wasn't really taking the threat seriously.

She was all nervous and jittery inside. She did not know what to do with herself. Nar was sending a private carriage just to pick her up. Quickly, she went upstairs to get ready because she knew the carriage would be here any minute.

Matilda had already sent the gown in a box. Simina put it on, and Olivia helped her put on a touch of makeup and did her hair. It wasn't put up or anything fancy. It was simply curled, and a part was pinned up in the back with a small hair clip. Simina didn't need much makeup. She was already naturally beautiful without it. Olivia only added a slight touch of eyeshadow to accentuate her lovely eyes, a gentle, subtle blush to her cheeks, and some simple lip gloss.

When Olivia finished, Simina took a glance at herself. She smiled, admiring herself, and wondered if Nar would find her beautiful. She couldn't wait to see him tonight. The ball started at eight. That's when people would be arriving. In fact, it was about fifteen minutes till. Olivia smiled and clasped her hands together.

"There. Now you're ready!" she said. The door opened, and Aunt Lyda popped in.

"Simina, your carriage is here." She looked at Olivia. "You should start getting ready, Olivia. We have to leave soon."

Simina rose and allowed Olivia to drape a shawl around her shoulders. Simina inhaled sharply and breathed out a slow, shaky breath. She left her room and slowly descended the stairs, holding up part of her skirt. Simina didn't see Gloria anywhere. Olivia and Aunt Lyda waved goodbye as she approached the door.

"Have a good time!" Olivia called. Simina waved back but said nothing. She walked out the door and boarded the waiting carriage to take her to the castle.

* * *

Upon arriving, Simina noticed quite a crowd entering the gates through the castle doors. Simina's excitement flared. She clutched the invitation in her hand, for she needed that to allow her access into the castle. Dismounting out of her carriage, she followed the crowd. Simina saw dozens of beautiful young ladies dressed up all fancy with an overzealous look in their eyes. She hardly saw any men, but she saw some here and there, swimming among the crowd of many women.

Light flooded the castle, streaming out into the night. Simina could hear the faint sound of music playing. The crowd formed a sort of line, and when Simina passed through the threshold, she saw Oliver standing inside, just to the right. He was dressed up fine in a suit, his white hair combed and swept back, his beard trimmed. He was taking invitations and putting them in a basket, and then he was taking people's coats and hanging them on a coat rack.

Oliver saw Simina, offered her a pleasant smile, and bowed his head. Simina curtsied and handed him her invitation.

"Good evening, madam." He greeted and took her shawl. Simina let him.

"Hello, Oliver," Simina greeted and smiled warmly. Then she passed on and followed the crowd through the foyer toward two great big double doors under the stairs. They were wide open, and that's where the music was playing. It was a pleasant sound, a jolly sound. Somebody played the violin, and Simina heard the gentle piano keys. She wondered who was playing.

She gazed out over the great expanse of the large ballroom. At the end of the long, wide, and vast room was a slightly raised platform with steps leading to two thrones.

The King was seated, dressed finely, looking his best despite the sickly pallor of his skin. The other throne, however, was empty, to Simina's dismay. The room gradually filled with people; some were already dancing to soft, romantic music. Through the crowd of people, Simina scanned around for Gloria. She's probably not here yet, considering she'd probably left a little after Simina. She did see Nar's uncle standing on the raised platform, speaking with the King.

Simina's dismay did not last long, for when she turned and looked to her right, she locked eyes with Nar, The Dark Prince. His eyes twinkled aglow, and a smirk gently tilted his lips. Simina's eyes were instantly drawn to his mouth. Her face flushed at the memory of them in the woods. Nar narrowed his eyes, and his smirk grew wider. He lifted his chin in a very esteemed way, and proceeded to stride over to her, confidence in his steps. It didn't take him long to reach her and close the distance between them.

"Simina, I'm honored that you accepted my invitation," Nar mused, voice wispy and silky, flowing sweet. He bowed with a distinctive flourish. Nar grasped her hand gently in his as Simina curtsied. He took in her appearance, eyes ravaging her, and Simina saw approval dancing in his eyes. He pressed his nose to her hand and inhaled her scent, closing his eyes.

"Mmm." A low sound resonated from his throat. Nar opened his eyes, locking them on Simina. Her breath caught at the intensity of the look in his glowing, purple eyes. She could not look away. Nar pressed his soft, feathery lips to the back of her hand, kissing it. He never took his eyes off her. She was too beautiful.

"You are radiantly lovely," Nar gushed as he pulled away, dropping her hand. Simina blushed and lowered her eyes. She only had the courage to gaze at him from under her lashes.

"Thank you," she responded coyly and took this time to take in his appearance. Like usual, he wore all black. His shirt was black linen, and over the top of that, he wore a black blazer. Simina admired the way his black leather pants fit tightly on his legs, hugging his thighs, making his long, graceful legs look breathtakingly sexy. Nar's shoulders were brilliantly broad, and his sharp collarbone peeked from under the lip of his shirt. A button or two was undone, and Simina saw part of his chest with a few hairs peeking out. His torso curved slimly as the jacket hugged his physique, spiraling down to a slender waist and hips. Nar was breathtaking and so handsome, and Simina lost all ability to think properly.

A soft, romantic melody simpered into the air and started playing. Nar's lips stretched up into a smile, and he offered Simina his hand, palm up. Simina noted the gentle, subtle, dark peach fuzz dotting his cheeks and chin.

"May I have this dance?" Nar asked softly, gazing intently into her eyes. Simina didn't take her eyes off him as she placed her hand on his.

"Yes," Simina whispered. Nar smiled and grasped her hand tightly, tugging her gently toward him. Simina placed a hand on his shoulder, Nar's hand coming swiftly around her waist. Simina's breath hitched at his touch, and her skin beneath the fabric tingled. Their other hands clasped together.

Slowly, they started to dance, moving swiftly, their feet in sync with the music. Luckily, they'd taught Simina how to dance at Etiquette School. Simina could hardly breathe at the moment. Her face was inches from Nar's, and she stared straight into his deep, luscious purple eyes. Simina's breathing turned shallow. Everything and everyone else melted away into the background. She was completely mesmerized by him.

Nar took in the awestruck expression on her face. Her lips were slightly parted, her breathing shallow and quick. Her eyes were clouded and dazed as she stared dreamily at him. Nar smiled at her, cocking his head to one side. His eyes narrowed curiously.

"You look lovely, Simina," Nar murmured, breaking Simina out of her daze. She blushed, and Nar grinned. He liked it when she blushed and was glad that he was the one who caused it.

"Thank you. Matilda helped me pick it out," Simina answered shyly. She cleared her throat, trying to clear her mind. Nar was amused. He enjoyed the way Simina looked at him. Her insides melted at their closeness, turning into a sweet, joyful goo. His warmth enveloped her like a fuzzy, cozy blanket. She stared at his full, luscious pink lips.

"You're handsome," Simina complimented, unable to take her eyes away. Nar smirked.

"Thank you. I know," Nar replied smoothly. He kept his steps light as he moved. Nar twirled Simina around in a slow circle.

He stared at her inquisitively. "Nothing suspicious yet. Keep your eyes open."

Simina nodded. "I know. I haven't seen Gloria yet."

Soon, the orchestra playing ended, and the music stopped. The piece had ended. Simina and Nar stepped away from each other, and disappointment followed at their separation. He bowed to her, and she curtsied to him in turn. Applause followed, and once the applause ceased, Simina saw the King rise from his throne. He held up a hand, silencing the buzzing of the excited crowd, drawing everyone's attention. The King smiled delightedly at them all.

"My friends. My people. It is such an honor to have you here tonight, joining us in welcoming our special guest: my brother. We gather here today to welcome him to our home and kingdom. But this party isn't just for him. I know you all must know I won't be here much longer. My son, the Prince, is soon to take a bride to be his queen. This ball will allow him to pick a suitable bride to marry for once I am gone." The King stopped for a moment and smiled at everyone. He sighed.

"But, please, continue to enjoy yourselves. This is a night meant for pleasantries and revelry. Please carry on, carry on," he urged. Finished with his speech, the King returned to his seat. The orchestra began to play again, and a soft but upbeat tune crooned melodiously into the air.

Nar turned back to Simina and held out his hand to her with a knowing smirk. Smiling, Simina retook his hand. Nar pulled her into his arms, faces inches apart, closer than before. Simina's face warmed as Nar's breath brushed against her cheek. A strange, pleasant feeling pooled inside her belly. She liked the closeness. A slight smirk kept his lips tilted and there was a deep, sensual look in his eyes as he stared at her from under thick lashes with beguiling eyes.

Simina couldn't help but stare at his lips. They looked plump, ripe, and succulent. She wanted to kiss those lips. They danced gracefully through the throng of people, dancing through the crowd.

"Can I ask you something?" Nar whispered. Simina smiled.

"Mmm. Yes," she answered. He pulled her closer.

"Are you in love with me?" Nar asked her, his voice growing deep and low. Her face heated instantly, and her breathing quickened. He pulled her closer, so close that his lips brushed against hers, his breath against her face. Her eyelids fluttered.

"And if I was?" Simina breathed. Nar spun her, holding her away from him a moment until he pulled her back to him, clasping her hands in his. He pulled her so close to him that their bodies touched. Their faces were so close that Nar's stubble gently scratched her cheek.

"Then you'd be mine." Nar breathed passionately into her ear, possessiveness filling his voice. Simina stifled a little sigh, and her breath quickened. Nar twirled her and dipped her low to the floor, arm around her waist. Her blood danced excitedly in her veins. Excited electricity sparked through her. Nar stared down into her eyes, and she stared up at him. Her belly clenched deliciously. He looked so hot, so delectable. Desire boiled deep within the pit of her stomach.

Nar pulled her back to him, and Simina put her arms around his neck. She gazed deeply into his enchanting purple eyes, swimming in everything that was him. Simina wanted to be a part of him. She wanted to lose herself in him. The music faded, and everything around her melted into the background. Simina wanted to be his, forever and eternally his. His scorching purple eyes burned hot, hot with desire. Nar wanted to be alone with her. They kept drawing closer and closer, slowly leaning into each other. Simina slipped the tips of her fingers into the ends of his soft, black hair. She ran her fingers gently through it, stroking softly through his hair.

Simina pressed her forehead against Nar's, taking in a deep breath, then breathing it out slowly through parted lips. They swayed slowly from side to side, in sync with the soft, sweet melody of the music. Nar brought his hand to the back of her head, tilting her head back ever so slightly. His lips parted. Simina's heart was pounding out of her chest. His lips grazed hers, and Simina fluttered her eyes closed, yearning for his kiss, waiting for it. He pressed a light kiss to her lips, and before he could deepen it, another man's voice ripped through their moment and tore it apart. Someone tapped his shoulder. Nar and Simina broke apart from each other, separating. Simina opened her eyes, disappointed and slightly disgruntled.

"Hey there, nephew. Mind if I cut in?" Simina heard the voice of Nar's uncle. Simina looked up to see him. He was squat and short, bearded and scary, and also ugly. Simina hated simply seeing his face. Nar seemed irritated, but Simina knew he was hiding it as he showed fake politeness.

"Oh, not at all, Uncle," Nar said politely. He turned to Simina, resuming his stature of grandeur.

"Please forgive my rudeness, Uncle. This is Simina. I never got the chance to introduce you to her earlier." Nar took Simina's hand, noticing her discomfort. Her body tensed, like a coiled spring. Simina relaxed just a bit when Nar took her hand and breathed in relief.

"Simina, this is my Uncle Julian," Nar introduced politely. Simina curtsied to him, and Julian smiled. He bowed to her and took Simina's hand.

"How do you do, Simina?" he greeted and bent to kiss her hand. Simina couldn't be sure, but she thought she saw a nasty, lustful desire in his eyes.

"I'm very well, thank you," Simina responded kindly. A waiter appeared seemingly out of nowhere, holding a tray with three glasses. Each glass was filled with sweet wine, the bubbles inside popping and fizzing. One drink was a clear and bright, vibrant pink, while the other two looked slightly cloudy.

"Sweet wine?" the waiter offered.

"Yes, thank you." Julian plucked the vibrant one from the tray, carefully holding the stem.

Prince Nar took one, and the last was offered to Simina. Gulping, she shook her head.

"No thank you, I'm not thirsty," she said.

"I insist." Julian took it from the waiter and practically shoved it into her hands. Simina stared into the dreary liquid, thinking of the poison she'd heard them talking about.

"A toast!" Julian exclaimed, turning his attention towards Nar. Simina took that chance to quickly pour the drink out onto the floor behind her back. Dancing patrons nearby stared at her oddly, but continued on their way. Simina held the empty glass in front of her.

"A toast to my nephew! May he find the noblewoman of his dreams tonight, so that he can finally marry!" Julian said boisterously. He clinked his glass against Nar's.

"Cheers," Nar said, smiling tightly. He slowly raised the glass to his lips.

Simina's mind went haywire. She couldn't let him drink that. She decided to spill it somehow using magic, but realized that she'd left the crystal at home. However, Simina had to channel her own. This was a matter of life or death. Staring hard at the glass of wine, Simina pulled hard on the magic energy deep inside of her. Energy zapped through her entire body, sharp and powerful. *Shatter.*

Just before the liquid could touch his lips, the glass cracked and shattered in his hand. The liquid spilled out everywhere, spilling on his blazer. Startled, Nar dropped the stem and the glass pieces tinkled to the floor. A waiter rushed over to clean up the mess, handing Nar a towel.

"It's quite all right," Nar assured the waiter, refusing the towel. He simply touched his blazer, and the liquid that soaked into the fabric dried up, leaving it just as it had been a moment ago.

"Oh dear," Julian said, faking concern. A look of dismay flashed in his eyes, but disappeared quickly. "That was unfortunate."

He downed his drink and handed his empty glass to the waiter. Simina did the same.

"I hope you don't mind, Nar, if I steal your lady for a quick dance," Julian requested, holding out his hand to Simina. Simina saw Nar's lips twitch uncomfortably. His brow seemed to flinch. But quickly, Nar composed himself, even though he despised the thought of his Simina in Uncle Julian's arms.

With a fake smile and pursed lips, Nar nodded. Simina gulped. She internally shuddered at the thought of being that close to Nar's gross uncle, who had just attempted to poison them. Simina wanted to glare at him, but she held it back.

"Of course," Nar agreed politely, smiling falsely. He turned to Simina, bowed to her, and drifted away, melting into the throng of people. Simina's eyes drooped, and her heart fell. She wished Nar hadn't left her with Uncle Julian. Simina turned to him and took Julian's hand. He pulled her to him, taking her waist. Simina flinched at his touch. She did not like it.

Simina put her hand on his shoulder, taking his other hand, and they danced. She looked anywhere but at his face. She did not want to look at his face. It was too much for Simina to bear, being around the man who tried to kill Prince Nar. He also stank, reeking of a terrible odor of something unclean, covered up with the stench of cologne.

"So, you're Simina. How nice to meet you," Julian greeted formally. Simina thought he sounded like a snake.

"Yes..." Simina responded dryly. Julian nudged her chin up with two fingers.

"Let me look at you. I'd like to see you better." Simina was forced to raise her head. He stared at her closely. Julian slowly took in her beauty, and immediate desire swept through him. He wanted her. He wanted Simina to be his. She was young, beautiful, and most likely a virgin.

Simina saw the lustful desire in his eyes and instant revulsion clumped in her throat, leaving a sour, nasty taste on her tongue. She yearned to be back in Nar's arms, dancing with him, staring into his wonderful purple eyes. Her stomach squirmed, worming around uncomfortably inside her.

"You are a lovely young lady, Simina," Julian complimented. Simina hated the blush that came into her cheeks. She looked down at her dancing, waltzing feet.

"I see why Nar has taken quite an interest in you," he continued. Simina scowled. *He hardly knows me,* she thought. How could he see why? It wasn't just her beauty that Nar liked. It was her personality, her kindness and understanding.

"Thank you." She tried to keep the bitterness out of her voice. Simina was half-minded about telling him that she was betrothed to Nar already, so that he'd back off.

"How old are you, my dear?" he crooned. Simina gulped.

"Twenty-one years," she answered quietly. Julian was surprised at this. *She is twenty-one and not yet married,* he thought. He could have her as his. Yes, no one had a claim over her. He assumed that she was a noblewoman or some sort of royalty because it was rare for a peasant to be this beautiful.

Meanwhile, Simina was scanning the dancing crowd for Nar. She could not spot him in the crowd of all the dancing people. Her eyes kept searching. Just seeing him would make her feel better, even a little. Looking for him took her mind off who she was dancing with. Finally, Simina spotted him among the crowd. He was dancing with another young woman, someone she didn't know. At the sight of him, her heart yearned to be by his side, to be with him.

"And you aren't married?" Julian's voice reluctantly brought Simina's attention back to him. She shook her head.

"No," Simina said with a sigh. This piqued Julian's interest even more since it confirmed his assumption. Simina hated the fact that he was interested in her. She didn't want him. She didn't love him. Simina loved and wanted only Nar.

"You are young and eligible, Simina. You should use that," Julian suggested. Unnerved, Simina looked up at him.

"What do you mean by that?" Simina sounded incredulous. He smiled at her in a very creepy way.

"Take advantage of it. Marry someone. With your beauty, you could woo any man into marrying you. Marry someone eligible, someone rich. There are so many eligible bachelors here. Like myself," Julian explained, voice a low, disgusting husk. Simina blinked at him. She couldn't believe this.

"If you're willing...would you marry me? You're so young, lovely, and fruitful; I'd be pleased to have you as my wife, Simina. Would you?" Julian asked, voice soft, sickly sweet, and placating. Simina's heart jumped into her throat. Revulsion swept through her. Disgusting. She couldn't imagine ever marrying this man. Soon after the revulsion, Simina was overcome with the sudden, overwhelming exhaustion that came with using magic. Her knees buckled, eyes fluttering and Julian held her up to prevent her from falling. Her stomach toiled in disgust at this, and coupled with the exhaustion, Simina couldn't stand to be near him any longer.

"Excuse me, please..." she pushed away from him, loosening herself from his slimy grip.

"Are you all right?" he asked, but Simina was already staggering away through the crowd. Simina needed air, and she headed for the exit.

It took longer for her to get tired. Usually, it happened immediately after using magic. But it had been a few minutes since she made Nar's glass explode. This was an improvement. The music slowly faded as she walked deeper into the foyer. Simina ran as fast as her heels would allow, picking up her skirts so she wouldn't trip. Finally, she burst out of the double doors and into the cold, wintry night. Breathing heavily, she rested a moment against the wall.

She gathered herself, and the exhaustion soon melted away into a soft tiredness. Feeling a bit more at ease, Simina walked through the snow to the garden, stopping at the bed of black roses. She caressed the petals gently on each flower. Footsteps crunched in the snow behind her, but Simina did not turn.

"Is everything all right, Simina?" Nar's voice interrupted.

She sighed. "I just needed some fresh air."

"It was you who made my glass explode, wasn't it?" He smirked.

"Perhaps," Simina answered vaguely, smiling slightly. "I didn't need the crystal this time."

"You're getting better." Nar stared at her with approval and admiration. "What are you doing out here?"

Simina frowned. "Your uncle is slime."

"What happened?"

"He asked me to marry him…" She suddenly regretted telling him as she realized that she wasn't sure how he would react.

Nar's eyes widened, then narrowed, filling with outrage. He frowned and gritted his teeth.

"What?" he hissed. His eyes began to glow.

"I'm not going to, of course," Simina said quickly.

"I'll kill him!" Nar growled, spinning around back towards the castle. The snow melted instantly where his feet stepped, a dark cloud trailing after him.

Simina grabbed his arm before he could reach the castle doors. "Nar, calm down."

He halted, taking a deep breath and turned towards her, purple eyes ablaze. She placed a hand on his cheek.

"This is not who you are," she whispered.

The glow in his eyes dimmed slowly, and he calmed. Taking her hand in his, Nar kissed the inside of her palm.

"I'm sorry," he apologized. "I forget myself."

"It's okay."

"You see right through me," Nar muttered. "You're the only person who's never treated me like a monster."

Simina squeezed his hand. "Because you aren't."

Prince Nar stared at her for a long while, completely silent. Then, without warning, he pushed his fingers into her silky hair, tilted her head back, and kissed her. Nar gently pressed her against the wall, arms around her.

Simina moaned softly, responding eagerly to his kiss. He moved his lips on hers, savoring her taste and kissing her deeply, passionately. Peasant or not. This was the girl he wanted to be with for the rest of his life.

Simina's fingers dove into his hair, curling around the short, wispy strands. She pulled him closer, reveling in this sensation, his heat. Simina loved the softness of his lips and the urgency, passion, and possessiveness of his kiss. Nar's hands slowly traveled higher, higher from her waist up to just under her breast line.

Simina's hand traveled down his face, stroking her fingers across his throat, his pulsing pulse trailing a sweet, sensual touch down to his shoulder, then his collarbone. His skin, hot with passion, yet soft. His muscles rippled, hard under her fingers. Simina traced her finger slowly across his collarbone. Nar moaned, lips breaking from hers. Simina just realized that her face was hot. Nar grabbed Simina's hand.

"Simina..." Nar murmured, his lips brushing gently against hers. The pit of her belly tingled with sensation. He pressed his forehead to hers, eyes closed, breathing in her lovely scent.

Her fingers skimmed across his skin at the edge of his shirt. He clasped her chin between his thumb and forefinger and kissed her once more. Simina slipped her arms around his neck, drawing him closer, enjoying the feel of his arms around her, his strength. She was utterly captivated by him. She grasped a handful of his coat in her fist. Nar cupped her face with a gentle caress, his fingers twisting into her soft, silky hair as he stroked through the tresses. He kissed her deeply, savoring her until he finally broke away from her.

Taking her face in both hands, Nar stared down at her with smoldering, blazing purple eyes.

"Marry me." It came out as a demand, not a question. Simina stared at him in shock, her mouth agape. He really wanted to marry her, a peasant? This had to be a dream, a fairytale. But it wasn't. It was better than a fairytale because it was real. The Prince, the imperfect prince with all his flaws, wanted to marry her.

"Yes," she answered, holding back tears. Then Simina hugged him tightly, pressing her face into his neck. Nar smiled and pressed his nose into her hair. He held her tightly against him, wrapping his arms around her.

"Mmm..." He sighed with content.

"I love you," Simina whispered into his jacket. She whispered it so low that Nar almost didn't hear her, but he caught it.

He smiled. "And I love you, Simina."

Simina thought that she'd never want to marry anyone, much less get married in the first place. She hadn't found anyone to interest her, until now. But she'd never actually been involved with a lot of men. She's only known and associated with three men in her entire life. Her father, Ernest, and now Prince Nar. The Prince who wanted to marry her.

After a long moment, Nar finally pulled away from her. He stared at her for another brief moment before saying, "We should get back."

Simina nodded in agreement. "I'm sure everyone will be wondering where you are."

Silently, the two of them headed back inside the castle, reveling in their newfound love.

Twenty-Five

The morning after the Royal Ball, Nar stood by his father's bed. He bowed to him out of respect, but did not kneel.

"Father," he said. The King struggled to sit up in bed.

"What do you want?" He frowned at his son, and then coughed.

Prince Nar took a deep breath. "I'm here to inform you that I have chosen to marry this woman. Simina Gorchev."

Simina stepped out from behind him, hands clasped behind her. The King's eyes bulged at the sight of her.

"Again with this nonsense?" he harrumphed. "She is no noble! She's a filthy *peasant.*"

"Peasant or not, I am going to marry her," Nar insisted.

The King's nostrils flared. "I forbid it. Do you hear me, boy? I forbid it!"

"I don't *care,*" Nar spat. "I'm going to marry her anyway."

"I am still the King!" he shouted hoarsely. "And you do as I say! If you marry this girl, you forfeit the throne! I'll give it to your uncle!"

Nar chuckled. "No, father. As long as I live, the throne will be mine. You know as well as I do that, unless I die, Julian has no claim to the throne."

"You have *disgraced* the name Darkla," the King hissed. "You are a disgrace!"

Rolling his eyes, Nar turned and walked out. Simina followed after him, ignoring the King's mad ravings.

* * *

Later that day, Nar and Simina departed for Autumnville. Using Nar's teleportation, the two of them arrived instantly. However, Nar had never been to Simina's house, so they took a carriage the rest of the way. Simina squirmed in the carriage next to Nar, unable to sit still. She was nervous about going to see her father. She did want to see him, but that's not what worried her. Simina was concerned that her father would not allow them to get married because of who Nar was, the Dark Prince.

Simina was mainly worried about his reaction. Would he hate her? Shun her? Nar was doing this properly, traditionally, by asking her father for permission to marry her. It was right. Why should he deny it? Next to her, Nar sat leisurely and relaxed, staring out of the window at the lovely landscape smoothly rolling by.

Simina reached her hand out and grasped Nar's. Alerted by her action, Nar turned and glanced over at her. He was met with two big, desperate, worried eyes filled with pleading. Nar offered a reassuring smile and stroked the back of her hand with his thumb.

"Don't worry, Simina. It'll all turn out just fine. Trust me," Nar tried to assure her. Simina squeezed his hand. Nar weaved his fingers through hers and squeezed back.

"Okay Nar. But I'm just worried." Simina's voice wavered.

"Why?"

"Because. My father...well..." Simina gulped and swallowed. She continued after taking a short breath.

"He doesn't really like the whole thing about...the Dark Prince. He thinks you don't exist and that you're something evil. He got mad when he found out that I was reading a book about you," Simina explained.

Nar understood why she was troubled. But the rumors about him in Autumnville just weren't true. He licked his lips, feeling slightly troubled now himself. Nar sighed. *This is what being a King means. Diplomacy.* Nar figured he'd have to negotiate with her father for her hand, just like a King would have to negotiate. *Just think of it as a negotiation.*

"Well, I'll have to explain to your father that I'm real and not evil. I promise, we will be married. Leave it to me."

He brought her hand to his lips and kissed it. "Let me worry about this. Just relax."

Simina took a deep breath, nodding. Holding Nar's hand, the two of them rode the rest of the way in silence.

* * *

Several minutes later, their carriage rolled to a stop. Simina glanced out of the window at her old house. She recognized it, but at the same time it looked so unfamiliar to her that she wondered if it really was her house. Simina couldn't believe she was back here after all this time.

"We're here," Nar said. Simina wrung her hands, then her stomach turned. This was it. Simina remembered sending a letter to her father telling him about Prince Nar. He'd never responded to it. Right now, that deeply worried her. Nar opened the door and stepped out, and took Simina's hand as she dismounted.

Without further delay, the carriage rode away. Simina looked around at the familiar little town. Of course, it didn't look as rich as Winterville, but it was nonetheless her home. Looking at it made her want to cry. She'd never realized how much she had missed the place until now.

Simina stared at the front door to her old house. She swallowed. Nar squeezed her hand reassuringly. Simina hadn't seen her dad in a while. She wanted to, but was scared he would have a bad reaction. Gathering her courage, Simina walked up to the door, pulling Nar along with her. Tentatively, she raised a fist and knocked on the door.

Simina waited in anticipation. She heard tromping footsteps coming to the door. Simina recognized that sound as her father's tromping big boots. The sound greatly calmed her and reminded Simina of those peaceful, happy days. The door opened. Simina held her breath. Gregory, her father, stepped out onto the threshold. Gregory's eyes widened when he caught sight of Simina. He blinked a few times, thinking perhaps that it was just him hallucinating or something. But she looked too real.

"Simina." Gregory choked. Tears sprang to her eyes, quick and merciless.

"Hi, Father." Simina sniffled. With great emotion, Simina ran to him and gave her father a great big hug. He hugged her back tightly, tears overflowing his eyes. He hadn't seen her in so long, it was so good to see her. He squeezed her tight, sniffling, trying to dry his tears. Gregory kissed her head.

"So good to see you again, Simina," Gregory rasped. He pulled back and held her at arm's length to look at her. He placed a hand under her chin and tilted Simina's head, inspecting her.

"You've grown since I've last seen you." He beamed. "You're growing up to be quite a woman, Simina." She smiled.

"Thank you, Father. I'm glad to see you too." Simina pulled back out of his embrace. Nar stared awkwardly at the two of them, thinking himself out of place as he watched their happy reunion. What also added to his anxiety was the constant weird stares people were giving him and Simina. He noticed that these citizens looked quite poorer than those in Winterville. They'd never seen people wearing such nice clothes.

Taking notice of the man standing behind Simina, Gregory gestured to him.

"Who is this young man you've brought with you, Simina?" His brow furrowed with curiosity. Simina looked over her shoulder at Nar. Nar offered her a shy, awkward smile in return. She held out her hand for him to take.

"Father, I'd like you to meet someone," Simina whispered. Nar took her hand. Nar stepped up to her father. Gregory was a little wary of this handsome man standing next to his daughter. Nar, gathering his courage, bowed to Simina's father.

"Pleasure to meet you, Mr. Gorchev. I am Prince Nar of Lazera, at your service," Nar wisped in his low, respectful, authoritative voice. Gregory's eyes narrowed suspiciously at his title. A prince? His daughter had brought a prince with her? What in the world could a prince want with Autumnville? He held his hand out to Nar.

"Nice to meet you, your Highness. Please call me Gregory," he said respectfully. Nar took his hand and shook it.

"Father, there's something we'd like to tell you," Simina murmured, twiddling her fingers. Gregory raised a wary eyebrow.

"Oh? And what's that?" Nar held a hand up, halting the conversation.

"Perhaps we should take this inside," Nar suggested. Gregory stepped aside, allowing Simina entrance, and Nar after her. This made Gregory more suspicious.

"All right. Come in and take a seat," Gregory said. The three gathered and sat at the small kitchen table. Everything evoked memories in her, yet it seemed foreign at the same time. Simina shifted in her seat uncomfortably. She hoped this went well. Gregory crossed his arms.

"What's this about?" He stared pointedly at Nar. Nar looked at Simina. She caught his eyes. He curled an eyebrow at her, silently asking, "Are you sure about this? Are you ready?" Simina nodded. Nar looked back at her father.

"I've come to ask for your daughter's hand in marriage," Nar answered respectfully. Simina's heart flipped, and she glanced at her father for a reaction. His face blanched, but other than that, he looked stone-faced. Her stomach turned, roiling with a deep-seated worry. Gregory sat up straighter and squared his shoulders. He set his jaw, then set his powerful glare on Prince Nar. Simina shivered. Uh-oh. She knew that look.

"You want to marry my daughter?" he asked Nar, voice loud and booming, much louder than it should be. Nar, however, seemed to be unperturbed. He answered sincerely and respectfully.

"Yes, Mr. Gorchev," Nar replied sincerely. Gregory looked at Simina harshly.

"Simina, outside," he ordered snappishly. Simina immediately stood.

"Yes, Father." She obeyed and went outside. Was it really that serious? Simina walked around her house to the stables to see if Winona was still there. To her liking, Winona was still there where she'd always been. Simina smiled and stroked Winona's mane. Winona neighed and nuzzled into her hand.

"Long time no see, huh, Winona?" Simina spoke to the horse. She hugged it for a bit, enjoying her reunion, and then fed it hay and water. Afterward, Simina saddled her up for a short ride.

"You wanna go for a ride, girl? Let's go for a ride and stretch those legs," Simina muttered. She swung herself up on Winona's back and steered her gently out of the stables. Simina whipped the reins.

"Ha!" she cried and trotted Winona out into town. Simina was slowly bouncing and trotting through town, enjoying the sight of her old hometown. It may not have been as rich and glorious as Winterville, but it was still her home, and she still loved it. Everything looked familiar, but it just seemed so different now. Maybe it's because she'd gotten used to Winterville. Or perhaps Simina had grown up a little in the past year. Nostalgia greeted her, reminding her of the person she once was and the person she'd now become. She reflected on her previous behavior, which she now considered childish. That's how she saw it now. Childish. The games. Ernest. So childish.

Simina reflected on those days and missed them, but did not yearn for them in vain like she'd done before. Such things were trivial. Simina had grown quite a lot since she'd moved away to Winterville, since she'd met Nar. But Simina couldn't focus on the past. She had to focus on the here and now. Nar was asking her father's permission to marry her. Something serious was about to happen

Simina took a breath and tried not to think about it. *Think about something else, think about something else. Should I go to the forest?* It was certainly an excellent place to frolic. Simina wanted to take Winona for a nice ride. So Simina headed toward the forest, once again feeling nostalgic. Once Simina hit the trail that led out of town and into the forest, she surged Winona forward.

"Hi-ya!" Simina cried. Winona neighed and charged down the trail with great speed. The wind billowed through her hair, billowing up her dress. As Simina ran, exhilaration breezed through her, making her feel alive. The forest looked as beautiful as ever today. The air smelled sweet with the aroma of wildflowers. The grass was so green in the summertime, leaving a crispy shade of jade. Everything looked so vibrant and alive.

Simina kept riding and riding and jumping over logs and other things until she got to the stream where she and Ernest used to play. It seemed so long ago, but it was only a year ago. So much had happened in a year; so much had changed. But Simina didn't regret it. She didn't regret anything.

Upon arriving at the stream, she dismounted Winona. Simina stood at the stream's edge. Holding up her skirts, she removed her shoes. Inching toward the rushing water, Simina gingerly put her toe into the cool water.

Simina waded into the rushing, cool water until it was up to her ankles. Simina sighed with relaxation. She stretched her toes. The cool water running over them was refreshing, giving her a brief moment of solace. Simina tilted her head back into the breeze. Her hair wisped about her face, and she closed her eyes. The breeze cooled her skin, sending pleasant tingles across her body. Simina enjoyed the steady flow of nature all around her. The lovely chirps of the birds. The buzzing cicadas. The soothing rushing of the stream's water. Simina loved nature. But she was slowly eased out of her reverie when she heard the clip-clopping of a horse drawing near. Simina opened her eyes, blinking them against the bright sun. She looked toward where she heard the sound. Simina watched as a lovely, luscious brown horse came trudging through the woods with a young man riding atop its back.

Simina couldn't believe her eyes. She recognized the young man. He had a light mop of red hair sitting atop his head and light peach fuzz on his face. His facial features were a little boyish still, even though Simina could tell he'd grown up a bit. She recognized him. The boy saw Simina, and before she could say anything, he did.

"Simina?" His voice was filled with shock. Simina widened her eyes and smiled.

"Ernest?" Simina's voice rose with excitement and surprise. Recognizing each other, they smiled. Ernest leaped from his horse, and Simina splashed vigorously to get out of the stream to reach him. They ran to each other and embraced in a big hug. Simina threw her arms around his neck, and Ernest hugged her tightly, pulling her close. Simina was so glad to see him after so long. She'd missed Ernest, her best friend.

"Simina, it's so good to see you. I haven't seen you in so long," Ernest sighed. Simina pulled back to look at him.

"It's great to see you too," Simina said with a smile. Ernest smiled and observed her. She had gotten lovelier than before. She really had grown.

"So, what have you been up to? What made you come back?" Ernest asked curiously. Simina blushed.

"Well, nothing much..." Simina explained to him in a summary what she'd been doing in the past year since she'd left. Ernest listened and focused intently on her every word.

Afterward, he nodded in understanding. "Ah. I see." Ernest stroked his chin. "So what are you doing here?"

"Well, Prince Nar is asking my father for permission to marry me," Simina told him. Ernest smiled and scratched the back of his neck. He couldn't believe that she was getting married.

"Wow, congratulations, Simina! I'm happy for you!" Ernest said joyfully. Simina beamed.

"Thank you so much!" She kissed his cheek.

"I am getting married soon, too," Ernest said shyly and blushed. He scratched the back of his neck. Simina grinned at him and squealed.

"Oh my gosh! Congratulations, Ernest!" she gushed. Ernest's blush deepened.

"Yeah..." he muttered and glanced away from her. Simina giggled at Ernest's shyness.

"Well, I'm happy for you. If Father agrees to my marriage, you can come to the wedding," Simina offered. Ernest nodded and offered a small smile in return.

"Thanks. You can come to my wedding too. I'll send you a letter notifying you of the date and time," Ernest said. He looked up at the sky as the breeze picked up. The wind tousled his floppy blond locks. He inhaled the scent of the air.

"Nice day, huh?" Ernest whispered. Simina nodded, watching him. "It is." She noticed the faraway, distant look etched across his face. Ernest closed his eyes for a moment and then blinked them open.

"Hey, Simina. What do you say we...play a game?" She barely heard him because his whisper was almost softer than the breeze. Simina's eyes widened.

"Huh?" Her brow rose. "You mean...like we used to?" Simina's heart skipped with excitement at the promise of a fun, thrilling game. Ernest tilted his head down and set his eyes on her.

"Yes. Just like we used to. How about it?" Ernest smirked boyishly, the way he always used to do when he'd challenge Simina to a bet when they were much younger.

"For old time's sake," Ernest added. Simina smiled, feeling slightly nostalgic. She agreed. Once again, they played their game of the Princess and the Witch just one last time, reliving the old days. Simina ran through the woods, tearing her dress like she used to, the wind flowing through her hair, splashing through water and mud puddles. They played for a long time until the games ended, as they always did, with Ernest catching and tackling Simina. Simina squealed with laughter and pushed Ernest off. They both rolled around on the ground laughing until their chests hurt.

They lay on the ground for a while, panting, trying to catch their breath while staring up at the blue sky filled with white, puffy clouds. Simina liked looking at the sky and the clouds. It relaxed her. Once they'd caught their breath, Ernest got up. He climbed a tree, picked two apples, and tossed one to her. She caught it and took a nice chomp. It was perfect and crispy and made a satisfying crunch. Juice dribbled down her lips.

Ernest jumped from the tree, landing on his feet. As Simina stared at the sky, she wondered how Nar's talk with her father was going. Her stomach clenched and swirled nervously. She hoped everything went well. But deep down inside of her, Simina had a bad feeling. Ernest noticed the troubled expression creasing up her face.

"Hey, whatchu look like that for?" Ernest asked, crunching his apple. Simina took another bite of hers, swallowed, and sighed.

"Oh. I'm just worried that...Father will say no to Nar's proposal. Then I won't get to marry him," Simina pouted. Ernest shrugged.

"And that's gonna stop you from marrying him?" Surprised, Simina looked up at him.

"If you love him, then...you love him. You should marry him even if your father says no," Ernest told her, finishing off his apple. He tossed the core off to the side. Simina finished hers and dropped it to the ground.

"Thanks, Ernest." Simina stood. Ernest stood as well.

"I should get back. It's been a while," Simina said, walking toward Winona. She and Ernest said goodbyes, and Simina rode away on Winona.

Simina was back at her house and put Winona into the stables in no time. She fed her some hay, gave her water, and brushed her fur. Just then, Simina heard shouting coming from her house. It didn't sound like Nar was shouting. She knew that shout. It was her father. The next thing she heard was her father's heavy footsteps thudding toward the door. Her heart jumped with fear. Simina knew what was going to happen next.

Her father, Gregory, busted out of the house, his face contorted with rage. Nar quickly strides toward him, emergence in his steps, alarm flashing in his eyes. Gregory's eyes were blazing.

"Simina!" Gregory roared her name. Simina jumped and shrank away behind Winona. Gregory caught sight of her. He gestured for her to come to him.

"Come here!" he shouted at her. With shaking legs, Simina slowly walked toward her angry-looking father, swallowing hard. Simina stopped a foot in front of him and maintained that distance, scared that he might strike her. Though he'd never hit her before, she still feared that he might if angered enough, and that he was. But he did not strike his daughter. He was furious at her for falling in love with this Dark Prince, for getting involved with someone Gregory considered foul and distasteful. *How dare she bring him to my house?*

"Yes, Father?" Simina's voice sounded so small and soft that he almost took some strange kind of pity on her. But no, instead, Gregory blew up.

"No! I won't allow it! I refuse to let you marry this man!" Gregory yelled, shaking his head. Simina's heart sank. She knew it. She knew this would happen. She saw Nar's eyes glowing dimly, and he attempted to go to her because being near her calmed him down, but Gregory stopped him.

"Don't you dare go near my daughter, you...you..." Gregory flailed for words. "You fiend!" He spat the words out at him like daggers. Nar took a step back, his expression disgruntled.

"Father, please!" Simina begged. She worried about Nar's temper, and his magic. She did not want him to lash out at her father. He glanced at her for a moment.

"No!" Then he rounded on Nar, eyes blazing.

"Did you deflower her?" Such an inappropriate question made Simina blush. Nar's eyes bulged wide in astonishment.

"No, of course not. I have done no such thing, Mr. Gorchev," Nar answered respectfully. Gregory's eyes now blazed with triumph.

"I won't allow you to defile my daughter!" He grabbed Nar by the shoulders. Tears started welling in Simina's eyes.

"Please, Father, I love him!" she cried. Gregory stopped a moment, and the action of shaking Nar halted. His eyes narrowed.

"You what?" he spat through gritted teeth. Simina gulped, now unable to speak.

"I refuse to let you marry him! You cannot!" Gregory yelled to Simina. Simina's body shook, and tears flowed down her cheeks. The sight of her crying sent a sharp pang of pain through his chest.

"My Lady." Nar outstretched his hand to her. He yearned to go to Simina to comfort her, but Gregory would not allow him. Gregory balled up a fist and punched Nar in the jaw. The blow sent Nar spiraling to the ground, his vision blurring around him. He winced, hearing Simina's wailing cries.

"Nar! No!" Simina screamed. "Stop it, Father, please!" Nar tasted the metallic tang of blood on his tongue. The sharp pieces of gravel dig into his cheek, and the dirt clumps up underneath his fingers. Nar's head spun, the world spun, and the ground below him began shaking as if an earthquake were happening. He stayed down for a moment, feeling his magic bubbling up inside him. He forced the anger down below, refusing to let it out. Nar didn't want to fight back against Simina's father; he could not allow his magic to get the better of him.

Simina tried to go to him to comfort him, but her efforts were in vain. Her father wouldn't let her go to him. Gregory held her back, held back her struggling, flailing body from Nar. She wanted to comfort him and make sure that his magic wouldn't get the better of him. She saw the black tendrils of mist curling out from his tense, stiff form on the ground, and the need to get to him only grew more urgent. She fell to her knees and started to plead with her father.

"Please, Father, don't hurt him!" Simina's voice cracked, tears streaming down her face. Gregory's face boiled and red with rage as he glared at her.

"No! I don't care! Take this filth away from me! I don't want him in my house! And I can't bear to look at you right now! Get out of my sight!" Gregory roared at Simina. She flinched, hurt, as Gregory stormed away and disappeared into the house. She waited a few moments until Simina was sure he wouldn't return. She hurried over to him on her hands and knees as he sat up from the ground. A string of blood ran from the corner of his lip. His cheek was swollen and red. Dirt was caked up on the other cheek. He pressed a hand to his cheek with a grimace, eyes laced with pain and distaste.

"Nar! Nar, are you all right?" Simina took his face gently in her hands. He breathed heavily, the ground rumbling slightly underneath him.

"I'm fine," he groaned and pushed her hands away. Nar noticed the townspeople nearby were staring, which only added to his growing anger. *Yes, stare at the freak.* He placed his hands on her shoulders.

"You should get away from me," he grumbled.

Simina shook her head stubbornly. "I'm not going anywhere."

"I could hurt you."

"You won't," Simina said sternly. "Just calm down."

"Let's go somewhere a little more private," Nar mumbled, nodding. Before Simina could react, Nar had already disappeared with Simina and reappeared in the woods. They were finally alone, crouched on the ground beside a light-flowing stream. Nar finally allowed himself to collapse. He fell against Simina, laying his head on her chest. Simina hugged his head to her chest, cradling him like a baby. She ran her fingers through his hair. Nar moaned in contentment, feeling his anger melt away. She kissed the top of his head.

"I'm sorry," she murmured, sniffling. Nar let his eyes flutter closed and buried his face in her neck, trying to calm the restless, violent power within him. He took comfort in her loving embrace, letting her warmth and care surround him. The blow from her father had given Nar a headache.

Nar lifted his head to see Simina's face.

"It's not your fault," Nar rasped, his voice a mangy croak. His eyes drooped with exhaustion.

"I hate it when you cry," he sighed, and kissed her jawline softly. Simina pulled back from Nar to inspect his face. She frowned at the bruise forming on his left cheek and his cut lip that leaked blood.

"You're hurt." Simina softly caressed his bruised cheek and skimmed across the cut on his lip. Nar winced and flinched away from her touch. Simina's eyes started brimming with fresh tears. Her bottom lip began to quiver. Nar's eyes narrowed. He grasped her chin fiercely, tugging her face toward him.

"No. Don't cry," Nar demanded, his voice stern. He touched his wounds, feeling the warmth of his magic as he healed them. Then he took his hand away, revealing a perfect, unscarred face.

"See? All better." He smiled half-heartedly.

Simina sucked up her tears until they were dry. Simina blamed herself for this. Guilt consumed her. Nar stared at her and watched the look of guilt on her face. He frowned and shook his head. Simina saw the look of disapproval, and she opened her mouth to speak, but Nar put a finger to her lips.

"No. Stop. Don't say anything." He stroked his fingers across her cheek and trailed them along her jawline.

"Let me be quite clear, my lady. This is not in any way your fault. All we want is to be married. What's the fault in that?" Nar snapped curtly with a fierce tone. He removed his finger from her lips.

"But we can't get married," Simina whimpered, pain filling her chest. Nar puckered his lips thoughtfully.

"Hmm, why can't we?" He quirked an eyebrow.

"Because my father won't allow us to; he said no."

She was getting irritated with Nar.

"Are you still living in his household under his rules? Have you been living there for the past year?"

Simina shook her head. "No."

"All right then. That's not going to stop me. I'm still going to marry you," Nar said with conviction. "I actually should be asking your aunt." His voice was a dark whisper.

"Nar, my father said we can't."

Nar glared at her. "I don't give a damn." Nar pushed her down gently until she was lying flat on her back on the ground. Startled, Simina tried to say something, but Nar cut her off with a fierce kiss. Simina responded quickly, her face heating. The kiss was short, yet passionate, and it took her breath away.

"I love you." He leaned close to her, and Nar trailed his lips along her jawline, smirking when she shuddered. "I am the Dark Prince, and I will do as I please."

Simina giggled at his response, nodding in agreement. "Yes, the Dark Prince takes orders from no one."

"That's right. And I will marry you," Nar whispered with a light chuckle. He kissed her forehead and then sat up.

"Anyway," he began softly, "I think that maybe your father overreacted just a bit." Simina looked up at him.

"What do you mean?" Simina allowed herself to feel a little hopeful. Nar shrugged.

"I don't know. Maybe...he was just angry and overwhelmed. Maybe he just needed some time to cool off and think it over," Nar suggested, casually playing with a few strands of grass. "You are his only daughter after all."

Simina shrugged and stood up. "I guess..."

"Are you ready? It's been a while. We should go talk to your father again," Nar suggested. Simina shivered, thinking about his previous reaction. Gulping, she nodded nervously.

"Okay," she muttered and took his hand. Simina closed her eyes. Nar and Simina disappeared out of the woods in a swirl of dark purple mist and reappeared standing in Simina's yard in front of the house. Everything was quiet except for the dull buzz of the townspeople walking by on the streets and the peddlers at their stands urging people to buy their items.

Holding Nar's hand, Simina walked to the front door. She raised a fist to knock, but hesitated. Once more, guilt filled her. Simina couldn't help but feel she'd somehow betrayed her father by falling in love with Nar, the Dark Prince. Simina was scared that he'd lose his mind again. Simina also didn't want to risk Nar losing control of his magic. She was unsure. Nar squeezed her hand in reassurance.

"It's all right, Simina. I'm right here; I'm with you. You can do it," he encouraged. Simina nodded and took a deep breath. She rapped her knuckles softly three times on the door. They waited, and Simina lowered her hand. They heard a noise coming from the inside and tromping boots or feet walking across a wooden floor, approaching the door. Simina's throat tightened. The doorknob turned slowly, and the door was furiously yanked open. Her father towered tall and fierce in the doorway. Nar stood bravely beside her on the front porch, holding her hand. Gregory glared at them.

"Hi, Father," Simina squeaked, unable to meet his glowering gaze. "May I please speak with you?" She gulped and stared at her feet, waiting expectantly. Gregory flicked his eyes over to Nar.

"I wish to speak to my daughter privately," he informed Nar calmly and respectfully. Nar bowed out of respect.

"Of course. I'll wait outside." Nar obliged and stepped off the porch. Gregory stepped aside to let Simina enter, and she walked in. Gregory closed the door behind them as Simina sat at the table. He sat as well. They both sat in awkward silence for a moment, Simina picking at her nails, feeling nervous and unsure.

"I'm sorry," Gregory apologized, feeling ashamed of himself. "I...I may have overreacted just a little bit."

Simina looked up, surprised.

"Really? You really mean that?" she asked, perking up a bit. Gregory even had the decency to look ashamed. He nodded.

"Yes. I'm so sorry, Simina. It was hard for me to fathom that you wanted to get married," he told her. Gregory looked at her and offered a small smile. He took her hand.

"Oh, Simina, how you've grown. I never thought this day would come," Gregory said with a sad sigh. Tears started welling in his eyes.

"Father, please don't cry," Simina whispered.

He sniffled. "Is he good to you? Does he treat you right?" His voice shook.

"Of course, father. He's always good to me."

"Do you love him?"

Simina nodded. "Yes. I love him."

Gregory sighed, defeated. "Well, you are of age. Go ahead and marry him. I'm not going to stop you." He looked away. Excited, Simina jumped to her feet.

"Really? Thank you, Father, thank you!" Simina ran up to him and hugged him tightly. She kissed his cheek. Gregory nodded and stood. Simina pulled away from him. She followed him to the door, skipping happily. When they exited, Simina found Nar sitting on an upturned bucket with Winona in the stables. Nar saw them and stood with a grand flourish. Simina went to him and hugged Nar.

Gregory went up to Nar and clapped him on the shoulder.

"You treat her right. Take care of my daughter. Understand?" Gregory's gruff voice returned, and he glared seriously at Nar with narrowed, stern eyes. Nar bowed his head and placed a hand over his heart.

"I will, Mr. Gorchev, sir. It's an honor. Thank you," Nar quipped diplomatically and respectfully. He looked toward Simina.

"Ready to go now?" he asked. They'd been here long enough. Simina nodded.

"Yes." She quickly said goodbye to her father, then she and Nar took their leave. He teleported back to Aunt Lyda's house, and Nar explained to her where they'd been and were getting married. Gloria heard the news and was extremely jealous. She wanted Simina dead so badly that her hatred flared to even greater extents.

However, when Nar was getting ready to leave Simina's house, he received terrible news from a Royal Courier. The courier stopped him and saluted.

"Your highness, I have a letter from your father for you. I'm afraid I have some disturbing news for you." The courier looked pale and grave as he handed the letter to Nar. Nar took it.

"What is this bad news?" Nar started to open the envelope. The courier cleared his throat.

"I'm afraid that...while you were away, your father, the King...passed. He's died, sir," the courier explained, solemnly. Nar's eyes widened. He looked up at the courier.

"What?" He must be dreaming. He couldn't believe his ears.

"I'm sorry, sir," the courier said. "He died from a mysterious illness. That letter is the King's Will." The courier pointed at the letter in Nar's hands. Cursing, Nar opened the envelope and took out the letter. He read it.

Dear Nar,

If you are reading this, then that means I am now deceased, and you have succeeded in killing me. Unfortunately, I have no other heirs and this means that you will be King. However, I still have hope for my kingdom. Your Uncle Julian will stop at nothing to acquire the throne, and I pray to Zormon that he challenges you for it. My brother is my last hope to keep my kingdom out of your dark, evil hands. Tomorrow, after my funeral, your coronation ceremony will be held to make you King, as the law states. Julian is my last hope to destroy you for good before that happens. You are an abomination and a disgrace. I never loved you.

Your father,

The King.

The letter infuriated him, but he did not ball it up, even though he wanted to. Instead of being sad, he was rather angry. Even dead, he still hated his father. Nar looked up and pointed at the courier.

"Make an announcement about the King's funeral and my coronation. Get it out to everyone that my coronation is tomorrow and make sure everyone is there," Nar ordered. The courier saluted and clicked his heels.

"Yes, sir," he said. With that, Nar disappeared into a dark cloud of purple smoke.

Twenty-Six

The next day was the King's funeral. Every citizen in Winterville was there to attend. A sick sort of pleasure consumed Gloria at the sight of the casket with the King's body inside. All the while, she and Julian had been planning. Julian knew that Nar's coronation would follow immediately after the funeral because that's how the law worked.

But Gloria and Julian had a plan. During the coronation, there would be a tragic "accident." Julian had gathered some mercenaries, at least three, to help him and Gloria take the throne. Gloria would be up in the stands, watching from above, waiting for Julian's signal to attack. During the attack, Gloria would use her mist magic, so the public wouldn't be able to see, and Julian's mercenaries, hiding in the crowd, would attack Simina. It would be the perfect assassination, and no one would see. When all the smoke from her magic would cloud everyone's eyes, Julian and Gloria would be killing the Prince. Gloria couldn't wait. She wished she had other magic, something more offensive, that could help Julian fight. But the mist magic was all she had.

All the while she was thinking about this, she stared with hatred at Simina, who stood next to the Prince, holding his hand and laying her head on his shoulder to comfort him, dressed in a modest, cute little black dress. Nar was dressed in a mournful black, tight-fitting suit to match Simina's black dress. It was slightly drizzling as they stood in the Royal Cemetery, listening to the mournful sermon of the preacher.

With a peculiar expression, Simina stared at Nar's face. It was blank and pure white. He stared, devoid of emotion, at the open casket with his father's body. His dark purple eyes were drier than a desert. Simina knew that Nar hadn't had the best relationship with his father. But it was still father, and Nar's aloof reaction concerned her.

"I'm sorry Nar," Simina said, just to be polite. Nar said nothing, only nodded. Simina decided not to say anything else, so she stayed quiet. She laid her head on his shoulder and closed her eyes. The preacher's sermon started to sound like a drone to her. Pretty soon, it faded, but Simina didn't realize it was over until Nar moved. She opened her eyes. Nar was pulling her along with him to stand before the King's casket. He turned to face the crowd. He was clutching fiercely to Simina's hand. With seemingly hollow eyes, Nar addressed the crowd.

"My humble citizens. Thank you all for coming today. I know you all are mourning the death of the King, my father, as I am. Thank you for taking this time to mourn with me." Nar took a strangled breath. When he spoke again, his voice cracked.

"I only wish I could have been with him in his last few moments. He was a truly great King and a fair ruler. I can only hope to be as great a King as he is. Thank you." Nar bowed his head respectfully, and the crowd murmured their agreement, faces drawn and haggard with grief. But Simina could see through the facade Nar put on, and saw that his "grief" was only an act. He didn't mean a single word of his speech. Nar cleared his throat, gathering the attention of the crowd. The murmurs were silenced.

"Despite this unexpected tragedy, I have pleasing news to share." The crowd buzzed with excitement. Nar held up a hand to silence them.

"I will be marrying soon," Nar announced, "to this beautiful, charming young lady next to me." Nar picked her hand up and kissed it, staring into her eyes with heart-thumping passion. Simina blushed. She couldn't believe he was doing this in front of a crowd. Nar turned back to the people.

"We will marry soon, and I will make her my queen. Shortly after my coronation, I will announce the date and time of my wedding. Again, I appreciate you all for attending my father's funeral. Thank you." Nar bowed his head and then waved over two undertakers standing to the side the entire time. They came over and closed the casket, and each undertaker took an end of the casket, picked it up, and lowered it gently into the ground. Then they began to bury him with their shovels, tossing piles of dirt after dirt until the casket was completely buried beneath the ground, six feet under.

Afterward, a sea of black moved away, dispersing. Then, Simina noticed a young, blue-haired man wearing a white cloak come up to Nar, extending a hand. He was a very beautiful man, tall and lithe. His hair was long and blue, flowing in waves to his shoulders. He had sharp features.

"Excuse me, your highness," the man said politely. Nar turned his head sharply in his direction. He narrowed his eyes.

"And you are?" The man bowed.

"My name is Blu Coloure, your Royal Adviser. Your coronation is prepared in the Ballroom. I've had the guests taken inside. Are you ready now?" the man, Blu, explained. Nar nodded curtly. He recalled his father's Royal Adviser, Sage. Blu looked remarkably like him and figured he must be Sage's son. He vaguely remembered Blu. He might have seen him once or twice in passing, but didn't really remember.

"I am."

"Then please, follow me." With a swish of his cloak, he turned around and strode toward the castle's main entrance. Nar spun toward Simina.

"I must leave you now, my love. Please follow the others into the castle and sit in one of the front pews," Nar instructed. He swiftly kissed her cheek in one fluid motion. Without further ado, he hastily strode after Blu. Simina did as he said without argument and followed the crowd into the castle. A sea of black-dressed guests filed into the Ballroom, dozens at a time. Pews had been set up in the room, and many other guests were already taking seats.

Simina strode confidently to the front of the room to the front pew on the right. The Royal Adviser, Blu, was already sitting, and there was a spot next to him on the pew. She took note of the sword strapped at his hip. Simina wondered how he'd gotten there so fast, but did not ask. Instead, she just sat next to him.

Twenty-Seven

As the coronation ceremony began, Gloria watched from atop the balcony, peeking through the curtain.

She looked down among the crowd as Nar held up the King's scepter. Everyone was focused on the preacher and Nar. Gloria spotted Julian in the crowd. From Gloria's vantage point, he sat in the front row on the right. Simina was seated on the left in the front pew, next to Nar's Royal Adviser, Blu.

Gloria clutched the folds of her cloak in her left hand, waiting for the moment to strike. Julian wasn't looking at her. He was paying close attention to the ceremony. Nar was kneeling before the preacher. The preacher held a book, and Nar placed his hand on it. Nar was now taking the King's Oath. Gloria gulped. Anxiety pulsed through her veins. Her heart hammered against her rib cage. It was almost time. She glared back at Julian. Still, he did not look up at her.

Gloria grounded her teeth. Come on! It's time! She was tired of hearing the senseless droning of that preacher! It had been about ten minutes. Even the crowd down below seemed restless. Gloria located the spot of each of Julian's mercenaries in the crowd. All of them shifted uneasily in their seats. Gloria started chewing on her bottom lip. All she had to do was use her mist magic so no one could see. Then, before the smoke consumed everything, she'd tackle the Prince, and Julian would aid her in killing him. While that was happening, the mercenaries would attempt to kill Simina. They could see through the thick mist with their special goggles.

Gloria smirked maliciously as she glared down at Simina. *You'll get what's coming to you; you and your little Prince.* She seethed with hate for Simina. *The little brat, I'll have the throne soon. It'll all be mine once you and Nar are dead.* Her vicious, hateful thoughts filled her with a sick pleasure.

"Almost time," Gloria mumbled eagerly to herself. She watched the audience, staring with awe at Prince Nar, soon to be their King. But not for long.

"...I must be a humble king," the preacher said. Nar recited,

"I must be a humble king..."

"...that respects the rights and laws of my royal citizens..." he droned.

"...that respects the rights and laws of my royal citizens..." Nar repeated.

"...not peasants..." the preacher read.

"...not peasants..."

"...I will be a fair king..."

"...I will be a fair king..."

"...that treats my citizens with respect..." And every sentence the preacher read, Nar repeated without fail. It was a long and dull process, and listening to it gave Gloria quite a headache. She glared down at Nar's kneeling form below her. Then she glared down at Julian, who sat calmly in the pews, looking bored. Why hadn't he given her the signal yet? Wasn't it time? Gloria gritted her teeth with impatience.

After a few more sentences, the oath ended. The preacher drew Nar's sword and tapped Nar on each shoulder with the blade's tip. Then he slipped the sword back into Nar's sheath. He carefully picked up the King's golden crown, holding it with both hands. He started to lower the crown onto Nar's head. Gloria flicked her eyes in Julian's direction. He still wouldn't look at her. Her eyes bulged. *Come on, come on! Give me the signal already!*

The audience began to applaud. Gloria's blood boiled. The preacher placed the crown on top of Nar's head.

"Rise, O' Honorable One. Face your people. You are now King," said the preacher. Nar rose and faced the audience. He waved at the applauding crowd. Simina blew him a kiss. Gloria looked at Julian, her heart pounding. Julian glanced up at her, and their eyes met. Julian nodded ever so slightly, indicating for Gloria to use her magic. Excited, Gloria slipped from behind the curtain. She sprayed the mist from her hands in thick waves in Nar's direction, and it wafted throughout the room, creating a bunch of dense, white fog. The preacher stumbled back, alarmed. Gloria jumped down from the balcony and landed right on top of Nar.

A startled gasp rose from the audience and a thick, white fog filled the Ballroom. Simina's vision immediately vanished. All she could see was white. Her eyes started to water. The mist filled her lungs. She coughed. Everyone else was coughing, too. *It has to be Gloria; she's using her magic.* Simina thought she saw a figure jump down onto Nar right before the fog engulfed everything. She wasn't sure.

Chaos filled the entire room. There were sounds of a struggle. People screamed. Everyone started running blindly, trying to get out, but instead tripped up over the pews. A little to Simina's left, there was a loud crash of people tripping and falling over pews. Simina remained still, not attempting to move around.

Nar expected this to happen, however. As the mist cloaked everything, someone tackled him. With a bang, his crown fell off his head and clattered to the floor. He hit the floor with a heavy thud, landing on his back. Someone was on top of him. Gloria pulled a dagger from her cloak. She attempted to stab him, but Nar could see through the mist with his magical powers. He grabbed her wrist, stopping her. Nar flipped her and, as he did so, twisted her wrist until she dropped it. He pinned her below him, restraining her. Someone grabbed Nar from behind, grabbing him around his waist. This person pulled him off Gloria and attempted to hold him back while Gloria tried to stab him. But Nar disappeared in a cloud of dark purple just in time and reappeared behind his Uncle Julian; the one who'd grabbed him. Nar unsheathed his sword and swung it at him in a wide arc. Julian turned around just at the right moment and jumped back. The blade barely bit into his right shoulder.

Julian grabbed his shoulder and winced as blood smoothly leaked out of him. He looked wildly about him, realizing the mist was starting to clear. He didn't want the rest of the general public to see him attacking the new King. So he ran off just as Nar swung at him again. Nar saw Gloria trying to run for it, too, but he would not let her escape. He disappeared and reappeared behind Gloria, restraining one of her arms as he held the blade of his sword at her throat. She wasn't going anywhere.

While that all happened, Simina was being attacked. She was attempting to get her bearings about her with the fog when a strong hand clamped around her mouth. An arm encircled her waist. Simina's eyes popped out of her head, and her heart rate increased dramatically. She started to flail and kick, and the heel of her foot met with someone's shin. There was a wince, and then a curse. The hand clamped over her mouth loosened, and she shook it off. Simina threw her butt back into the gut of her attacker, throwing him off her.

"Dammit! Stop fooling around! Just kill her already!" an unfamiliar voice hissed. Her blood froze as if touched by ice. Her face blanched. Someone was trying to kill her. Simina turned tail and attempted to run, but she tripped over a pew since she couldn't see where she was going. Her knees hit the hardwood of the pew, and her momentum threw her forward, crashing all over and across the pews, knocking over quite a lot.

During the fall, she injured and probably bruised most of her body. A throbbing, aching pain zapped through her nerves. On the way down, she whacked the side of her head on a pew, and her head started to spin. Black spots flickered in the white fog as a woozy feeling filled her clouded mind. The noises and all the sounds began to fade around her. Her head started throbbing, pulsing. Her body slammed on the floor hard, the impact shaking her to her core. Simina now lay on the cold, hard floor, everything in her head swirling terribly, everything moving.

Someone got on top of Simina and pinned her legs down with their hips. Someone else grabbed her arms and held them down so she wouldn't be able to flail. Simina flailed as much as her little body could manage, but it didn't get her anywhere.

"Stop writhing," that same, unfamiliar voice said through gritted teeth. A hand wrapped around her neck and slowly squeezed. Something sharp and painful cut into her left cheek and red-hot pain lanced through her face. Simina squeezed her eyes shut, gritting her teeth, attempting to breathe despite the hand slowly trying to crush her windpipe.

A terrified, hopeless scream ripped out of her throat and into the air, mixing with all of the other loud ruckus and commotion around them. Through the pandemonium, Nar didn't hear her scream. He was also fighting off two people who were trying to kill him.

Luckily, Simina had practiced magic enough to know how to cast a defensive spell. Drawing energy from the chaos around her and her own adrenaline, power surged through her. She croaked the incantation with the little breath she had left, and instantly a whirlwind formed out of Gloria's mist. The man on top of her was ripped off by a huge gale, his body flung across the room. The sharp blades of wind tore through the other three men, tearing through their flesh like butter. Simina's wind cut them down mercilessly. When it was finally over, all three of their mangled bodies fell to the floor, blood leaking from the various gashes. Simina opened her eyes. She sat up and observed the carnage her magic had caused. She stared in awe at what she'd done, and couldn't believe that she'd conjured such magic. Just as the exhaustion set in, she realized that the misty fog was clearing, and Blu was standing over here, holding a bloodied blade.

Blu reached a hand down to her. Simina looked up at the Royal Adviser. He offered her a kind smile.

"Here, young lady," Blu said softly. Simina took his hand, and Blu helped her get to her feet. She stood, brushing herself off.

"Thank you, Blu," Simina said with a curt nod. Blu nodded.

"Of course." He re-sheathed his blade. Blu looked toward Nar, the new King, who stood on the raised platform before the crowd. Simina followed Blu's gaze. She saw Nar restraining Gloria, one arm around her waist, his sword under her chin, at her throat. Simina's heart leaped. He must have caught her in the act!

After the fact, everyone else was all dazed and confused. In the crowd, Simina heard Aunt Lyda and Olivia's gasps and exclaims. Stumbling over fallen pews, Aunt Lyda rushed forward, Olivia dogging at her heels.

"Oh, my Zormon! What is the meaning of this?" Aunt Lyda exclaimed shrilly. The Royal Adviser, Blu, stepped into their path, stopping their pursuit, and held up a hand.

"Please, madam, do not come any closer," Blu said calmly. Aunt Lyda's mouth hung agape.

"But-but t-that's my daughter he's got, good sir; please let me pass!" Aunt Lyda cried, trying to find a way around Blu, but he would not let them pass him.

"I'm sorry, miss. But you must stay out of the King's way," Blu said. He gestured to an upturned pew that had gone unscathed during the craziness.

"Please. Have a seat." With pursed lips, Aunt Lyda sat, unwilling to argue another word, as Olivia sat beside her.

Gloria writhed to be free of Nar's restraint, but it was futile. Nar looked toward Blu.

"Blu! Arrest this girl immediately! She tried to kill me!" Nar growled as he wrestled with Gloria's struggling body. Blu strode swiftly over, waving over two guards who seemed to appear out of nowhere. Simina hadn't noticed them before. One guard handed Blu a pair of shackles, which he took silently as he clasped them around Gloria's wrists and fastened them as Nar restrained her. Once firmly apprehended, Nar released her, and Blu dragged her away by the arms.

"You are under arrest in the name of the King for treason against the throne," Blu stated in a robotic tone. She was handed over to two guards, each taking an arm. Blu waved a dismissive hand.

"Take her to the dungeon," Blu ordered. The guards saluted and went off to carry out their duty, dragging Gloria with them. Simina watched them carry her away with a significant amount of glee.

Blu turned to Nar. "Is there anything else you wish me to carry out for you, your Majesty?" An aura of authority wafted around Nar. A cold look was in his eyes, something Simina had never seen before.

"First, I want you to escort my Lady Simina to the Queen's quarters and have two guards posted at her door. Then, I want you to find my uncle. He also attempted to assassinate me, but he got away. Send out search parties, find him, and arrest him. You are to carry out these orders immediately and without fail. Do I make myself clear?" Nar ordered. Blu bowed.

"As you wish, my King." Blu swiftly turned and strode to Simina to carry out his orders.

"Please, follow me, Miss. As the King ordered, I will escort you to the Queen's quarters." Blu bowed to Simina. Simina followed him without question.

"Lead the way." Blu slipped a casual hand around Simina's waist and led her out of the Ballroom. Simina listened to Nar bark out orders.

"Everyone else, please go home! You there, soldier! Find and arrest anyone who had anything to do with overthrowing my throne!" Nar shouted.

Blu and Simina exited the Ballroom and entered the foyer. As he led her through the foyer and up the stairs, Nar's voice faded more and more until she got so far away that she could no longer hear his shouting.

Twenty-Eight

Gloria had been Nar's prisoner for a few weeks, her fate still to be decided by Nar, who was now the King. Nar had been interrogating her, trying to figure out the whereabouts of Julian, but she wasn't speaking a word about it. Search parties had been sent out, many search parties, but they found no sign of Julian anywhere. Gloria really didn't know where Julian had gone. He could've been anywhere on the entire planet.

Besides Julian's whereabouts, Nar had interrogated her about their reasons and motives. She refused to say anything about that until Nar snapped. He lunged for her, grabbing her around the throat. Gloria gasped as the rest of her breath rushed out of her. Nar slammed her head against the hard concrete wall. Gloria cried out in pain as stars danced in her eyes. Nar put his lips really close to her ear.

"Look, you disgusting, filthy, treacherous, jealous bitch," Nar spat hatefully. Gloria tried to breathe, but Nar had a firm grip on her neck as he squeezed. She made a strange, strangled choking noise. Nar glared at her, pinning his eyes to hers.

"I'm so tired of playing the quiet game with you. Tell me what it is I want to know, or so help me, I will kill you right here without thinking twice. I'm not in the mood today," Nar growled. Gloria managed a nod, and Nar released her. He gave her a minute to regain her breath. She coughed, sucking in rattling breaths through her mouth, letting the air fill her lungs. Nar drew his sword and put the tip just under her chin.

"Start talking. Now!" Nar hissed, purple eyes glowing bright and vivid with lividity. His eyes seared her. Gloria gulped and started talking.

"Julian wanted your throne. He wanted to be King. He was jealous of you and your father since you inherited the family powers, but he hadn't. He thought he deserved the throne after his brother died, not you. So, he planned to overthrow you by killing you, and I helped him," Gloria sputtered, her words stumbling out of her mouth in a jumble. She had to repeat some of it because she was shaking so much.

"Why were you a part of it?" Nar asked smoothly.

"I was jealous," Gloria gasped. "I was jealous of Simina. She always had your attention, she's so much prettier, when I wanted you. Everyone always chose her over me. I hated it. I hated her, and I still hate her. I wanted to be queen. Then I met Julian. We connected through our jealousy and hate. He told me of his plan. I offered to help him, but in return, after you were dead, he'd marry me, so I'd be queen. We were supposed to

"

kill you and Simina at the ball. But your drink spilled. So we made another plan and Julian hired some mercenaries. That's why I became part of it."

"And where is Julian now?" Nar asked again, for the millionth time. Gloria shook her head.

"I don't know. I really don't know. He has no way of contacting me," Gloria said.

"What are the names of these mercenaries?"

Gloria told him the names. Satisfied, Nar sheathed his sword. He thanked her and promptly left the dungeon. He sent out guards and soldiers to find the people with the names Gloria had given.

Soon, Nar's dungeon was filled with many traitors.

Twenty-Nine

A month later, on the day of the wedding, a lovely dress was sent to Simina's house with a note attached.

Simina recognized Nar's fancy handwriting. Before looking at the dress, she opened the note and read it.

Dear Simina,

I hope you like this wedding dress. It was my mother's. I bet you'll look absolutely divine in it. It has been altered to fit your dimensions.

Love,

Nar.

Simina couldn't help but smile as she took out the gown. She, Olivia, and Aunt Lyda gasped in unison at its beauty. Silky fabric caressed through her hands and fingers. It was sleeveless, with only large, ruffled straps that would rest on the shoulders. Its white bodice was studded with little crystals, and the skirt flowed all the way to the floor, smooth and pure, shining white. Of course, a veil came with it.

A few minutes later, they'd gotten her into the dress, which fit her perfectly. It was snug in all the right places. Olivia added a touch of makeup while Aunt Lyda touched up her hair. She didn't put it up. Instead, she left it down and brushed it. Simina's hair became wavy and curly. Her aunt pinned the veil in her hair and gave her a bouquet of white roses.

A carriage arrived to take Simina, Olivia, and Aunt Lyda to the church. When Simina arrived, she became nervous once she saw all the people there. Her stomach churned, and she almost started hyperventilating. Her father, there to walk her down the aisle, assured her it would be okay.

Most of the people there were commoners, but some were family. She only wished her mother was there to see her getting married, and to a King! Speaking of the King, Simina spotted Nar standing at the altar in front of Blu, the Royal Adviser. Her breath caught when she saw him. He looked so handsome, dressed in his black suit and matching leather pants. Nar looked very dapper, and Simina's heart began to ache. Desire pooled in the pit of her stomach. She just wanted to be alone with him instead of going through all of this.

You already know the wedding proceedings, so I will skip that bit so as toas not bore you with my rambling.

Simina and Nar wanted a quick wedding, and that's exactly what it was: quick. In thirty minutes, the entire wedding procession was already finished. There would be a reception, but the bride and groom would not be present for it.

They wanted such a quick wedding so they could hurry up and be married. Simina wanted to be alone with Nar in his castle so he could hold her tight. She didn't want to be around all of those people; she just wanted to be alone with Nar.

Simina slipped her hand into Nar's and gripped it tightly. Nar squeezed her hand gently back, stroking her hand with his thumb. Simina gazed up at him with love-filled eyes. Nar smiled at her and pulled her close to his side. Nar smiled at the crowd and waved. He thanked them all for coming and told them to treat themselves to the refreshments previously set up. He turned to Simina.

"Are you ready, my Simina?" he asked sweetly. He stroked her face with the back of his fingers. Simina leaned into his touch and took his hand in both of hers, holding his hand there.

"Yes," she breathed. "I want to be with you." Nar put his arms around her.

"Hold on tight to me," he whispered. Simina grabbed him and snuggled her head into his chest, arms around his back. She closed her eyes. In a puff of swirling purple smoke, Nar and Simina disappeared. They reappeared in the castle, alone in Nar's quarters, the King's Quarters. Nar stroked her hair.

"We are alone now, love. Open your eyes," Nar murmured to Simina, pulling back from her. Simina pulled away, staring up at him. He caressed her face, taking in her beauty. Nar smiled. She was finally and fully his. Blood rushed into his loins. He took a breath. He wanted her.

"Turn around for me," Nar said seductively, brushing a finger down her arm. Simina did as he said and turned around. Simina heard something drop to the floor. Nar was undressing. He removed his suit jacket and unbuttoned his shirt. He threw it to the floor. Nar dropped his pants and kicked them away. Taking the zipper of her dress in his thumb and forefinger, he tugged it down, unzipping.

Simina noticed the dress loosen on her, and her breath quickened at the intimacy of the moment. Nar revealed her luscious skin beneath and pushed the sleeves off her shoulders. It fell to the floor around Simina's feet. Simina stepped out of it, standing bare in front of Nar. Nar held back a growl of seduction at the view of Simina's naked body in front of him.

Simina enjoyed Nar's hands on her, caressing her curves, touching her waist, feeling her hips, groping her thighs. Simina closed her eyes, her breathing growing heavier and more rapid. She leaned into Nar as he pulled her against him, bodies touching, skin touching skin. He touched her all over, enjoying the feel of her skin, of her warm body against his. Simina's face heated. Nar tilted her head back and swept her hair back from her neck. He leaned forward and pressed his lips softly to her throat, kissing her. Nar kissed her neck, lips moving all over her warm skin. A pleasant, tingling sensation spread through her skin. Simina let a small, soft sigh escape from her lips and the sound aroused Nar even more.

"Ah…" Simina breathed. Nar continued planting hot, sticky, wet kisses all over her neck, enjoying the sound of Simina's pleasure.

"Will we…you know?" Simina sighed out through heavy breathing. Nar ran his nose along her skin.

"Mmm. Yes. But only if you want to," Nar murmured. A shiver ran down her spine.

"Yes."

Nar's hand traveled up Simina's side and caressed the side of her right breast. He inhaled deeply.

"You're so beautiful, Simina. Every inch of you." Nar turned her to face him and saw her blushing. He brought his lips to hers and kissed her, grasping her thigh, pressing her body against his so her breasts were flush against him. Simina became acutely aware of Nar's erection against her thigh.

"Let me love you," Nar murmured against her lips. He swiftly picked her up and cradled her in his arms like a baby. He carried her to the bed.

* * *

Sometime later, Simina lay naked beside Nar in the King's Grand Master Bed. She rested her head on his bare chest, running her fingers through his chest hair. Nar lay with his eyes closed, resting.. Simina kissed his cheek.

"I love you," Simina murmured. Nar opened his eyes and turned his head to look at her.

"And I, you, my love," he replied. Nar leaned in and kissed her sweet lips.

"Mm. You're sweet." Nar nuzzled his nose into her hair. He leaned back and kissed her ear. Simina giggled as the soft peach fuzz on his face brushed against her chin.

"Do you remember when we first met?" Nar asked, stroking a finger down her arm. Simina let her mind wander back to that fateful day.

"Yes." She remembered seeing him for the first time. Simina laughed.

"I hated you back then, when you locked me up in your dungeon," Simina said with a chuckle. Nar grinned at her.

"You hated me? Really?" He couldn't believe how much that had changed. She nodded.

"Really."

"Well now, we see how that changed. What made your feelings change?" He quirked a quizzical eyebrow. Simina shrugged.

"I don't know," she sighed. "I just ended up loving you." Simina snuggled close to him, burying her face into his neck, breathing out with contentment.

"So tell me. How does it feel to be my wife?" Nar asked her.

"Ecstatic," Simina breathed out, and she smiled.

"Good. You're now my Queen. You are now royalty, my Queen Simina. All hail the Queen." Nar smirked.

Thirty

Simina fully moved into the castle when Nar ordered her things to be brought there. Three months had passed since the wedding and Simina was happy in her new life with Nar. Since Nar was now King, he took care of his Kingly duties, and sometimes, Simina helped him, knowing that since she was Queen, it was her duty to do so. Her father visited once, and she also went to Ernest's wedding. Sometimes, commoners even came to the castle with offerings and gave Simina baked goods.

One day, Simina and Nar were sitting in the Throne Room. Simina quietly knitted while she sat, and Nar watched her. She'd been learning how to knit with Matilda's help, and she was getting pretty good at it. Suddenly, the two great doors flew open. A disheveled, angry, ugly-looking man strode in, a pair of guards hot on his tail. Nar stood up, alert. Simina was startled, but she did not stand.

The man was short and squat, but very bulky. Brown, thinning hair hung down in greasy strands around his shoulders. Simina recognized the muddy boots, the fur cape, and the dull lavender eyes. She knew exactly who it was, and her blood curdled. He drew his sword from its sheath as he approached Nar. Simina's heart jumped. She stood. Julian pointed the tip of the blade at Nar's throat. Nar remained very still. Julian's eyes turned into slits, filled with determination.

"I challenge your throne," Julian hissed through gritted teeth. Nar raised an eyebrow, then his eyes narrowed, and his lips tightened. Nar drew his sword and pointed it at Julian's throat.

"You dare challenge my throne?" Nar whispered dangerously. Julian smirked.

"Yes. I dare."

"I accept your challenge," Nar said coolly.

"Three days?" Julian quirked an eyebrow. Nar nodded.

"Three days," he confirmed. Nar waited for him to withdraw his sword first. Satisfied, Julian withdrew his and re-sheathed it. He turned on his heel and strode out of the Throne Room. The two guards followed him, and the two doors slammed shut. Nar re-sheathed his sword, intensity etched on his face. Simina walked over to him.

"Nar? What was that all about?" Simina asked, getting a bad feeling. Nar glanced at her.

"He challenged my throne," Nar stated.

"What does that mean?" Simina's voice quivered. Nar sighed.

"I have to fight him. He's going to fight me for my throne," Nar told her. Simina knew that couldn't be good. Nar decided he better explain in more detail.

"You see, when a challenge is accepted, both competitors must wait three days before the challenge to prepare. During the fight, anything goes. There are no rules. The winner is only decided once the other dies," Nar explained to Simina. Pallor washed over her cheeks, chasing away the usual warmth. Simina couldn't believe what she'd just heard.

"What?" Her voice was a raspy croak.

"It's a fight to the death." Nar turned away from her, so Simina faced his back. He didn't want to see her expression. Simina rushed to him and grabbed his arm.

"Oh, Nar, you can't! Please, don't risk your life!" Simina pleaded, trying to talk him out of it. He turned his face away.

"I've already made my decision," Nar stated calmly. Simina shook her head.

"You can't!" Nar ignored her.

"My uncle must be destroyed. This is my only chance. If I win, Julian dies, and everything will go back to normal. But if I lose..." Nar trailed off.

"Don't say it!" Simina couldn't bear to hear it, even though she needed to. She didn't want to imagine what would happen if Nar lost.

"If I lose," he continued, "I will die. Julian will then take my throne, my land, and become King, taking everything that is mine." Nar finally looked at Simina and stared her right in the eyes. Something like heartbreak filled them. "Including you."

Everything around Simina faded, and her mind tried to picture herself as Julian's wife. The mere thought disgusted her. She'd have to kiss him, have sex with him, and be his. She didn't want that. Simina didn't want to be Julian's. It revolted her, and she wanted to vomit. Simina wildly shook her head.

"No! I'd rather die!" Simina cried, eyes flooding. Nar quickly grabbed Simina and held her tight in his arms and allowed her to cry into his jacket.

"I won't lose. I promise you. I don't care about the throne. I don't care about the land. He won't take you from me," Nar assured her with a fierceness. He pulled her back from him.

"Now. Listen. The Queen, which is you, has to be present for the fight." Simina opened her mouth to protest, but Nar held up a hand. Simina shut her mouth.

"You have to be there. If you like, Matilda will be there with you. If I lose—"

"Don't—" Simina began. But Nar put a finger to her lips, silencing her.

"If I lose...I want you to run far, far away from here. Run. You will go with Blu; he'll help you escape if something goes wrong. I don't care where you run. Just run, get as far away from him as you can. Promise me that you'll run." Nar removed his finger from her lips.

"I'll run. I promise I'll run," Simina mumbled and nodded her head. She looked down, sulking. She wanted to cry but wanted to be a strong Queen for her King. Nar tilted her chin and looked at her with a stern expression.

"Don't sulk. I already promised you that I wouldn't lose. And besides. We still have three days." Nar pressed a soft kiss to her lips. He pressed his forehead to hers and looked straight into her eyes.

"I won't fail you, my Queen. Never," Nar vowed passionately to her.

* * *

A day before the duel, Matilda made Simina take a pregnancy test. Matilda suspected she might be pregnant because the day before she had thrown up during morning hours and she hadn't bled for a while. So Simina, with Matilda's help, performed a spell that would let her know if she was indeed pregnant. Upon completion of the spell, Simina's tummy glowed bright gold.

"What does that mean?" Simina asked her. Matilda smiled at Simina.

"It means you're pregnant," she said. Simina's eyes widened and her mouth hung slightly open. She couldn't believe it.

"What?" Her voice became an inaudible whisper. Matilda hugged her.

"Congratulations! I think you should probably tell Nar about this," Matilda suggested. Simina composed herself, trying to come to terms with this big news. She nodded and cleared her throat.

"Y-yes," she stammered and went in search of Nar. As she stumbled through the halls to his study, Simina's eyes began to burn with tears. Her vision blurred. On weak legs, Simina stumbled through the study door. Nar stood from his desk, alerted by the way Simina stumbled in. He rushed to her in a few quick strides. Blubbering, Simina pointed a finger at him.

"Nar, don't you dare lose tomorrow!" Simina shouted, voice cracking. Nar stood in front of her, eyebrows raised in concern.

"I told you, I won't lose," Nar assured her.

"You better not because I'm...I'm with child!" Simina blurted out. Her anger flared up out of nowhere. She grabbed the folds of his jacket and clenched the fabric in her fists. Nar's eyes flashed and widened. He was silent for a moment. Slowly, Nar raised a hand and placed it on her stomach, gently letting it rest there.

"I..." Nar swallowed. "I will not only live just for you now. I will now live for you and our child." Nar kissed Simina's brow. "I promise." Simina bawled and sobbed hard, clutching onto Nar with everything she had left.

***

The duel took place in the foyer at twelve. Blu conducted it to ensure everything was right and fair. Julian and Nar stood at least two feet apart. Blu stood in the middle of them, wearing a placid expression. He looked cold, like ice. He raised a hand and gave each man a sharp, calculated look.

"Draw your swords," Blu ordered with a flick of his wrist. Simina gulped, sweat trickling down her brow. Nar and Julian drew their swords at the same time. Blu raised his hand, palm down, just above his head.

"Raise your swords to the top of my palm, blade points touching," Blu instructed. They did so, and neither of them broke eye contact. Intensity radiated within the atmosphere, thick and ruthless. Blu lowered his hand but instructed them to keep their swords raised. The two swords formed an arc of steel in front of Blu. Then, he took out his sword and raised his tip to the same level as theirs.

"This is a duel. Both of you must keep fighting until one of you dies." Blu then looked over at Nar. "Nar. If you win, you will remain King and your throne, land, and Queen shall remain yours." He looked over at Julian. "Julian. If you win, you will become King, and the throne, the land, and the Queen shall become yours. Do both of you understand and accept these terms?" He glanced at them both. Nar and Julian nodded in unison.

"No one is allowed to aid you during this battle. Remember, this is a fight to the death." Blu lowered his sword and took a few steps back.

"You may begin," he stated calmly. At once, they rushed at each other, swords clashing with a loud clang. Simina's heart leaped. Matilda stood next to her and placed a hand on her shoulder reassuringly. Despite Matilda's efforts, Simina did not feel reassured.

Nar swept-kicked Julian's feet, pulling back from him, off-balancing Julian, and then lunged at him, slamming into him so hard that he stumbled back. Using his weight, Julian pushed back against Nar, shoving him back. Both swords clashed in midair, steel biting steel. Simina's nerves racked and jumped with each clang of their swords.

Simina hadn't taken notice of Blu standing beside her because of the fight. She didn't notice him until she heard his voice whispering in her ear.

"Don't worry, my Lady Queen. Nar is strong. Trust in him," Blu murmured sweetly to Simina, soothing her. His sweet, soft voice eased Simina's nerves and made her feel less tense. Matilda stared with awe, entranced by Blu. Blu pretended not to notice the look Matilda gave him because he was used to it.

Simina focused herself back on the battle, watching Nar and Julian's movements, but watching Nar's a little more closely. In the middle of a clash, Nar used his powers. He disappeared out of sight and reappeared behind Julian. Julian's eyes popped open in surprise. Moving fast for such a heavy person, he turned just in time to avoid the full blow of Nar's sword. Instead, Nar managed to slice him deep across the chest, cutting through his shirt and deep into his skin. A sharp, red line opened in his chest.

Julian howled with pain as the blood dripped, seeping into his torn shirt. Julian charged forward, seeing a spot Nar left open on his person. He raised his sword and sliced the blade deep into his right arm, the arm that wielded his sword. Nar cried out and stumbled back, a deep gash sliced nicely into his arm. Simina whimpered and put her hands over her mouth. Blood seeped out of the wound, gushing over his left hand as he clutched it.

Blu leaned close to Simina, whispering, "Don't worry, my Queen. If things go south, I am prepared for what must happen."

Julian smirked, seeing his advantage. He lunged at Nar, blade at the ready for a final blow. But Julian should have known that it wouldn't be that easy. Nar's left hand shot out and a gust of purple, misty smoke blew Julian back. Julian landed hard on the ground a good two feet away, his sword clattering to the floor with a clang. He skidded across the floor on his back. Julian grunted at the impact. Nar made his sword disappear and reappear in his left hand using his magic. He strode forward toward Julian, an angry grimace stretching his face. Alerted by Nar's pursuit, Julian scrambled to his feet and grabbed his sword just in time to engage with Nar's.

Nar's grasp on his sword was not as strong as before, since his right arm had been hurt, and he could barely move it. Sweat trickled down the side of his face. Using Nar's weakness against him and his strength, Julian pushed back against his nephew so hard that it threw Nar off balance and left him open for attack. Before Nar could raise his sword to defend himself, Julian sliced Nar across his chest, tearing his shirt and cutting deep into Nar's flesh. Nar let out a yell of pain and fell to the floor, his sword falling out of his hand and landing uselessly a foot away. Nar's chest and arm stung with hot, biting pain.

Simina screamed. "Nar!!!"

Nar's vision started going black at the edges. He could feel the blood seeping out of his body. It slowly began to pool on the floor around him. As he lay there, he looked at Simina across the way. She was crying and reaching for him, sobbing out his name. Blu was restraining her from going to him. Simina kicked and thrashed against Blu's hold, eager to get away from him and help Nar. She didn't care about the rules; she had to help Nar. Blu was holding her around the waist, clutching her small, writhing body against his, trying to still her flailing arms pushing on his hands.

"Let go! Let me go, Blu!" Simina shouted, tears streaking all over her cheeks. Blu gritted his teeth as Simina stomped on his foot.

"Simina! Stop it! You cannot!" Blu warned. Simina grunted, straining, and somehow managed to escape his hold. She pushed him back with her butt, elbowing him in the side, thrusting her hips back. Blu grunted, releasing her, and Simina ran out into the foyer that had turned into a battle arena. Blu cursed to himself.

"Nar!" Simina called and ran to him. Nar heard her voice, but it only sounded like an echo. She fell to her knees next to his limp form on the floor and picked up his head, cradling him.

"Nar, oh Nar, please don't die," she pleaded, tears flowing. Nar looked up at her.

"Simina...get away from here," he rasped. Julian was approaching, the look of pure outrage on his face.

"Simina! Get back here; you are not supposed to interfere!" Blu shouted and strode across the foyer floor toward Simina and Nar. Blu reached her and grabbed her by the arms. He began to drag her away, but Simina lost it.

"No! You let me go!" Wooziness flooded her brain, her vision blurring over with dark yet sparkling spots. At the sight of Nar's blood, Simina fainted, her arm still outstretched, reaching for him. Matilda gasped. Blu caught her before she hit the floor and held her limp body in his arms. Matilda ran up to Blu as he held Simina.

"Take her to the Queen's Quarters," Matilda said in a rush, flustered and worried. Blu hurriedly carried her away, out of the foyer.

Seeing Simina faint like that renewed Nar's resolve. No matter his blood loss, he would defeat Julian once and for all. Nar saw Julian's pursuit, about to give the finishing blow. Using what little strength and magic he had left; Nar made his sword appear in his left hand in a delicate swirl of purple mist to block Julian's oncoming blow. Nar raised his sword just in time as it clashed against Julian's. The impact was so great that it reverberated through the bones in Nar's arm and all throughout his body, causing him great pain. Nar gritted his teeth and grunted. Julian pushed, straining.

Nar used his remaining strength to shove him back, and then, while Julian was momentarily stunned, Nar disappeared out of sight in a collection of smoke and reappeared on his feet behind Julian. Before Julian could even turn around or react, Nar ferociously drove the blade through Julian's back, impaling him. Julian gasped in surprise; eyes wide with pain. Nar shoved the blade deeper, up to the hilt. Julian coughed out blood, sputtering. Nar leaned up close to his ear.

"Goodbye, Uncle," Nar spat. With a swift motion, he yanked out his sword and watched his uncle collapse to the floor. Julian glared at Nar one last time before the light finally died from his eyes. He bled out all over the floor. As soon as it was over, Nar collapsed, dropping his sword. He landed with a thud and passed out. Matilda rushed to him, concerned. Blu returned and went to help. Luckily, Nar was still alive; he'd just lost a lot of blood. Blu carried him to the King's Quarters. He ordered some soldiers to clean up Julian's body and the blood, which they did with haste.

Once in the King's Quarters, Blu stripped off all of Nar's clothes, revealing his wounds. Blu quickly used his healing magic to stop the bleeding, then cleaned and dressed his wounds. He let Nar sleep, to heal the rest.

Epilogue

Simina woke in the Queen's Quarters. The room was dark, and she couldn't see. Simina remembered the reason she fainted. She remembered seeing Nar on the floor, bleeding, dead, or almost dead. She'd rushed to him. The blood was all over the floor, slipping out of Nar and dripping onto the floor. It might have just been her imagination, but there was so much blood. She remembered Blu tugging at her, lifting her away from Nar, from the blood. Her body rose as Blu lifted her up, and she started flailing, struggling, but the stench of the blood was too much. There was too much red, too much of the smell of blood. It overflowed her nostrils until she couldn't take it anymore. She remembered fainting.

Was he dead? Simina started crying, bawling. Did she now belong to Julian? Would she have to run away? Simina stared at the ceiling, choking on her sobs, tears running down the side of her face. She buried her face into a pillow, muffling her sobs, soaking the fabric with her tears. The salt from her tears leaked to her lips and she tasted their saltiness on her tongue. Her chest ached, and she could not take the pain. Even though she was not in the foyer anymore, she could still smell the blood and the iron's stench. Her stomach churned at the memory, almost feeling ready to vomit.

The door to her room creaked open, and a soft light streamed into the room. Simina was too distraught to hear the door open. Nar softly padded into the room, his arm and chest tightly bandaged. It'd been a good five hours since the fight, which is how long they had been asleep. Nar figured Simina thought he was dead, so he went in to see her to prove otherwise. He came and knelt by her bed. A gentle finger stroked her cheek, cajoling and assuring. She flinched.

"What? What's that?" Her voice was hoarse. Nar pressed a kiss to her temple. The wetness on her cheeks greeted him as he took her face in both of his firm, rough hands.

"You've been crying, my love. It pleases me not when you cry," Nar murmured, nuzzling his nose into her hair. Simina gasped.

"Nar," she choked. Simina sat up. She could make out his silhouetted form in the dark, with a little bit of light streaming in from the open door. She grabbed him and hugged his head to her bosom, running her fingers through his hair. Nar slipped his arms around her waist and closed his eyes, enjoying her smell and warmth, engulfed by her love. Nar breathed out slowly in relief and content. She was so soft, so warm. He heard her heart beating deep within her chest, beating a mile a minute. Nar trailed his hands and fingers up and down her back, feeling her muscles, strength, and liveliness.

"Oh, Nar, I thought you were dead," she sobbed. Nar slid onto the bed with Simina and held her in his lap. Simina held tightly onto him and curled up in his lap, resting her head in the crook of his neck. Gloopy, wet tears dribbled onto his neck like a soft, tiny rainstorm. He held her tight, trying to calm her shaking by petting and stroking her hair. Simina slowly sucked in breath after breath, breathing in all that was Nar.

"It's me. I'm here, Simina. I'm not going anywhere. I promised you that I wouldn't lose, didn't I?" Nar said, smiling, stroking through her hair. Simina nodded and smiled.

"Yeah," she said with a sniffle. Nar kissed her eyes, her nose, and finally, her lips, each with a sweet softness.

"I love you." Simina held onto Nar and never wanted to let go.

* * *

Six months later, as Simina held her infant son, she thought about all of the books she used to read. They had all been fairytales of some sort, with happy endings and happily ever after. The more she reflected on these stories, the more she realized that they were indeed hogwash, like her father had once told her. Fairytales were simple, easy, and black and white. But real life wasn't so simple. Darkness doesn't mean evil. Light isn't always good. While there were similarities to the worlds in those stories and this world, like magic, Simina decided that she didn't want to live a fairytale after all. She wanted the ugly, the raw, visceral reality that was her world. Nothing is simple, and princes aren't perfect. If she hadn't accepted that, she may have never seen who Prince Nar truly was. A tormented, brooding, and misunderstood kind soul.

The End.

First and foremost, I'd like to thank you, the reader, for choosing to pick up my book. However you got your hands on it, I'm grateful you chose to give my book a chance, and I really hope you enjoyed it. I'd like to thank my publishing and editing team who helped make this possible; all of your advice and help really made this story shine. Thanks for your hard work! Special thanks goes to my younger sister Emma, my number one fan and supporter. Thank you for always rooting for me and constantly listening to me drone on and on about my stories. Without your continued encouragement, I may have stopped writing a long time ago.

Rachel E. Croxton has been writing since the young age of eleven. She fell in love with it, and hasn't been able to stop since. She enjoys writing all kinds of genres from fantasy to sci fi, horror and romance. In her spare time, she enjoys watching her favorite tv shows. Her inspiration comes from a lifelong interest in magic, folklore and the paranormal.